It had all been for her.

For Faith.

For her approval, her respect. For her love.

"Take off your clothes."

Faith whirled around. His command, the croak of his voice as he issued it, the intensity in his eyes and the hard set of his jaw left her shivering, and not from the chill of her wet clothing.

He seemed taller, broader, certainly more imposing as he came toward her, presumably to enforce what had seemed like a practical directive. There was nothing menacing in his demeanor, which encouraged her to dare a step in his direction. And to obey him.

Zander had no delusions that what had initially been a practical concern was now something far different. Her clothes were surely uncomfortable, but once her soggy top was in a heap on the floor, he acknowledged the bare truth: After years of dreaming and wanting, he wouldn't wait another minute to have her.

TEMPTING FAITH

CRYSTAL HUBBARD

Genesis Press, Inc.

INDIGO LOVE SPECTRUM

An imprint of Genesis Press, Inc.
Publishing Company

Genesis Press, Inc.
P.O. Box 101
Columbus, MS 39703

All characters in this book have no existence outside the imagination of the author and have no relation whatsoever to anyone bearing the same name or names. They are not even distantly inspired by any individual known or unknown to the author and all incidents are pure invention.

ISBN: 13 DIGIT : 978-158571-288-5
ISBN: 10 DIGIT : 1-58571-288-4
Manufactured in the United States of America

First Edition 2009

Visit us at www.genesis-press.com
or call at 1-888-Indigo-1

DEDICATION

To The League of Ladies Who Love Extraordinary Gentlemen, especially Flaming Star, Viper, Serenity, Eve of Construction, Voracious, Dr. D, and Cyborg—super smart, super caring, and super talented supervixens all.

ACKNOWLEDGMENTS

Thanks to my California crew of Chele and Troy, Lauren, Douglas, John and Trinity, who shared their experiences and knowledge of how the cogs and wheels of Hollywood fit together. I offer special thanks to the Beverly Wilshire Hotel and the guest with the twin ocelots, who gave me the idea for Candy.

I'd also like to thank the National Mining Association and the West Virginia Department of Environmental Protection, as well as the kind residents of Dorothy and Whitesville, West Virginia.

CHAPTER 1

"Mr. Baron!"

A shrill voice climbed above those of the reporters assembled in rows of folding chairs before him. The voice turned out to be rather melodious and pleasant once the clamoring of the other reporters stopped to allow the first question.

"Mr. Baron," the owner of the voice said, now standing. "What high school did you attend?"

The rustle of clothing, the scritch-scratch of pens on note pads, the clicking of camera equipment—the music of the press conference played on as the media awaited his response.

More experienced reporters cast envious glances at *Personality!* magazine correspondent Faith Wheeler, whose innocuous question had incredible implications regarding Zander Baron, the actor they had come to the Renaissance Hollywood hotel to interview.

Faith's gaze flitted to Zander's publicist and agent, the beautiful platinum blonde mother and son duo of Olivia and Brent Baxter. Faith's question had not ruffled Olivia's frosty exterior, but Brent coughed nervously into his loosely curled fist.

"I went to Lincoln High," Zander said, his voice every bit as deep, smooth and commanding as it sounded onscreen.

Not bothering to record his answer, Faith pushed on with a second question.

"Did you have any hobbies growing up, Mr. Baron? Sports? Tinkering with cars?"

Sitting comfortably in a padded folding chair at a long, cloth-covered table centered on a low dais, Zander had been idly drumming the fingers of one hand; Faith's second inquiry stopped the drumming. Zander leaned forward, his right thumb and forefinger going to his right earlobe.

Faith smiled tightly, suppressing the urge to weep.

Brent Baxter hastened to Zander's side, but the actor's upraised hand stopped him from running interference.

"Girls," Zander answered with a smirk. "That was my hobby in high school."

Faith's mouth tightened into a little fist, earning a smug grin from Zander.

"Who gave you your first real kiss?" Faith boldly pressed on, raising her voice over that of the *L.A. Times* reporter poised to ask the next question.

"I think you're a little confused, miss," he told her, a sharp glint in his Atlantic-blue eyes. "When my studio invited you here to discuss *Reunion*, they meant my latest film, not junior high."

Amid laughter, Faith sat, still stubbornly refusing to write or record Zander Baron's responses. Arms crossed over her chest and her left leg hanging stiffly over her right, everything about her posture suggested hostility, even contempt.

Zander studiously avoided looking directly at the dark-eyed beauty in the middle of the third row, the reporter who had aggressively asked the very questions he and his handlers usually avoided. Such questions, harmless in and of themselves, could easily lead a resourceful reporter to secrets Zander wanted to keep.

Most of the reporters, photographers and cameramen sat spellbound in Zander's presence, their only movement that which was required to record his short, vague responses to their questions. The female reporters—all but Faith—gaped at him with an expression he'd become all too familiar with over the past few years.

Hunger.

The rookie scribbler from the *L.A. Times* blushed fiercely every time he glanced at her, and her pink-painted fingertips would flirt with the plunging neckline of her sheer blouse. Margo Bruckner, the veteran entertainment columnist from the *San Francisco Tribune*, unconsciously licked her lips as she listened to his answer to her question about working with his pretty co-star, former *Lifeguards* star Kyla Randall.

The reporter in the third row had a predatory stare of a different nature. She looked as though she wanted to devour him, but not in a carnal way. Her eyes, a peculiar shade of dark golden brown that reminded him of polished topaz, were wide, bright, and perfectly complemented the toasted warmth of her complexion.

The sleeves of her white shirt were rolled up to her elbows. The stubborn tilt of her head matched the scornful sneer she aimed at him beneath the heavy black frames of the glasses perched near the tip of her nose.

Every reporter had received a media kit, which contained everything they needed to know about his latest movie, *Reunion*, and the three-picture deal it trumpeted. The press conference, one of the few he'd ever sat for, was intended to promote his films by providing quotable tidbits to enliven the stories that would be written about him and the film.

The reporter shooting visual daggers at him showed a definite lack of interest in his words. This was troubling, because it meant that she probably already had the answers she wanted. More troubling still was Zander's unshakable sense that she seemed familiar.

Pretty girls came with the territory he inhabited, but he was certain that he would have remembered the reporter if she'd been one of his many—probably too many—conquests. Zander had the urge to get closer to her, to breathe the air around her and discover if he knew her scent or the texture of her flawless skin.

He couldn't keep his gaze from swinging back to her, not even when Brent coughed loudly to redirect his attention to the latest question.

"I'm sorry," Zander said, shaking his head slightly. He scanned the room to figure out who had last spoken. "Could you repeat the question?"

"You've been linked with the female co-stars of each of your films, Mr. Baron," said a male reporter in the back row. "Are you currently seeing anyone?"

Zander zoomed in on the middle of the third row. His cool, disinterested demeanor vanished, replaced by pop-eyed, slack-jawed comprehension. He was seeing someone all right, but not in the way the male reporter meant.

"I'm sorry," Zander said, rising. Unable to look away from Faith, he clumsily backed into his chair, knocking it off the dais. He exited the room through one of its many side doors. With the carriage of a queen, Olivia followed, effectively barring the way of pursuing photographers.

Straightening his maroon silk tie, Brent went to Zander's abandoned microphone and said, "Mr. Baron is finished answering questions for the day. Thank you all for coming out, and we look forward to your articles."

"That was weird," a freelance photographer remarked as he packed up his equipment. "I've never seen Baron freak like that. He's always so cool. He walked out of the Viper Room one night and right into a brawl on the sidewalk. Some guy threw a punch at him, and he blocked it and kept going. It was the coolest thing I ever shot. *Whisper Magazine* won the bidding war for that pic."

A few rows away, Margo Bruckner weighed in on Zander's uncharacteristic display of nerves. "He's seeing someone really ugly or really underage," she speculated. "Or both."

Or he's seeing a ghost, Faith thought, pulling her hemp satchel from beneath her chair. She slung it over her shoulder and worked her way over to her photographer.

"Are you working on a different approach or something?" asked Daiyu Lin, Faith's tattooed, bespectacled photographer. The pair had started at *Personality!* at the same time, almost two years ago. Managing editor Magda Pierson had teamed them, and the result had been so successful that neither Faith nor Daiyu could imagine working with anyone else. Better than anyone, Daiyu recognized that Faith's behavior had been totally out of character.

"Are you from a different planet or something?" Faith asked. She had arrived at the press conference thirty minutes early to pick her seat and was just now getting her first look at her photographer. Daiyu was barely more than five feet tall, but with her straight hair dyed yellow with white tips and styled in a spiky swoop straight out of the pages of a manga comic book, and five-inch platform combat boots, she had added eight inches to her height.

Smiling behind big, black wraparound glasses, Daiyu passed a hand over her spikes. Each sprang right back into place. "You don't like my *Yu-Gi-Oh!* look?"

"It makes you look like a kid," Faith said. With her black leather wristbands, chains dangling from her black cargo pants, and her black bra showing through her white wife-beater, Daiyu looked like the rebellious oddball at an alternative high school, not an award-winning photographer for a national magazine.

"Good," Daiyu said. "That's what I'm going for. I get better access when people think I'm pipsqueak paparazzi. I can't keep losing good shots at premieres to eighth-graders whose moms drive them to the events."

"If you can't beat 'em, scare 'em. I get that," Faith said.

They left the conference room and entered the luxurious lobby of the hotel. Passing the front desk, they saw a woman wrapped head and shoulders in a gauzy yellow scarf. Black Juicy Couture sunglasses covered half her face and gave her the look of a generic space alien. Her right hand cupped her left elbow; her left hand worried a white bandage covering her nose.

"Who do you think that is?" Daiyu whispered to Faith, both slowing to study the woman trying so hard to go unnoticed.

"Could be anybody," Faith said.

Soon after her arrival in Los Angeles, she had been struck by how small most female celebrities were in person. Daiyu was short, but her proportions were average. The woman at the front desk was Daiyu's height and forty pounds lighter. Her loose silk pants looked as if they were wearing her instead of the other way around.

"Who needed a nose job?" Daiyu asked, stopping to fiddle with what looked like a cellphone. Standing close to her, Faith shielded what Daiyu actually was doing—adjusting the lens of her smallest camera to shoot the mystery woman.

"None of them *need* nose jobs," Faith said.

"I'm going to shoot her over your right shoulder, so don't move," Daiyu told her.

"We don't even know who she is," Faith said. "Why waste time on the shot?"

"Better to have the shot and not need it, than to need it and not have it," Daiyu said, clicking rapid-fire images of the woman, who had received her room key and was having her Louis Vuitton steamer and garment bags carried by a tall, handsome bellhop.

Daiyu slipped her camera into her wristband, and she and Faith started for the gilded revolving door. The bright, welcoming sunlight on the opposite side was suddenly blocked by a wave of photographers and reporters, many of whom had just been at the Zander Baron press conference, pouring through the front doors and rushing past the columns in the lobby.

Faith and Daiyu scurried out of their path to avoid being trampled.

"My source says that Whitney Carver checked in ten minutes ago," a female reporter said, talking on a cell-phone as she hurried past Faith and Daiyu. "She had her nose done, maybe boobs, too, but I've got no verification."

The hotel manager appeared, and with his hands raised and arms outstretched, he tried to quiet the invasion. "I won't allow the privacy and security of any of my guests to be compromised by your presence," he announced. "If you are not a guest of the hotel, I must ask you to vacate the premises before I'm forced to call the authorities."

Invited to the hotel to cover the Baron press conference, Faith considered herself and Daiyu guests of the hotel, so they ignored the manager's request. Some of their best scoops had come from just waiting and listening.

"Is Whitney Carver here?" called a voice from the crush of reporters and photographers.

"Miss Carver maintains a residence suite at the hotel," the manager said. "I do not know if she's here at present."

"Can you check your guest list?" someone asked.

"I can assure you I have no guest registered under the name Whitney Carver," the manager said.

Daiyu leaned close to Faith and said, "You know what that means."

"She's registered under a fake name," Faith said.

"Do you want to talk to her?" Daiyu asked. "We got the photo. We might as well get the story, too."

Faith sighed. "I don't have to file the Baron piece right away, so I guess we could ferret out Whitney Carver."

Daiyu threw an arm around Faith's shoulders. "The Dynamic Duo strikes again! Magda will be so proud of us. So how're we gonna do this?"

Gazing at the reporters and photographers still harassing the hotel manager for information, Faith tapped her chin as she considered and then discarded one approach or another. Even though she had a good relationship with the hotel manager, a direct appeal would not work in this instance, not with so many other reporters around.

"We could pretend to be housekeeping and knock on all the doors of the residence suites," Daiyu suggested.

"That's too involved," Faith said. "We have to go simpler."

"Let's hang around outside," Daiyu said. "Her boyfriend will try to sneak in at some point."

"Tons of paparazzi with the same idea will be waiting outside," Faith said. Then she snapped her fingers. "I know. Room service."

"Room service?" Daiyu echoed.

Faith grinned. "We are *so* in."

Daiyu's chains noisily rattled as she bounced around Magda's cluttered office, regaling the managing editor with the tale of how she and Faith obtained an exclusive interview with Whitney Carver.

"We ran that story on celebrity weight loss secrets, and Faith remembered that Whitney Carver is on the Darwin mint tea diet," Daiyu said. "So Faith and I go out back of the hotel, and we wait until one of the kitchen jockeys comes out for a smoke break. Faith tipped him a twenty and the guy sang like a canary. She only had to ask him one question: Which room ordered Darwin tea?" Daiyu clapped her hands as if she were a magician who had just made a coin disappear. "It was that simple. He gave us the room number, we went up and Whitney answered the door herself."

Magda, her matronly figure clad in jeans and a simple white shirt, sat back in her leather office chair. "How did you get her to talk about her surgery?" she asked without removing the pen she was gnawing on.

"I told her that if I was able to find her, it was just a matter of time before one of the vultures in the lobby figured out which room she was in," Faith said, taking a seat in one of the chrome and leather chairs facing Magda's kidney-shaped desk. "I also told her that millions of little girls look up to her, and that if she'd give me thirty seconds—"

"The ol' Faith Wheeler Thirty-Second Interview," Daiyu said proudly.

"—of her time," Faith continued, "I'd write a piece that would give her the chance to explain her surgery before other rags put out whatever scandalous version of the story they had cooked up."

Magda spent a moment giving the pen a serious chewing.

"How's the smoking-cessation program coming?" Faith asked.

"Fine. I'm down to three ballpoints a day." She tossed the pen onto her desk. "I'm impressed, Faith. You're the only scribbler on my staff whose human approach actually works. I'll give you fifty-five lines for our little songbird and her new beak." She looked at Daiyu. "You get a two-page photo spread to accompany the story."

Daiyu raised her fists in triumph. "Thank you kindly, Mags!"

"Don't call me Mags," Magda said, turning to Faith. "What do we have on the Baron piece? Anything good, or was he his usual self?"

"He was usual," Daiyu said, burrowing through Magda's Italian crystal candy dish. "Answered questions without giving real answers. Faith was weird, though."

"No, I wasn't," Faith said defensively. "I got three questions in."

"Weird questions," Daiyu remarked, her mouth stuffed with grape sourballs. "Freaked him out a little bit."

Magda picked up a fresh pen. She used it to give Daiyu's greedy hand a sharp tap, and then popped it into her mouth as though it were a cigarette. "Leave my balls alone," she said.

"Is that a confession?" Daiyu joked.

"Get outta here before I reduce your two pages to a quarter-page vertical banner," Magda threatened.

Daiyu swiped a handful of Magda's "balls" before skipping out of the office. Faith was right on her heels, but Magda stopped her. "Not you, Scoop."

Faith froze in the doorway for a second before returning to her seat.

"You volunteered—actually, *insisted* would be a better word—when I asked for someone to cover the Baron press conference," Magda said. "After Daiyu's report, I gotta ask. Is there something you want to tell me?"

"No," Faith answered, grateful for the wiggle room Magda's phrasing had given her.

Magda slowly unwrapped a yellow sourball and toyed with it. "Okay. But I'm here if there's anything you want to discuss."

"Thanks." Faith shot out of her chair and back into the newsroom. She worked her way through the maze of nondescript cubicles until she reached her own. Taking refuge in her leather swivel chair, she spun around so that her back was to the entryway.

She put on her headphones and pretended to listen to her tape of the Baron press conference so that she wouldn't be disturbed.

Most of the other day staffers had gone. The night crew had arrived, but there wouldn't be much to do until photos and reports came in much later from L.A.'s hot spots. A spirited game of office beach volleyball was going on around Faith, but she politely passed on invitations to participate.

Her mind was still on the Zander Baron press conference, which had been one of the most intense experiences of her reporting career. Of her life.

There were so many unanswered questions about Zander Baron. Where was he from? How old was he? What was his real name? In an Internet age, he had managed to exist as a deliberate unknown, keeping the most basic details about himself totally secret even as his star shone brighter with each of his films. With one film, he'd gone from a nobody to the most popular of somebodies. It was as though he'd been created by his studio specifically to occupy the role of film superstar.

His studio, agent and publicist guarded his privacy ferociously; lawyers seemed to stand at the ready to file suit against anyone, or any organization, that dared print any kind of unauthorized information about him.

His mystique certainly increased the public's interest in him, but his good looks and talent guaranteed that he would not become a one-film wonder.

A multicolored, inflatable beach ball landed on Faith's desk, scattering a few of the Baron photos spread over it. She tossed the ball back and rearranged the photos. Zander Baron's ruggedly handsome face stared back at her from each one, as well as from the magazine covers, newspaper clippings and movie advertisements.

He had changed. He was just as handsome, perhaps more so since he was older. He was leaner, looked wiser, and somehow seemed sadder. But Faith was unmoved by the sadness, refusing to spend a shred of sympathy on a man who had broken her heart and scattered the pieces.

She removed her headphones and shoved them into the deep drawer on the right side of her desk. Glancing around furtively, she drew an old yearbook from her satchel. She set the book on her lap, and it fell open to a page she had visited frequently over the past decade.

She looked at the yearbook photo, and then at an eight-by-ten glossy of a movie still from *Reunion.* Zander had changed all right, but not enough to deceive her. His hair had been lightened from coal black to sun-burnished wheat; his teeth were straighter and whiter. He was taller because of improved posture. But he had done nothing to alter the stormy blue eyes that still made her heart beat harder and faster every time she looked into them.

With a frustrated sigh, Faith slammed the yearbook shut and returned it to her satchel. She sat back in her chair, slowly spinning from left to right. The volleyball game was growing noisier and more boisterous, but Faith scarcely noticed. Her mind was three thousand miles and ten years away.

Faith sat in a corner booth, her geometry textbook and a spiral-bound notebook opened, but neglected, on the table. Calculating the area of a trapezoid would have been much easier if her full attention had been on her homework. Instead, Faith kept stealing glances into the kitchen, hoping to see Alexander Brannon standing at the stainless-steel sink, his apron tied around his hips and a commercial sprayer clutched in his hand.

Alex wore the same dingy whites as the other two kitchen workers, but he filled them out much differently. His nineteen-year-old body was trim, with a lean, sinewy toughness, like an alley cat in human form. Black hair, which he kept rather too long, framed his face. His complexion was unbelievably perfect, probably from the daily steam facials he got from washing plates smeared with runny egg, ketchup, mustard and the various other leavings of the residents of Dorothy, West Virginia. Faith didn't know what his teeth were like because she'd never seen him smile.

He shifted his gaze from the sink full of dishes and winked at Faith. Exhilaration jolted through her, and she smiled into the pages of her book.

Even though Alex had graduated from Lincoln the previous summer, he and Faith had struck up a friendship in her junior year. On her way home from ballet class, her car, an old Bronco II her father had purchased from one of his employees at the mine, had broken down in front of Red Irv's. She'd gone into the diner to call AAA, but Red had sent Alex out to take a look at the car. He'd used a pencil to choke the carburetor and the car had started right up. Alex had refused to take money from her, and had only accepted a ride home from work because Faith had made such a scene outside the diner insisting on repaying him in some way.

For Alex, home was a rusting, unkempt single-wide trailer at the base of Kayford mountain, the very mountain Faith's father's company mined.

Stark and bleak, the neighborhood was bereft of the touches that made Faith's cul-de-sac on the other side of town so inviting. There were no nylon banners hanging like family crests advertising the residents' hobbies, new births or favorite sports teams. A big metal tub splotchy with rust patches served as a swimming pool, and no professional landscapers had ever touched any of the tiny lawns, which were overrun with dandelions, crab grass and clover.

A scrawny orange tabby with bald patches was licking the inner rim of an empty sauerkraut can on the patch of yellowing lawn in front of the Brannon home. The old Harley that Alex usually rode around town was up on blocks, a pan beneath it filled with a thick black substance Faith assumed to be oil.

Alex was about to thank her for the ride when angry voices came from inside the trailer. A man and a woman were arguing violently, but it ended abruptly with her shriek of rage, pain—or perhaps a combination of the two.

"I don't know why you make me so mad!" the male voice wailed in his Appalachia-flavored accent. His voice softening, he said, "Let me get you some ice, baby girl."

"You ain't got no right to be takin' my smokes, Orrin," the female voice sobbed, the notes climbing higher. "Jimmy Earl, gimme that carton! I didn't have to spend one red cent on 'em!"

Silence. When the man responded, his tone was low, menacing. "Jimmy Earl Latcherie don't give nobody nothin' for nothin'. You paid him somehow. You sure as hell better tell me now before I hear it from somebody down the mine."

She continued sobbing, the sound growing more piteous as it progressed.

"Tell me!" The violent command startled Faith and Alex. It was accompanied by a sharp smack, followed by the crash of something made of glass, and then a heavy thud.

Alex threw open the car door and leaped out, scaring away the hungry tabby. He drew up short, Faith right behind him, when the screech of the woman's garbled curse words, a sufficient sign of life, hit his ears. His shoulders slumped, he hung his hands loosely on his hips, his face turned up to the darkening sky. His chest rose and fell with his deep breaths.

Faith lightly rested a hand on his forearm, silently offering what comfort she could.

"You don't belong here," he said quietly, facing her but not quite meeting her eyes.

"Neither do you," she replied.

"You'd better go," he said. "They don't always keep their arguments behind closed doors. They'll both be looking for a piece of me once they finish with each other."

"I don't want to leave you." Her grip tightened on his arm.

"I can take care of myself."

Faith eyed the raised scar tissue curving an inch away from the outer corner of his right eye. She also scoped out the big burn scar on his left forearm, a souvenir of a wound she knew had not been sustained at the diner, according to town gossip.

Seeming to read her mind, he said, "I'll be fine."

"If I came in with you, maybe he would calm—"

He took her by the shoulders and gave her a little push toward her car. "If you want to help, just get in your car and go home. Please."

His tone was firm, but his eyes . . . his troubled, lovely eyes telegraphed his need. But she had no choice but to do as he asked. She had moved through the rest of that night and most of the following day convinced that he would never speak to her again.

So she was delighted and surprised the following Saturday when he cornered her in the regional history section of the Whitesville Public Library.

"I want to talk to you," he said in a whisper. Even though they were alone in the research section of the small library, he kept his voice low, as if fearing the librarian would kick him out if she found him there.

"Okay," she'd managed over the piece of her heart plugging her throat. Either he had been off work or he'd skipped the diner to come find her. And he'd dressed for the occasion in clean but very faded jeans, work boots and a blue chambray shirt with the sleeves rolled up. He might have even passed a comb through his long black hair, but six miles on his Harley had undone its work. Faith liked him windblown, but she found herself wanting to reach up and brush the hair from his forehead to better see his eyes.

"What d'ya got there?" He nodded at the three books in her arms.

One by one, she displayed them for him and read the titles aloud. "*Celebrating Freedom: African-Americans in West Virginia 1865 to the Present, African-Americans in Raleigh County,* and *A Timeline of West Virginia: The Black Experience.* The last one is kind of old."

"Looks new to me," Alex said, tapping the unbroken binder.

"I'll bet I'm the first person to ever check it out."

"Are you working on a school project?"

"Term paper. For Mr. Taylor's class."

"What's your paper on?"

"The role African-Americans played in West Virginia's coal mining history," she answered.

"Seems like your dad would be the best resource for that information," Alex remarked.

"My father knows the history of the mining company he bought and the business of running it, but he doesn't know all that much about the role African-Americans played in one of this state's vital industries," she said. "Mr. Taylor seemed really interested in my thesis. He says no one has ever covered this topic in his class." She sighed and glanced at her books. "I can see why. There's not a whole lot of information in the library system here. My parents are taking me to Chicago next weekend to do some research at the Newberry Library. It's right near Washington Square Park and Michigan Avenue, so we're going to make a weekend of it. Mom wants to take me shopping on the Magnificent Mile, and Dad wants to bore me senseless with a tour of the historic architecture of the houses surrounding the park."

"Sounds nice, actually," Alex said wistfully.

"Have you ever been to Chicago?"

He lowered his eyes and shook his head. "Farthest I've ever been from Dorothy is Roanoke. Went there after graduation last year to see about a job as a rigger. Decided not to take it. Found a reason to stay in Dorothy for a little while longer," he said, raising his eyes and meeting hers.

Even though he hadn't given his specific reason, Faith blushed deeply, her skin warming in a new and exciting way.

Alex changed the subject. "Taylor is such a hard-ass. Is he still assigning four term papers a year to his honors American history class?"

"How do you know that?" Faith leaned against one of the bookstacks. "And how did you know I was in honors American history?"

"You've been in honors everything since you started at Lincoln," he said. "And I had Taylor for honors history my junior year."

Her eyebrows shot up. "You were in an honors class?"

The left side of his mouth lifted in an adorably shy half smile. "Don't sound so surprised. I'm not stupid, you know."

"I never thought you were stupid," she said hastily. "What have I ever said or done to make you think that—"

"You're right, and I'm sorry," he said. She started out of the aisle, but he took her by the arm and spun her back. "I'm sorry, Faith. Really. Would you hear me out? That's kind of why I came here to talk to you."

She stared at the books in her arms, afraid to look at him for fear her expression would reveal she'd do just about anything he asked. "So what did you want to talk about?"

"That thing last week, what happened at my house," he began. He shoved his hands deep in his pockets and hunched his broad shoulders.

Faith smiled at the uncharacteristic display of nerves.

"That's not me," he said. "I'm not like that. I don't . . . I would never do that."

"I know." She moved closer so he wouldn't have to speak above a whisper.

Straightening his shoulders, he blew out a long breath of air. He raked his fingers through his hair, and then he did something Faith had never seen. He smiled.

Faith's heart began to beat so fast it seemed to whir against her ribcage.

It seemed to stop entirely with Alex's next words.

"Can I give you a ride home?" he asked.

"Sure," she blurted. "Yes. Absolutely." She threw her thumb in the direction of the table where her other books, notebook and backpack were spread out. "I have a little more work to do here, but it won't take long for me to finish up."

He followed her to her work station and took the chair opposite hers. "How did you know my car is in the shop?" she asked him.

"I figured your dad wouldn't waste time getting that busted carburetor fixed," he said. "And I do a little work at Brody's Auto Body from time to time. Your Bronco was on his work roster this morning."

"I take ballet lessons across the street from Brody's," Faith said. "I've never seen you there."

Resting his left elbow on the table, he propped his chin in his left hand. "I'm usually in the service bay under a car. You're usually upstairs at Miss Lorraine's, dancing in front of that big mirror."

Another blazing blush baked her cheeks as she stared at him. *He watches me dance.* She might not have seen him, but clearly he'd seen her.

Knowing that she'd never be able to decipher her handwriting later, she raced through the last chapter of the book she'd been working from and put her notes away. With her backpack zipped up tight and strapped to her shoulders, she put on Alex's spare helmet and mounted his Harley behind him. Eager yet hesitant, she slipped her arms around his waist.

Alex started the bike, and the roar of the engine scared Faith into holding him as tight as she could. Framing him between her legs, she pressed her body into his. Alex sat with the bike growling beneath them for a long moment before he revved the Harley and took off down Coal River Road.

"Would you like to grab some dinner?" he asked, pitching his voice below the roar of the engine so she could hear him without yelling.

To cover her shock at his offer, she pressed her cheek to his shoulder. "Sure," she finally said, managing to sound indifferent.

"We don't have to," he said, having had time to reconsider his hasty invitation.

"I'd like to," she said. "Really."

"It's Saturday. You probably already have plans to do something fun."

"My father always tells me that there's more to life than fun. Where would you like to go?"

"I haven't thought that far ahead."

They rode another mile or so in silence before he had to stop for a red light. "Do you want to sit down or get take-out?" she asked.

"What?" He was suddenly very warm, and very aware of her body pressing into his.

"Do you want to go to a drive-thru or sit down in a restaurant?"

"I don't care." He was surprisingly nervous. "I don't know."

"I know a place," she said after they had gone another mile or so cruising toward Booger Hollow. "One complaint and I'll pop you in the windpipe."

She directed him along winding side streets and a sparsely populated main road until they came to a tall laurel hedge bordering the south side of a grocery store parking lot. Zander parked, and they dismounted. Faith's legs were quivery from the long ride as they passed through a narrow opening worn in the closely trimmed hedge. The hedge had concealed a tiny building decorated with neon paint and bright lights forming the name Calliope Grill.

"So this is what became of Pee Wee's Playhouse," Alex cracked as they approached the small eatery.

Two naked mannequins in the foyer of the building met Alex when he opened the outer glass door for Faith. The mannequins were spray-painted in neon shades of kiwi, canary, tangerine and coral and draped from head to toe with dark-green variegated silk ivy.

"Say hi to Hillary and Laura," Faith said, holding the inner door for Alex.

"Hello, gorgeous!" called a man standing between the long mirrored chrome grill and the wide pink laminate counter. The grill chef wore a white T-shirt, a pink-speckled apron and a sky blue nylon hairnet. Faith returned his greeting as she led Alex to the counter.

"Who's this?" the cook asked, smiling widely.

"Alexander Brannon," Faith said. "Alex, this is Fennel."

"Fen, to my friends." He wiped his hands on a chartreuse towel. "Good to meet you." He extended his hand, at the same time bouncing his eyebrows and bobbing his head toward Alex while mouthing *Boyfriend?*

"Stop it," Faith warned sweetly.

Alex stared up at child-sized mannequins dangling by their ankles from the ivy-covered rafters.

"Is Dill on tonight?" asked Faith.

"Like you wouldn't believe," said Fen. "You want a table?"

She nodded.

A full-figured woman in a strapless flesh-colored cat-suit guided them through a narrow corridor and into a dining room that was only slightly bigger than the counter area. The walls, floor and ceiling were painted in garish Crayola shades of red, blue, yellow, green, orange and purple.

Four pens, two pencils and six crayons were stuck in the hostess's unruly nest of upswept hair. She seated them at a silver Formica table that had two red and two peach vinyl chairs. None of the other tables and chairs in the room matched, either.

"Dill decorated the place," Faith said as Alex pulled her chair. "He says he's a student of the Helen Keller School of Interior Design."

Alex took his weathered leather jacket and her light poplin coat and hung them over the back of an empty chair. "How did you find this place?"

"I was driving around one weekend, right after I'd had a big fight with my dad over some stupid thing at school. I got lost. I came in here to ask for directions. I got found, in a way." She waved at a tall thin man dressed in black. He was carrying a big round tray of food to a table of four. "This place is as out of place in Raleigh County as we are."

"Faith!" the man squealed. He set the tray on his patrons' table and skipped over to Faith and Alex. The abandoned diners served themselves, apparently accustomed to such indifferent service.

"Where have you been keeping yourself, sugar lump?" crooned the man in black. "Oh, I just love what you've done to your hair." He energetically ran his fingers through Faith's curls and leaned over to take a deep whiff of them. "Did you rinse in tea rose or spring rain? I can't tell. I've been here since dawn and I can't smell a doggone thing except gorgonzola." He paused to give Alex a wolfish grin.

"Honey lamb, you look better and better every time I see you," he waxed merrily, cupping Faith's chin in his slim hand. "You've lost a pound or two, yes? No? Angel, I'd die to have your bone structure."

He sucked in his cheeks. With a grand flourish of his hands and a toss of his head, he did a Gloria Swanson-*Sunset Boulevard* impersonation that made Alex recoil. "Maybe I'll get implants." With one hand on his hip and one on the table, the man in black turned his back to Faith and eyed Alex. "And you are ... ?"

"Dill," Faith said, easing him around to face both her and Alex, "this is Alex."

"Alex?" Dill's tone was deceptively friendly. "Just Alex?"

Alex became increasingly uncomfortable under the judgmental glare of Dill's grasshopper-green eyes. After a terribly long time, Dill smiled. Alex relaxed. Dill turned his scrutinizing gaze to Faith and said, "Sweetiekins, he is not your type."

Alex's jaw dropped.

"Dill, behave," Faith said. "Alex is just a guy from town. We came here for a nice dinner. That's all."

"I'll return for your orders," Dill said with a dismissive roll of his eyes. Squaring his narrow shoulders, he switched into the kitchen.

"'Just a guy from town?'" Alex asked.

Faith cleared her throat and paid unusual attention to unfolding and refolding her napkin.

Alex stuck his face behind a menu. Plastic ants formed a meandering line from the top of one page to the bottom of the next. "You could have said former schoolmate. Or friend. And what did Dill mean by saying that I'm not your type?" He demanded indignantly.

"Dill doesn't know what my type is. I'm not sure myself."

"Did I do something to offend him?" He closed the menu and returned it to the Statue of Liberty holder between the Washington Monument salt and pepper shakers.

"He might be jealous."

"Because I'm here with you?" The thought gave him an unexpected twinge of pride.

"Because I'm here with *you*."

"Dill is gay?"

"You couldn't tell? He's very open about it. I think all the men here are, except Fennel. He hasn't decided what he is yet. Fen was married for a few years, but he's dating a UPS deliveryman now. I'm not sure about Pepper, either."

"Who's Pepper?"

"She's the one in the catsuit. She owns the place with Dill and Fen. She's always here. I don't think she has time to date anybody, male or female. Does their sexual orientation bother you?"

The diamonds sparkling in her eyes almost made him forget her question. "Not at all," he answered. "I'm very secure about my sexuality."

Faith felt anything but secure as she gazed into his eyes. "You have sexuality?"

"That remains to be seen," said Dill. He had reappeared with a pad and pencil to take their orders.

"I'll have the quiche special," Faith said. "Without the attitude, please."

"That comes with an arugula and radicchio side salad," said Dill. "Ranch, thousand island, bleu cheese—"

"The basil vinaigrette, please," said Faith.

"To drink?"

"Water."

"Colonial or bottled?"

"Bottled," Faith said.

"Excuse me, but what's colonial water?" Alex asked.

"Tap," said Dill.

Alex patted the wad of cash in his pocket. His weekly pay would be a lot lighter after treating Faith to dinner, and there would be serious fallout to deal with when he turned the lighter pay over to his father. Alex pushed all that to the back of his mind and placed his order, determined to enjoy a normal date with Faith. "Buckwheat pancakes with home fries, scrambled eggs, a side of turkey bacon and a large orange juice, please."

Dill frowned at him.

"And a bran muffin," Alex added.

Dill continued staring.

"That's all," Alex said uncomfortably. "Thanks."

Dill grabbed his head as if he were in pain. "You're dinner, Faith. Just Alex is breakfast. Meals should never mix!"

"How dare you discriminate against intermeal eating, Dill," Pepper chastised as she glided by to seat a group of six.

Dill stopped at Pepper's table on his way to the kitchen. "Mark my words," he said loudly, commanding the attention of every diner. "This relationship will never work." He winked and disappeared into the kitchen.

Alex leaned across the table. "Was that for me or for you?"

Alex's bike heralded their arrival at the Wheelers' five-bedroom house. By the time he had cut the engine in Faith's wide, circular driveway, Emiline Wheeler was rushing outside. Simple introductions were made; Alex was polite and well-spoken. Faith knew her mother well enough to know that behind her forced smile resided a thousand versions of the same question: What the hell was she doing on the back of Alexander Brannon's motorcycle?

The longest dinner of her life had followed.

"Are you crazy?" Justus Wheeler had asked, so angry that he hadn't touched a bite of his favorite dinner, grilled beef tenderloin with asparagus and new potatoes. "Or are you just determined to embarrass me?"

"Jefferson called for you while you were gone," her mother had cheerily informed her in an attempt to diffuse the argument brewing between daughter and father. "He wants you to join him at the club for tennis after services on Sunday. You like Jefferson, don't you? He's such a nice boy."

"He's the only other black kid in my class," Faith had muttered sullenly. "Everyone is always trying to push us together."

"That Brannon boy has no future!" her father had shouted.

Matching his volume, Faith had fired back with, "He gave me a ride home, that's all. He didn't ask me to marry him!"

"Oh, my God," her mother gasped. "Faith, you're far too young and you have far too much ahead of you to be thinking about marriage." She brightened, looking from her husband to her daughter. "You know what would be a good idea?" With father and daughter glaring at each other and ignoring her, she answered her own question. "I think it would be a good idea for us to drive out to Charles Town for a visit. We could take a look at the dance school there, and if you like it, Faith, maybe we can visit the high schools and see which one you like best."

Faith shot up in her chair. "I'm not switching schools in the middle of a semester! Why on earth would you want me to live in Charles—" Her mother's logic hit her then. "If you want to send me somewhere with more black people, send me someplace cool, like Harlem or New Orleans. I'm not moving to Charles Town!"

"You'll live where we tell you to live, little girl!" her father bellowed.

"You want me to live in Charles Town, Daddy?" she asked, her eyes shimmering with tears.

"Hell, no!" Mr. Wheeler yelled, and then he turned on his wife. "Emiline, have you lost *your* mind?" he asked, forcing his voice lower. "I am not sending my seventeen-year-old daughter three hundred miles from home to go to school in the Eastern Panhandle."

"Well, we have to do something," Mrs. Wheeler whispered fiercely. "Before—"

"Before what, Mama?" Faith asked. Her tears evaporated in the heat of her growing anger. "Exactly what do you think I plan to do with Alex Brannon?"

Mr. Wheeler threw up his hands and slumped back in his maple Windsor chair. "She's calling him Alex. Is that your pet name for him?"

"It's his *name* name, Daddy!" Faith wailed.

"Faith, honey," Mrs. Wheeler started, her voice quivering. "You're known by the company you keep, and Alexander Brannon isn't the sort of person you should be associating with."

"You're such a snob," Faith mumbled.

Mr. Wheeler slammed his hands on the table, forcing plates, glasses and cutlery to jump. "Don't you disrespect your mother! We haven't raised you to call your mother out of her name, or to run around with the town hoodlum!"

"He's not a hoodlum!" Faith shouted, showing that she had inherited his quickness to anger along with his rich brown skin and expressive eyes. "You don't know him! You've never even talked to him!"

"I don't have to talk to him to know that I don't want his ass fooling around with my daughter!"

"You're so unfair, Daddy," Faith wailed, her tears reappearing. "You, of all people, should know how hard it is to live in a place where people cast you as a stereo-type."

Mr. Wheeler eyed her suspiciously, caught off guard by her savvy observation. "Don't you dare try to compare my experience as a hard-working black business owner in this town with that trailer trash Alexander Brannon. Our people have lived and worked here for generations, since John Brown's raid. That Brannon kid is one generation out of the hills, and he's gonna end up a drunk like his daddy or crazy like his mama. You are strictly forbidden to see him again."

"Daddy!"

"It's for your own good, baby," Mrs. Wheeler said in the placating tone Faith hated most.

"It's for *your* reputation," Faith said derisively.

She and her father stood at the same time, Mr. Wheeler knocking his chair over in the process. "Go to your room!" he ordered, his words overlapping Faith's, "I'm going to my room!"

Just as she had when she was eight and had been sent to her room for farting at the dinner table, she stomped out of the dining room, through the living room, into the foyer, up the carpeted stairs, and into her pretty pastel-hued bedroom. She paced angrily, like a panther in a cage far too small.

How dare her parents tell her with whom she could be friends! How dare they forbid her to do anything! Faith was a good student, she was popular, she never broke curfew, and no matter what, she never embarrassed her parents. As the wealthiest family in town and one of only a few black families in Dorothy, the Wheelers were always careful to adhere to a higher standard of behavior. It wasn't enough to be better; they strived to be the very best.

Faith loved and respected her parents, but their order completely fled her mind the next time she saw Alex—almost a week after her blow-up with them. She had been in ballet class in the studio above McGill's Pharmacy. Executing a textbook arabesque penchée, she caught sight of Alex standing just inside the garage at Brody's Auto Body. He was wearing a bluish-gray striped jump-suit with Brody's embroidered across the chest. Automotive grime smudged his chin and the backs of his hands. He appeared to be busy patching the inside of a tire, but he wasn't watching his work. His face was tilted upward, and his eyes were on Faith.

His gaze was so intense, Faith broke her perfect position. It had been impossible for her to concentrate on class after that. Afterward, she hurried downstairs and out of the building, hoping to run into Alex. And she had, literally; he'd been waiting for her.

Without a word, Alex had taken her hand and pulled her into the shadowy gap between McGill's and the Pearl S. Buck Community Book Exchange. That brief, secret meeting was the first of many between them, and they had managed to keep their innocent contact under wraps until the Thanksgiving Day football game between Dorothy and its archrival, Marsh Spring High.

Everything changed that day because that was the day they gave each other everything that mattered.

Faith stuck her foot out to stop the turning of her chair. She'd seen Zander Baron's first movie, *Burn*, while on a blind date with some guy Daiyu had set her up with, and the poor fellow had suffered the misfortune of being in her company the night she rediscovered the boy she had loved and lost in high school.

Alexander Brannon, the bad boy of Raleigh County, was alive and thriving in Hollywood as Zander Baron, movie star.

It had taken a few days and every skill she possessed as a reporter, but she now had no real doubt that Alex and Zander were the same person. The absence of any verifiable personal information about Zander Baron only confirmed her suspicion.

A part of her had never gotten over the loss of Alex, and that part had roared to life with a vengeance after she'd seen *Burn*. The movie's poster featured cars and weaponry rather than the characters in the film, and the studio had released no advance stills to the press. Since Alex was an unknown, the movie had been given a "soft" opening, showing in only a few theaters in New York and Los Angeles prior to its nationwide release on New Year's Day.

He'd shaved his head for his role, but the absence of his dark, silky hair had only drawn more attention to his eyes. His eyes were the feature she'd studied most, had learned best. In that darkened theater, she realized that her fondest wish had come true: Alex was still alive.

Maybe she had known it all along. Perhaps that was why she had never fallen in love or experienced a serious relationship. For ten years, she'd believed her heart had been lost along with Alexander Brannon.

Now she knew better. Zander Baron had had it all along.

Two teams of her co-workers were chasing the inflatable beach ball from cubicle to cubicle, and as the playful chaos around her intensified, Faith focused more sharply on the materials covering her desk.

The box-office success of Zander's first film had been phenomenal; *Burn*'s box-office receipts had set a record for a New Year's Day opening. The film continued to hold the number-one spot two months later. Zander had two new movies set for release—*Reunion* in the next month and *Miss Wright*, which was slated for June. *Burn*'s success had convinced studios that Zander Baron was the answer to James Dean, someone whose star had begun to burn well before most of his work had even caught the public's notice.

Zander was poised on the verge of superstardom, and the entertainment media hungered to turn him into their latest hot commodity. In just the past eight weeks, he had been on the covers of *People*, *Rolling Stone*, *Entertainment Weekly*, the *National Enquirer*, the *Star* and *OK!*

Photos were pretty much all the magazines had to offer. Team Baxter had done a very good job of doling out small doses of information to widespread sources. Faith admired Olivia Baxter's cunning. Zander had been interviewed by regional newspapers and magazines well before the release of *Burn*. Major media had picked up those stories and regurgitated the information, lending it credibility.

Faith knew it was all false.

She was sitting on a scoop that could send her career into orbit. If she told the world the truth about Zander Baron, she could write her own ticket. She had no desire to be the next great gossip maven, but a scoop was a scoop, whether it uncovered an actor or a political scandal. Writing a story that no one else had would give Faith the leverage and reputation she needed to get a job with a serious news agency, reporting stories that actually meant something.

All she had to do was kill Zander Baron just as he had killed Alexander Brannon.

CHAPTER 2

Olivia worked from her million-dollar Bel Air mansion, having turned the room with the best view into her office. From her platinum bob and steel grey eyes to her snow white pantsuit, Olivia favored the color palette of the proverbial ice queen. Her thick carpeting, which was the pale, barely blue hue of a glacier, muffled the sound of Zander's heavy black motorcycle boots.

Sitting in an office chair ergonomically designed to coddle her lower back and ease her occasional sciatic pain, Olivia watched Zander, only her eyes following his slow, measured steps.

"You know, Zander, you really haven't changed that much since we first met," she began in the clipped, patrician accent that exposed her boarding school background. "You still have that discomforting energy about you, that sense of a caged tiger yearning for escape."

He forced himself to stand still, choosing a place near the floor-to-ceiling window. Staring at the picturesque Santa Monica mountains, Zander tried, unsuccessfully, to quiet the restlessness that had plagued him since the press conference the day before.

"You know her."

It wasn't a question, so Zander didn't answer. Keeping one hand in the pocket of his black leather motorcycle jacket, he raked the other through his hair. It had been Olivia's idea to strip it of some of its color. She'd been convinced—correctly—that lighter hair would make his eyes appear more intense. Five years later, he still wasn't quite used to it. There were times when he caught his reflection and saw a stranger.

After yesterday's press conference, he had accepted the fact that he *was* looking at a stranger every time he caught his reflection.

"She certainly seemed to know you, Zander," Olivia said.

She hadn't raised her voice above her usual conversational purr, but Zander knew that she was worried. Concerned, rather. In the years she'd represented him, Olivia had never worried about anything.

"A crisis is merely a problem for which one is ill-prepared," she'd told him early on in their relationship. "I'm always prepared."

Zander doubted that Olivia was prepared for the appearance of Faith Wheeler. He certainly hadn't been, although he thought he had played off his initial reaction very well. His carefully cultivated image would have taken a dramatic hit if he had passed out from the shock of seeing her.

Even thinking about her now, his knees weakened, and he might have actually slumped against the windowed wall if he hadn't caught himself.

The past decade had been more than kind to Faith. She still had the silky skin that always put him in the mind of hot cocoa with just the right amount of marshmallows melted into it. He hadn't recognized her voice at first. The shrill, native cry of the story-hunting reporter was nothing like the voice he would hear in his deepest, most vivid dreams over the years.

If warm honey had a voice, it would sound like Faith.

"She writes for *Personality!*," Olivia said, pulling him from his reverie. "She took the job there close to two years ago after spending the prerequisite time at daily papers in New York City and Chicago and stringing for a few rags in San Francisco and Los Angeles. She graduated from New York University with a master's degree in journalism, and although she comes from money, she earned a partial scholarship and paid for her schooling herself."

Her information had no effect on Zander. So far, Olivia hadn't told him anything he hadn't already Googled himself.

"Her father, Justus Wheeler, is something of a self-made millionaire, having purchased the Duchess Waverly Coal Company in Dorothy, West Virginia, with part of the fortune he made after Proctor & Gamble bought the patents for two household detergents he developed. Justus renamed the mine for his wife, calling it the Lady Emiline Coal Corporation."

The admiration with which Olivia recited Mr. Wheeler's accomplishments increased when she spoke about his wife. "Emiline Wheeler was a stay-at-home mother who now fills her days with volunteer work at a hospital and an assisted-living facility in Raleigh County. She also chaired a committee that supported the Mine

Improvement and New Emergency Response Act a few years ago. I'll bet that made for a few chilly nights in the Wheeler bedroom."

Zander threw one of his characteristic dark looks at Olivia, who seemed proud of the reaction she had elicited.

"You knew her. Before?"

"Before . . ." Zander repeated. "Before" was Olivia's name for the time preceding their meeting, and it encompassed the entirety of his true history, not the one Olivia had manufactured.

"Yes," he said, "I knew her before."

Neither Zander nor Olivia reacted when her door flew open and Brent rushed in. Where Zander and Olivia were two versions of the same type of reserved composure, Brent was all color, hurry and noise.

Olivia's preference for wintry pastels had not been passed on to her son. Perhaps in response to her aversion to color, he always wrapped himself in it from head to toe. Impeccably dressed in the custom-tailored clothing he favored, he looked like a macaw on an ice floe when he stepped into his mother's office.

"I thought you were going to wait for me," Brent said to his mother, taking a seat in one of two white leather chairs facing her desk.

Zander pinched back a smile as he watched Olivia's pale eyes scan her only child.

Brent's short hair with its razor-sharp right-side part was a few shades darker than Olivia's, but still lighter than it would have been if he spent less time on his surfboard and more in a temperature-controlled office like his mother's. Everything about Brent was Southern California—his sun-bleached hair, perfect teeth and the surfer physique he kept dressed in every style from avant-garde Japanese couture to classically tailored Armani and Calvin Klein. Brent had the looks and charm to succeed in Hollywood as an actor. But he didn't have the heart. In fact, he had too much, although it had taken Zander a while to realize it.

He had been in the middle of a session with a dialect coach when Brent, freshly graduated from the University of Southern California, had bounded into his mother's study.

"Another one of Olivia's strays?" he had asked the coach in a tone that had made Zander self-conscious about his worn-out work boots and the crescents of auto grease that seemed permanently imbedded under his nails. "I hope this one is housebroken," Brent had added.

Zander had approached him, and perfectly mimicking his coach's Australian accent, he said, "You must be Ms. Baxter's pampered, pedigreed poodle of a son."

Weeks of traded insults eventually formed the foundation of a fast friendship. Brent had come to respect Zander's talent, particularly his chameleon-like ability to fully inhabit his characters, becoming them so convincingly that even veteran actors with whom he worked were impressed. And Zander had come to admire Brent's determination to carve a niche of his own in Hollywood rather than coast on the reputation his mother had spent most of his life building. He was his mother's equal when it came to business, which was perhaps why he opted to call her by her first name in all business matters.

Exceptional business acumen was all the mother and son had in common. They were as different in personality and dress as a spark is from a snowflake.

Brent's light jacket was as red as fresh arterial blood, and Zander remembered Brent's joy at its arrival from Japan, where artisans had hand spun the cashmere thread used to make the fabric. His black collared shirt was vintage GAP and his resin-rinsed blue jeans were Marithé+Girbaud. His shoes, though, were the conversation piece, and by the way he slowly set his right ankle on his left knee, Zander knew that Brent was waiting for someone to notice them.

Olivia did the honors. "Son," she began evenly, "did you skin Bart Simpson to have those shoes made?"

"That's an awful thing to say, Olivia," Brent chuckled.

Zander thought Olivia's question was fair. Brent's latest kicks looked like they had been cobbled by a master but dyed by Dr. Seuss. Most of the upper was dark mustard-yellow leather; the outer side of the vamp was blue and the inner side was the same bright bloody red as his jacket.

"Italians," Olivia sighed, shaking her head.

"So how are we going to handle Faith Wheeler?" Brent asked, turning their attention from his wardrobe to business.

Zander turned his attention to mother and son. "What do you mean, 'handle?' " he asked. "You sound like you're planning to put a hit out on her."

"I hope it won't come to that, but I certainly can't rule it out," Olivia said blithely, slowly rising from her chair. "With one *Personality!* headline, that pretty little minx could undo an image it took me years to craft and destroy a product perched on the edge of superstardom. I won't have it all ruined because of some reporter trying to make a name for herself."

"Faith isn't like that," Zander said.

"So you *do* know her," Brent remarked. "Mom pulled her bio. What else can you tell us about her?"

It had been years since Zander last felt the urge to flee an uncomfortable situation, but the old instinct flared as he contemplated the best way to answer Brent's question. If he would at all.

Zander absently switched places with Olivia, moving closer to her desk while she went to the bar near the office door. He let the majestic sight of the mountains carry him to another one in another time, a dying mountain overlooking a terminal town on the opposite side of the country.

Marsh Spring really didn't have a chance, not with quarterback Rafe Hatchett at the helm for Dorothy. As if playing in the shadow of Kayford Mountain didn't make the Marsh Spring Cardinals feel small enough, with a full quarter left to play, the Lincoln Black Bears of Dorothy led them by twenty-four points. Ordinarily, Black Bears coach Hiram Benton would not have run up the score, but the annual Thanksgiving Day game between Lincoln and archrival Marsh Spring was one of the few games that drew scouts from major collegiate football programs.

Rafe was having a good season, and a good "Turkey Bowl" performance was sure to earn him a four-year ticket out of Dorothy.

From the far end of the uppermost bleacher bench, Alex watched the game. Even though most of the town had turned out for it, Alex still managed to isolate himself. He was the only spectator dressed in black instead of Lincoln's gold and blue on the sunny but chilly November morning.

His shoulders hunched against the cold in his worn and scarred motorcycle jacket, he rested his elbows on his knees. The smoke from the Marlboro pinched between his thumb and forefinger curled upward, mingling with his condensed breath to shroud his head and shoulders. His right knee bounced as if he were apprehensive over the outcome of the game.

Alex could not have cared less about the game. He'd come to watch Faith.

She seemed immune to the frigid air blowing off the mountain, although in deference to it, she and her cheermates were outfitted in their winter uniforms—fitted, long-sleeved jerseys in Dorothy's colors of gold and blue—and blue skirts trimmed in gold with white spanky pants underneath.

Faith wasn't head cheerleader, but she certainly stood out most. Her ballet training softened the stiffness of some of the signature cheerleading moves. A little punch of a shoulder when she raised her arms for the "V, V-I-C" half of the Victory cheer, followed by a saucy shift of a hip when she twirled into the V-I-C-T-O-R-Y part set her performance apart from the more robotic movement of her fellows. Even her tumbling moves were as elegant as they were powerful, and Alex wanted to applaud along with everyone else after she completed a roundoff-back-handspring-back tuck tumbling pass that was so polished, even Marsh Spring fans cheered.

She bounded back to the cheerleaders' bench afterward, her smile warming the chilly Thanksgiving Day.

Alex had no idea what was happening on the field, but he could have provided a detailed play-by-play of Faith's every smile, laugh, shiver and wave. The other cheerleaders had an eerie sameness—blue eyes, strawberries-and-cream complexions, and blonde or light brown hair pulled into severe ponytails adorned with blue and gold ribbon curls.

Faith was the one true individual among them, her fuller figure and distinctive hair setting her apart. The cheerleaders sat on their bench with their backs to the bleachers, and it was impossible for an onlooker's eyes not to pause at the head of spiral curls in the middle of the bench. Untethered by satin ribbons, Faith's curls bounced with her laughter and danced in the cold breeze. The ponytails on the other girls looked like dead things compared to the liveliness of Faith's curls, which caught the sunlight and gleamed in a spectrum of browns ranging from dark gold to sienna.

All the cheerleaders were about five and a half feet tall and probably no more than a hundred and twenty pounds, but Faith seemed taller because she stood straighter, her hair giving her another several inches over the other girls. Her arms and legs seemed longer and certainly more graceful. As easy as thought, she lifted her right leg in a high kick that left Alex blushing.

A wolf whistle forced Alex's attention from Faith to the group of young men sitting nearest him. They were natives, Dorothy High alumni home for the Thanksgiving holiday. Alex recognized all three of them because they had graduated in the same class.

The thought made him chuckle. Socially, he wasn't in the same class. Justus Wheeler was the richest man in Raleigh County, but the three guys leering at the cheerleaders and whispering about them were the offspring of Dorothy's few well-to-do families. Leland Birch, Travis Gates and Ritchie Platt had gone on to college—Leland and Ritchie to Montgomery University and Travis to Mountain Valley Bible College. Of all his classmates, these three were his least favorites.

"Al Brannon," Leland said enthusiastically, displaying a smile crammed with crooked yellow teeth. "Man, what is up?" He held his hand up and out and waited for Alex to slap him a high five.

Alex left him hanging.

Leland lowered his hand and returned it to the pocket of his plaid flannel hunting jacket. He exchanged a shifty glance with Ritchie before he said, "Been keepin' the home fires burning, man? I hear you're working at Red Irv's."

"Brody's," Travis chimed in. "Uncle Brody says Al's the best he's got in the shop."

"Good game today, Al," Ritchie added. "Scenery's not bad either."

"I'd tackle that curly-headed Black Bear in a red hot second," Leland said. He pointed a gloved finger at the cheerleader's bench, where Faith was sipping a steaming beverage from an insulated Dorothy Black Bears bomber cup clutched in her mittened hands.

"Faith Wheeler," Ritchie said, following up with a lascivious grunt. "Talk about hot cocoa. I wonder if she'll be at any of the parties tonight."

"Your dad would shoot you if he caught you with Justus Wheeler's daughter," Leland laughed.

"Justus Wheeler would shoot you if he caught you with Justus Wheeler's daughter," Travis retorted.

"Hey, Al," Ritchie called, "is Faith Wheeler with anybody these days?"

With deliberate slowness, Alex took out another cigarette and lit it. By the time he'd taken his second draw on it, the college boys had figured out that he had no answer or just plain wasn't going to answer.

"Dot's a small town, Al," Leland said. "Between the diner and the ding shop, you gotta know everybody's business. Who's Faith screwing? Jefferson Winslow?"

"I'll bet she's doin' Hardy Ketchum," Ritchie said. "He's a senior, he's always had game and he's got a thing for black girls. Remember when he got busted last year, driving ninety miles an hour into Comfort to see that black girl at Stonewall High?"

"He got some comfort, all right!" Leland laughed. "I've got a thing for hot girls, and little Faith Wheeler's all grown up and fine! I'm gonna talk to her after the game."

Alex made a sound that was something between a laugh and a snort.

"Something funny to you, man?" Leland asked coolly.

"I'm just minding my own business," Alex said through a long exhalation of smoke.

"Ignore him," Ritchie said.

Leland lowered his voice, and muttered something to his friends, who laughed. ". . . loser . . ."

Up until that word reached his ears, Alex had been able to ignore them. "What did you say?" he asked, his eyes pinned on Leland.

"Nothing, man," Travis said quickly. He put a hand on Leland's shoulder. "Come on, guys, let's show the Black Bears some support."

Travis began clapping, and other spectators joined in, but Leland was still trying to win a staredown with Alex.

"I said you're a loser, Al," he taunted. "I thought you were rock bottom in high school, but you're even more of a loser now. I'd kill myself if the highlight of my life was watching high school girls cheer at a football game."

"Guys, it's freezing out here," Travis said, again putting his hand on Leland's shoulder. "Let's go back to my house and catch a game on television."

Leland shook off Travis's hand. "I was never scared of this stupid thug in high school and I'm not scared of him now." Sneering at Alex, he said, "What are you doing for dinner today, Al? Gonna get drunk with your pa over a bowl of corn nuts at Buzzy's Tavern? Or are you gonna be taking your ma to the vet's office in Charleston to get stitched up, like last year?"

Ritchie snickered, pretending to hide it behind his hand.

"Quit it, Leland," Travis urged. "We're not in school anymore."

Alex calmly ground out the butt of his cigarette under the heel of his heavy black boot. "I never beat your ass for you in school because I didn't want to get expelled. You might want to listen to your buddy Travis, because he's right. We're not in school anymore."

Leland laughed. Ritchie scooted a safe distance from him, no longer amused. Travis continued appealing to Leland, looking anxiously from his friend to Alex.

"I'm not scared of Alexander Brannon," Leland announced, drawing the attention of their nearest bleacher mates. "What're you gonna do, Al? If you lay a hand on me, I'll have you arrested for assault."

"Dang it, Leland, can we all just watch the game in peace?" Travis pleaded.

Throwing off Travis's hand, Leland stood and approached Alex. Leaning over him, he jabbed a finger at Alex and ranted, "I'm not backing down from Al Brannon. What's he gonna do in front of all these people? Nothing! A loser like—"

Leland's fingertip brushed Alex's forehead, and Alex heard nothing past that moment. The sudden rush of blood to his ears deafened him to Leland's taunts, the roar of the crowd cheering Rafe's latest touchdown pass and Travis's attempts to pull Leland back.

Alex's left fist was connecting with Leland's jaw before Alex even knew what he was doing. His blow sent Leland hurtling over the back of the bleachers, and his momentum carried him after him, and both young men fell eight feet to the frozen ground. On his hands and knees, Leland tried to scramble away, but Alex grabbed his ankle and yanked him back, flipping him over. Straddling him, Alex let his fists speak for him, finally answering every taunt, jeer and joke that Leland and others like him had subjected him to from kindergarten right up to this moment. Every derogatory comment hurled at him about his mother, every nasty comment about his father, even the pity from people like Travis was answered with a blow to Leland's head and face.

Oblivious to the people who had climbed the bleachers to watch the fight from above and those who had circled around them for an even closer look, Alex didn't pause until he looked up and saw Faith at the front of the crowd.

A different kind of humiliation gripped him, and he sat back on his heels, his chest heaving. Leland wriggled away from him, his forearms and elbows still protecting his face.

"You had that coming, Leland, and you know it," Travis admonished his friend. "Show's over, folks. Did y'all come out for a game or a fight?"

His eyes fixed on Faith, Alex couldn't move until the murmuring started. Voices, all of them so low he couldn't identify their owners, overlapped and drove him to his feet.

". . . such a shame . . ."

"His daddy has a short fuse, too . . ."

". . . poor boy . . ."

". . . white trash . . ."

Alex shouldered his way through the crowd and hurried to the parking lot.

"Wait!"

He recognized that voice, but he kept walking.

"Alex, wait!"

He hopped onto his Harley and turned the key in the ignition. The ferocious roar of the Harley's rebuilt four-cylinder engine scared most people, but Faith showed no fear as she straddled the front wheel to stop him from leaving.

"Don't you ever make me chase you again!" she shouted over the bike's growl.

He tightened his hands on the handles, his only indication that he was leaving. With or without her. Faith understood him perfectly, because in the next instant she had mounted behind him. Once her hands had knotted themselves securely at his waist, he took off, the wheels of his bike spraying gravel behind him.

He drove with no destination in mind, and it was all he could do not to keep going until he hit Interstate 64. He had everything he needed right there with him, and there was nothing to stop him from heading west and driving until the road ran out.

His vision of escape vanished when Faith began to shiver behind him. His denim jeans and heavy leather jacket protected him from the wintry wind, but Faith was far more vulnerable. He couldn't take her to his house, and he didn't dare take her home, so Alex brought her to the one place he could call his favorite in Dorothy.

The Harley climbed Kayford Mountain only as high as the trails that had been cut by the heavy machinery used by the Lady Emiline Coal Company. Alex parked the bike in the shelter of the boulders that had been cleared after a recent blast on the mountainside. He took off his jacket and wrapped Faith in it. Her teeth stopped chattering the instant he zipped it up around her. The jacket was big on him, so it all but swallowed Faith.

Holding her hand, he helped her pick her way a bit higher on the mountain, to an area that hadn't been deforested by her father's strip mining operation. Most of the larger wildlife had been frightened off by previous explosions, but the smaller, friendlier animals could still be heard darting in and out of the underbrush. A white pine that had fallen because of weather or the concussion of a mining blast made a cozy bench for them, once Alex had brushed it free of leaves and smaller branches.

"You come here a lot, don't you?" Faith asked as she sat crosslegged on the log.

"What gives you that idea?" he responded.

"There's no moss growing on top of this log and the brush is flattened in front of it."

"I like the way you notice things," he said. He sat close to her, hoping to steal a little of her warmth.

"I noticed Leland Birch provoking you into a fight." She pushed back the sleeve of his jacket so she could take his hand in hers. She turned it over, wincing at the sight of his bruised knuckles and the blood caked in their creases.

"Birch came off the worst for it." Alex stared beyond the trees and onto the quiet town far below them. "Dorothy looks so much better from up here. I can see your pool."

"It looks like an ice mint Jelly Belly."

"Can I have that back?" he asked, indicating his hand with a tip of his chin.

"No." Faith held his hand tighter, and he made no move to take it from her. "Why did you let Leland get under your skin? He's a total ass."

"He thinks he's so much better than me," Alex said.

"Do you think he is?"

"Hell, no."

"Then if it isn't true, who cares what he thinks?"

Alex chuckled. "I wish it was that easy to let go of stuff like that."

"It is," Faith assured him. "You think I don't get crapped on? Every time Leland Birch calls me Brillo Head, or Bethany Brewer tells me that there are no black prima ballerinas, I just think about where I'll be in ten years and where they'll be. Leland will be running his dad's used car lot, and he'll probably have the same terrible comb over. Bethany will find a way to trap Travis Gates into marriage, and she'll be living the soccer mom life with a frooty bigger than the mayor's wife's."

"Where will you be, Faith?" Alex asked.

"Anywhere but here," she answered wistfully. "I hate it here sometimes."

"You've got it made, princess. You don't have any problems you won't outgrow."

"I won't 'outgrow' being black in an all-white town," she said. "I can't 'outgrow' being thought of as the spoiled rich girl."

"Those aren't real problems," he said.

"They're as real as yours."

"You've got the whole world out there for you, Faith," he said passionately. "I was born in this town, and I'm gonna die in this town. There are only two Brannon family traditions—alcoholism and dying in the mines. My dad's got the alcoholism sewed up, so I guess I'll end up dead in a mine like my granddaddy."

"Then I guess you have to get outta Booger Hollow," Faith said dryly.

Alex laughed, and the sound echoed off the trees. "You always know the right thing to say."

"You have a nice laugh," she told him. "It's a shame you don't do it more often."

Rubbing his hands together to warm them, he shrugged. "Yeah, well, I don't have much to laugh about most days."

Faith unzipped his jacket and slipped out of it. "Put this back on," she directed, handing it to him.

"I'm good," he said, refusing it. "You're only half dressed."

"Just put it on," she said.

He did so, and she switched position on the log, sitting with her back to him and scooting back until she was nestled between his legs and cradled against his chest.

"We can both keep warm this way," she said, pulling his arms around her.

"I'll say," he sighed, nuzzling her soft curls with his nose and chin.

"Let's not go back," Faith suggested. "We could just stay up here forever."

"It might be a little noisy with your dad blasting the mountain away to get to the coal."

"Don't mention him," she said. "You'll ruin the fantasy. Did you ever read a book called *My Side of the Mountain*?"

"Didn't catch that one."

"It's about a boy who spends a year living in a hollow hemlock tree in the Catskills," Faith said. "Any hollow trees around here?"

"I think there's an old pine stump somewhere nearby, but a family of raccoons has dibs on it."

She playfully drove an elbow into his ribs. "Don't make fun. It's a good book, and I'm serious. I'd love to get away from Dorothy and start life somewhere new and exciting."

"I'd settle for new," he said.

"Take me with you."

"Where?"

"When you leave, take me with you."

"I wish I could." He brought his legs to the top of the log, forming a cocoon of warmth around her with his body. "You don't know how much I wish I could, Faith."

"Zander, you've not heard a word we've said, have you?"

Olivia's cool, calm inquiry gently pulled Zander from his warm memories of Faith Wheeler. "Forgive me," he said quietly. "I was thinking."

"I would ask what has you so completely absorbed, but I believe I already know," Olivia said. "The very person we've been talking about for the past twenty minutes."

"Faith just might expose me for a fraud," Zander said. *And I wouldn't blame her for one second.*

"Don't underestimate your publicist," Olivia said. "There's nothing I can't spin. Alexander Brannon's story is far better than Zander Baron's."

"I don't ever want anyone to know who I really am!" he stated with a bit too much vehemence. "If it gets out, I'll disappear again. For good."

"There's obviously more to your past than you've told us," Brent said. "What are you hiding?"

"Your mother did a very thorough background check on me before I moved into your house," Zander said. "You don't have to worry about any skeletons falling out of any closets."

Zander took his earlobe between his thumb and forefinger—the nervous mannerism *Entertainment Express* magazine recently credited with stealing the heart of every female moviegoer in America over the age of nine. The motion had no effect on Brent, other than letting him know that Zander wasn't ready or willing to supply new revelations about his past as Alexander Brannon.

"There it is, then," Olivia said lightly.

"So we're in agreement?" Brent said.

"Yes. I'll phone *Personality!* now, and then I'll call you with a date and time."

"Hold on," Zander said, raising a hand. "Who are you calling? What are you up to?"

"I'm saving your career," Olivia said, clipping her phone headset onto her right ear. She spun her chair to face her glorious mountain view, effectively dismissing both her only son and favorite client.

"Paula," she said, speaking to her assistant through the headset, "conference me in to Magda Pierson at *Personality!*"

"I'd rather you didn't," Zander said, stepping toward the desk.

Brent caught his arm and silenced him with a wave.

"Tell them that I'd like to set up a tête-a-tête with Faith Wheeler and one of my clients, Zander Baron," Olivia continued. "Off the record, of course."

Brent signaled for Zander to follow him as he exited his mother's office. Olivia's entire house had been decorated in her signature snow queen shades of white, faded blues, greys and silver. Zander had done some amazing drops and car chase stunts in his films, but nothing daunted him more than navigating his way down Olivia's "floating" spiral staircase. Constructed of narrow six-foot planks of silvery-white marble, the gently spiraling staircase had no visible means of solid support.

Zander always felt as though he were hovering in midair when he went down the stairs.

"What does she hope to accomplish by shoving me right under Faith Wheeler's nose?" he asked once both feet were safe on the gleaming white marble floor of the foyer.

"Mom is worried," Brent said, grabbing the long, stylized chrome handle of the frosted glass front door. He swung it open for Zander. "She's managed every detail of Zander Baron's life and choreographed his rise flawlessly. That *Personality!* reporter really threw her for a loop."

"Yeah, she kinda surprised me, too," Zander admitted, stepping into the bright February sunshine.

"You're doing it again," Brent said in a warning tone.

"Doin' what?"

"Your Appalachia is creeping in."

Zander grinned. Of all the things Brent policed him on, his native accent was the one Brent monitored most closely. When he got tired or stressed, two years of diction coaching gave way to his West Virginia origins.

"Sorry," Zander replied in the Midwestern accent Olivia had paid for. "I've got some things on my mind."

"Some things or some *one*?" Brent asked, following Zander to his bike. "And why didn't you ever tell me about her?"

Zander scratched behind his ear. "No reason to. She's someone from a long time ago. From another life."

His answer was really no answer at all, but he knew Brent would understand.

When Olivia discovered an unformed lump of West Virginia mountain clay and brought it home to shape into Zander Baron, Brent's first instinct was to resent the intrusion of the country-bred stranger who had become his mother's latest project. But Brent's head for business had prevailed, and he had accepted Zander's role in their lives, with the two ultimately becoming friends. Truthfully, Brent was Zander's only friend, and he felt guilty for not having shared the one good thing in his past with him.

Brent's hybrid car, a sunset-orange Lexus GS, was parked alongside Zander's motorcycle. He paused at the driver's door, toying with his keyless remote. "It's all gonna come out someday, you know, probably sooner than later. And you don't have anything to be ashamed of."

"I know," Zander said hastily, mounting his bike. He absently ran his hand over the handlebar. The Confederate Hellcat, the first thing he'd purchased with his very first big paycheck, had been hand-built in Alabama to his specifications. Having money in his pocket for the first time, he'd gone a bit spend crazy, but the silver and black beauty beneath him was far and away his favorite purchase. He'd often thought about driving into Dorothy, announcing his return with the roar of the Hellcat. But there was no reason to return to Dorothy now, not with Faith in Los Angeles.

"I'll give you a call after my mother finishes working her magic," Brent said, getting into his car. "Hopefully, what she comes up with won't be too painful."

"I can handle it, whatever it is," Zander said. "I'm the strong, tough movie star, remember?"

CHAPTER 3

"I can't do this," Zander said, the heels of his boots wearing a path in his living room carpet. "I won't."

Brent snorted. "What happened to Mr. Tough Guy? I've never seen you like this. Zander Baron, scared of a woman."

Zander glared at him. If some other man had made such an accusation while reclining on his dark-brown leather sofa he would have found himself bleeding profusely, but Zander realized Brent's baiting was deliberate.

"I'm not afraid of her," Zander insisted. "And she's no ordinary woman. She's . . ."

He left his response hanging. He had no idea what Faith was anymore. She had been in the deepest reaches of his heart and head for years, but he hadn't seen or talked to her. The Faith Wheeler who had hurled angry questions at him at the *Reunion* press conference was not the girl he'd known in Dorothy.

Or was she?

"The only way to take control of this situation is to meet it head on, find out what the reporter wants—"

"Faith," Zander interjected. "Her name is Faith."

"Once we find out what Faith wants, maybe we can turn this situation our way," Brent said.

"I don't see how." Zander drained the last of his Ned's Pale Ale. His fondness for the West Virginia Brewing

Company product was one of the very few things he hadn't left behind when he left Dorothy. At Olivia's hypocritical insistence, he had given up smoking, but he refused to abandon his home state brew. As if doing something illegal or illicit, he had to order his beer from the distributor through Brent, so that nothing connected him directly to anything associated with West Virginia.

"You two have history, right?" Brent asked. "There are a couple of approaches you can take. One, appeal to her memories of the friendship you two once shared, or . . ." He raised an eyebrow and tipped his head in some wordless communication Zander was meant to understand.

"Or what?" Zander said, failing to translate Brent's expression.

"Or use your considerable appeal to win her silence," Brent answered. "It's not like you've had any trouble seducing any woman you've set your sights on. I've seen some of the coldest broads in Hollywood turn to putty once you smile their way."

"Faith was never like that. It'll take more than my rebuilt face and dubious charm to turn her to putty. As for friendship, I don't think her memories of it will be that good."

"What did you do to her?"

"Nothing," Zander said defensively. "What the hell kind of question is that? Why are you automatically assuming that I did something to her?"

"Calm down, Zander," Brent said. "It was an innocent question. Or so I thought until your reaction just now."

"I—" His words snagged in his throat. He couldn't look at Brent as he admitted, "I hurt her."

Brent sat up, his concern evident in the serious set of his features. "What happened?"

Dropping heavily onto the sofa, Zander rubbed his palms over the stubble covering his cheeks. "I left her alone in Dorothy."

Brent relaxed, sitting back and sighing with relief. "Don't scare me like that, Alex. I thought you were gonna tell me that you killed somebody."

"I did, in a way," he said. "You don't know what it was like for me and Faith back there. We were freaks."

"I don't doubt your memory of your childhood, bro, but I have to tell you that Faith Wheeler isn't anything close to what I'd call a freak. That woman is beautiful, and she's obviously smart. If Mom wasn't so frustrated with her right now, she probably would have tried to get me to sign her as a client."

"Freak isn't the right word," Zander said. "We were outcasts. We couldn't have been more opposite, but we were still in the same boat. She was black and rich, I was poor white trash. Her dad owned the biggest coal mining company in southwestern West Virginia. My dad was the town drunk. She was an honor student and a cheerleader—"

"You're right," Brent chuckled. "She was a freak."

Zander ignored him. "I was the local waste of space working two minimum wage jobs to keep the trailer over our heads and my mother's antidepressant prescriptions filled."

"And you two were friends?"

"I can't tell you exactly what we were because I don't know. But it was more than friends. It was better than friends. The only time I was ever happy in Dorothy was when I was with her. She treated me like . . . like . . . like I mattered."

"I don't get it," Brent said, wrinkling his brow. "Why did you leave?"

"I had to." Zander stood, his quick and decisive motion making it clear that he wanted to change the subject. "So when and where am I supposed to meet Faith?"

Brent gave him a tiny smile. "Ten tomorrow morning at Krasco's Deli."

"Krasco's Deli. Are you kidding?"

"Would I kid about a thing like that?"

"If your mom is trying to tell me something, I wish she'd just come out and say it and not play games with me."

"You know Olivia," Brent sighed. "She only plays games she knows she can win. Sending you to Krasco's might just be her way of trying to teach you a lesson."

"What kind of lesson?"

"Hell if I know," Brent chuckled. "I gave up questioning Olivia's methods years ago when she got me out of summer school by flipping my trigonometry teacher a walk-on in *Ally McBeal.*"

Zander sat in a booth in the back of Krasco's. Five years ago, he'd come to the same deli—the same booth, in fact—for a meeting with Olivia Baxter. That meeting had changed his life, and now he was back full circle to meet another woman who had the power to change his life again. For better or worse.

Nursing a cup of Krasco's signature black coffee, Zander picked at a crack in the blue vinyl seat. Krasco's was the real deal, a genuine 1950s-era diner that had been run by the Krasco family for fifty-five years. It was so authentic, in fact, that Zander's stomach had twisted a little bit upon walking through the door and inhaling the aroma of fried meat and onions cooked on an open grill. The scent reminded him so much of his years spent at Red Irv's, and it reminded him of nothing good.

Except for Faith.

There was no doubt Olivia had been a godsend. In the years since that first meeting, Olivia Baxter had taken control and given him a life he had never imagined.

He'd made his way from Dorothy to Los Angeles a few bucks at a time, hitchhiking when he dared, walking when he didn't. Finding work had never been any trouble, but keeping it proved problematic when he couldn't provide a social security card or any ID other than an expired out-of-state driver's license.

He was Alex Brannon back then, and home was a pay-by-the-hour or -week motel. He'd been earning a meager living as a part-time mechanic and day laborer when he had run into Olivia—literally.

One of the few perks of working for a custom garage in Los Angeles was delivering cars to their owners once the work on them was completed. On a clear and sunny

June day, he'd been cruising along Roxbury Drive in a champagne-silver Jaguar belonging to an actress when Olivia Baxter, her face partially concealed by oversized Dolce & Gabbana sunglasses, shot out of the driveway of a big Tudor house hidden behind birch trees.

Alex hit the brakes, managing to lessen the Jaguar's impact on the front passenger door of her white Mustang convertible, spinning it in a half circle. Shock, embarrassment and fury sent him into the wide, tree-lined street, where he shouted at Olivia.

With her benevolent yet playful smile and perfectly coiffed hair, Olivia reminded him of actress Betty White, and for a moment, he'd thought he had crashed into a *Golden Girl.*

To her credit, Olivia had calmly exited her car and leaned against it, her steely gaze dissecting him as he had ranted about cats, women and how neither should ever be allowed behind the wheel of a car.

When she reached into her damaged car to retrieve her handbag, Alex was sure she was about to give him her license and insurance information, which pressed his panic button. The garage paid him under the table, and he was driving uninsured on an expired license. If he'd been alone he might have wept at the irony of a day that had started so beautifully finishing with him in jail—the very place most people in Dorothy had expected him to end up.

But instead of accident information, Olivia had flipped out a thick cream-white business card pinched between her impeccably manicured index and middle fingers.

"Call me," she had said, pressing the card into his hand.

The black crescent of his thumbnail stood out starkly against the pristine white card, which read:

OLIVIA BAXTER
Founder & President
Baxter Publicity and Promotions

In the lower corners of the card were phone, fax and cellphone numbers newly smeared with traces of automotive grime from his fingers.

"The accident was my fault," Olivia had said with the same concern she might have shown in reporting the time. "Once your boss calms down after you tell him what happened to Robia Hart's Jaguar, have him call me and we'll work out the arrangements for the repair of the car."

Alex looked up from the card. "How did you know who this car belonged to?"

"Robia Hart is one of my clients," Olivia said, smiling serenely. "She bought that car with the paycheck from her first film. I look forward to hearing from you, Octavio."

"Hey, lady, my name isn't—" But Olivia had started her car, spun her wheels, and peeled out of sight.

Tucking the card into a front pocket of his borrowed jumper, Alex circled the vehicle, inspecting the damage. The front of the Jag was scratched and dented, but the Mustang had come off the worse for its encounter with the British import. The vanity license plate Alex hadn't noticed earlier now made sense: RBAHRT.

His boss had been livid when he saw Alex returning with the freshly battered Jag, but his rage vanished within the first twenty seconds of his phone call to Olivia, who had verified that the accident had occurred exactly as Alex had claimed. Alex had no idea what she'd said, but from what he gleaned from his boss's end of the conversation, Olivia was paying triple his rate to have Robia's ride repaired as soon as possible.

As for Robia Hart, Hollywood's reigning period-movie princess had been royally pissed about the accident, but even she had come to Alex's defense when told that Olivia Baxter had caused the new damage. Evidently, every licensed driver in Robia's neighborhood knew to literally steer clear of Olivia's white Mustang when they heard it roaring down Roxbury Street.

His boss had flung Olivia's business card at him—after firing him. Even though he had praised Alex's skill at working with cars, he couldn't take the risk of keeping on an employee with no social security card and no driving insurance.

With Olivia's business card and his last day's pay in his pocket, Alex walked the four miles home to his motel. Everything was so expensive in Los Angeles, and he already felt the sting of unemployment. His weekly rent of one hundred and forty dollars was due, his Harley was sitting idle because he lacked the money to purchase the parts he needed to repair it, he was down to his last package of ramen noodles and the six dollars cash and eighty-five dollar check he had in his pocket was all the money he had in the world.

He walked past his motel and went to the corner bar, Jose's Hideaway, to drown his sorrows in one-dollar shots of watered tequila. He allowed himself six shots to figure out his next move.

There were other repair jobs, but the last one had been relatively close to home, and he'd enjoyed his coworkers. By his third shot, he had just enough of a buzz to convince himself that things wouldn't look so bad in the morning. Two shots later, when he realized he needed his last buck to tip the barkeep, renewed anger at Olivia Baxter killed the warm fuzzies he'd talked himself into.

He was out of a job, he'd soon be without food, and unless he could talk the motel manager into letting him do odd jobs around the building, he'd be homeless, too. In one careless strike of her hot Mustang, Olivia Baxter had seriously dented his pathetic life. Insurance would take care of the Mustang and the Jag, but who would compensate him for the damages *he* had suffered?

Searching his pockets, hoping to find a stray bill hiding somewhere, Alex patted a stiff wad of paper in his hip pocket. He smoothed it out on the water-marked counter.

Olivia's card.

Call me.

Alex had gone back to his room. In his old jeans, work boots and ribbed undershirt, he'd sat on his sunken mattress, his head and shoulders propped against the stained wallpaper, staring at the little card in his hand.

And then he'd stopped staring. He'd picked up the phone, dialed the number and, the next morning, he'd met Olivia in a back booth at Krasco's.

He'd left Alexander Brannon in that booth, and the rough lump that would become Zander Baron had walked out with Olivia Baxter.

And now Zander Baron was there to meet the one woman Alexander Brannon had ever loved.

It was easy to admit that while masquerading as Zander Baron.

"Quit it," he whispered to himself. "Only crazy people talk about themselves in the third person. Or is it the fourth person, since I'm talking about someone who doesn't really exist. Or—"

Noticing the pretty waitress watching him mutter to himself, Zander slumped deeper into the booth and turned his face toward his cold coffee.

He glanced at his watch, a heavy silver and black Oris that one of the producers had given him at the close of filming for *Burn*. A simple Timex would have been more in line with his tastes, and certainly easier to read. He had to angle the numberless face of the watch just so to catch enough light to read the time.

It was 9:55, and knowing that Faith would soon walk through the door sent a surge of anxiety through him. He didn't want to watch the door, but he found himself staring at it, his eyes fixed immovably on it.

His palms began to sweat, so he wiped them on the legs of his jeans. Afraid to blink and miss the moment she came into view, his eyes went dry. Without realizing it, he clamped his jaw hard enough to compromise the integrity of the smile Olivia had bought for him. Even though he had later reimbursed her for every penny she'd spent on his transformation, she still referred to his smile as hers.

The tense agony of waiting left him rigid enough to snap, but then the glass door swung open, and Faith entered the deli.

Zander sat up straighter.

She seemed to move in slow motion, which gave him the time to take in everything about her.

She looked taller, but that might have been a trick of her shoes, black pumps with ankle straps that drew his eye immediately to her legs. A slim-fitting black skirt hugged her hips and complemented her white blouse, which was buttoned low enough to instantly make his mouth water. She removed her black sunglasses, a pair of sensible plain RayBans, and slipped them into her over-sized handbag. With a flip of her shoulder-length hair, which she now wore straight, she zeroed in on him, her dark eyes narrowing.

Zander's heart pulsed in one hard, painful beat, and a low moan escaped him. Meeting her at Krasco's was agony enough without seeing that the pretty cheerleader he couldn't forget had grown into an impossibly beautiful woman.

She slowed a step when he stood. He opened his mouth to greet her, but no sound came out. "Hello" didn't seem to be adequate, not after ten years, and certainly not considering the conditions under which they had separated.

Faith took the initiative. "Mr. *Baron*," she said pointedly.

She plopped her bag on the booth seat and slid in beside it. After placing a slim, stylish microcassette recorder on the table, she laced her fingers and studied Zander.

Her knuckles whitened under the effort it took to keep her hands from trembling. She fought the urge to chew a corner of her lower lip, one of her most obvious signs of nerves. She had so many things to say to him, but she dared not open her mouth until she was sure she could do so without screaming, crying or kissing him.

"Can I get you something to drink, or—"

The appearance of the waitress startled both Zander and Faith, and their sudden jumps in turn alarmed the waitress, who leaned heavily against the table behind her, clutching her order pad to her chest.

"I'm sorry," she laughed nervously. "I didn't mean to scare you."

"You should be scared," Faith said, keeping her eyes fixed on Zander. "It's not every day you get to serve a dead person."

"Uh, could I get a fresh pot of coffee, black," Zander requested hastily. "And a three-egg white omelet, no salt, no oil, with spinach. Fresh spinach, not frozen." He turned back to Faith. "Would you like something?"

"No," Faith said, the lone syllable as friendly and warm as the snap of a crocodile's jaws.

Zander swallowed hard. "Thanks," he said to the waitress. "I think we're set."

"I'll be back in a few with your order," she said brightly.

She started off, but turned back twice to peer at Zander before disappearing behind the swinging door to the kitchen.

"I think she recognized me," Zander said quietly.

"That makes two of us then," Faith responded. "Egg white omelets? No salt or oil? You're all kinds of California now, aren't you? It couldn't have been easy giving up Red Irv's 'psghetti and patabas.'"

He loudly cleared his throat. "The coffee's good here. You—"

"The coffee at Red Irv's was good, too," Faith said stubbornly. "He still talks about you, you know. Every time I go home for Christmas or Thanksgiving, the two of us sit in the diner and talk about you. My old dance teacher Miss Lorraine still talks about you, and so does Art Brody."

"I was his best grease jockey," Zander said. "And I worked cheap."

"I'm not the only one you left, Alex," Faith said. "I'm not the only one who missed you."

Zander grimaced. He had no right to expect her to make this meeting easy, but he had hoped that she wouldn't make it so hard, either.

"You hated Booger Hollow as much as I did, so don't—"

"Back then, yes!" Faith said. "I was a kid itching to get out into the world I saw on MTV! But guess what, Alex? I'm not a kid now. And every time I go to Booger

Hollow, I'm going home. My parents are there. The dance studio I loved is there. The guidance counselor at Lincoln High invited me to speak on careers for writers two years ago, when I was still at the *L.A. Times*." Unshed tears strained her voice as she quietly added, "All my memories of you are there, and that makes Booger Hollow very special to me."

Zander plucked a napkin from the container resting against the leather-covered wall, and he mopped his damp brow.

Faith watched his every move. She had noticed the subtle changes in his appearance at the press conference. His lower teeth were no longer slightly crowded. His nose had been broken twice in Dorothy, but it appeared to have been rebroken and properly set to remove the tiny bump he'd once had. His hair was much lighter, brightening his face and softening the intensity of his gaze. The old scar near his right eye was virtually undetectable.

The one thing he hadn't been able to alter, the one thing that had given him away, remained achingly the same. His eyes, as vivid and captivating as the last time she'd looked into them, had been left unchanged, a blessing for which she offered a silent prayer of thanks.

"Look," she began, refocusing her attention, "I know who you are, and—"

"That makes one of us then," he interrupted.

"Please. Drop that phony accent. It's not you."

"My accent isn't fake." He leaned across the table. Lowering his voice, he seamlessly reverted to his native

West Virginia dialect. "Zander Baron was born in Australia. He was left an orphan when his parents were killed in a motorcar accident. Young Zander was taken and raised by an American uncle in Wyoming, where he learned to ride horses and rope cattle and—"

Her hands clenched into fists, Faith cut him off. "I've read your biography. I don't need that fiction recited to me."

"What do you want from me, Faith? Money?"

"Are you dumb?" she asked, incredulous at the suggestion.

"Then what are we here for?"

"A damn explanation!"

"For what?" he hissed.

She slammed her palms on the tabletop. "For everything! For leaving, to start with! For letting everyone believe that you were dead!"

"Making a scene here will hurt your career far more than mine, Faith, so calm down," he warned. "Lower your voice and I'll answer your questions, if I can."

Her appearance had changed, but she was still the straightforward, stand-up Faith he had known in another life.

"Did you ever think of me?" she blurted, frustrated with herself for losing her cool and exposing a wound that had never quite healed.

"Yes," he answered immediately.

She dropped her eyes and blinked back tears of relief that threatened to give away how much of her heart she had invested in his response. She lightly cleared her throat. "Zander Baron is a puzzle wrapped around a secret, but I've pieced most of it together," she said. "I know enough about Olivia Baxter to recognize her fingerprints all over your transformation. The cosmetic work must have been easy, but it's a lot harder to weave the facts of your life into the fabric of your fictional one. She didn't hide the seams well enough."

"Really? Enlighten me."

She leaned back, inadvertently giving Zander an inviting view of her décolletage. "Olivia has a knack for finding talent for her son to represent. Her boys aren't just easy on the eyes. Most of them can actually act, too. She collects stars the way other people stumble upon good luck pennies, only she *makes* her stars what they become."

"She's a good publicist," Zander said. "You make it sound like it's a crime."

"If my research is at all accurate—and it is—here's what happened," Faith went on. "You left West Virginia for whatever reason and came out West. Olivia Baxter saw you at some point. I can't begin to guess where, but the when is a bit easier. You had surgery to correct your nose and at least one procedure to straighten your chompers. Then there was the removal of the scar from your face, but the coaching probably took the most time. Dialects, foreign languages, deportment, etiquette and acting. Have I missed any?"

"No," he said, grudgingly impressed. "Do continue."

"Once you were remodeled, buffed and polished, Brent sent you out, and you were cast in *Burn* as part of a ten-million dollar deal. It's been skyward and onward since. If *Reunion* performs as well as forecasted at the box office, chances are pretty good that you'll become the newest member of the twenty-million-a-movie club. Not bad for the bad boy of Raleigh County. From mountain boy to superstar in . . . five years?"

He tapped the table with his knuckle. "Just about to the day. You're a good researcher, Faith."

"I'm surprised that Brent has gone along with this deceit. As agents go, he's pretty decent. He's got a great reputation for genuinely caring about his clients and for having a conscience. I think Olivia relied on that to give substance to the crap she's been peddling about you."

"Before we go any further, let's get one thing straight," he said sternly. "Brent is my best friend. He's my only friend. It was never my intention to deceive . . . to misdirect anyone in any way."

"Then let me tell the truth about who you are. It's going to come out anyway."

"Are you threatening me?

"I'm warning you." She sat forward, reaching for his hand, but then withdrawing her own quickly. "I've been assigned to write a story on Zander Baron. It would make the cover if . . . if I wrote it in full. It would be my biggest cover story, and given the public interest in you, it would garner a great deal of publicity. For both of us."

The waitress returned and set Zander's meal before him, but he no longer had any taste for what little taste the omelet had. "Do you really hate me that much?"

She winced. Her nostrils twitched, another telltale sign that tears were close. "This is the nature of the business, Alex," she said softly.

He shoved his plate aside. "Don't call me that."

"That's your name."

"Not anymore. It's all legal. I can even show you a driver's license to prove it."

"I know," Faith said. "It was issued in Cheyenne, Wyoming, five years ago."

"How long have you been planning this grand exposé?" he asked.

"That first close-up in *Burn* . . ." She shook her head and smiled wistfully. "I felt like I was having a heart attack. I knew it was you. I asked my editor to let me cover your *Reunion* press conference. I wanted to see you."

"I've wanted to see you too, Faith. You have to believe that. My memories of you were the only things that kept me going at times when—"

"Zander Baron has no memories of me," Faith cut in, her tone jagged. "Don't you dare pretend that you're the same person I knew back home."

"Home," he repeated with a bitter laugh. "Home to you was hell for me, and you know it."

"Is that why you ran?" Her voice broke. "Is that why you left me?"

He rested his elbows on the table and covered his face with his hands for a moment. "I didn't—" He sighed sharply and tried to explain. "I saw a chance to start over that night, and I took it."

"What about all the days and nights after that, when you could have called or written me just to let me know you were still alive?" She couldn't stop her tears this time, and she angrily swiped them away. "Did you even know when your mom died? You hadn't been gone two years when she was rushed to the medical center with her head split open—"

"I was living on a lettuce farm, sleeping in a bunk with twenty other guys," he said through gritted teeth. "I was in no position to help anyone else, especially a woman whose idea of quality childcare was to strap me to my bed so she could hang out at Buzzy's Tavern. Don't criticize my choices until you have all the facts. It was easy to leave Dorothy, but it killed me to leave you." He reached forward to brush away her tears. "I never wanted to leave *you*."

She pushed his hand away from her face, but he took hers and held onto it. "But you did! You left me behind. I wanted out of Booger Hollow just as much as you did back then, but I wasn't willing to kill to do it!"

"I was willing to die," Zander insisted. "Not kill."

"You got rid of Alex Brannon just the same, though, didn't you? You must have thought you'd hit the lottery when you met Olivia Baxter. You had your very own fairy godmother to turn you into a whole new person."

"I never begrudged you your rich parents," he said. "Don't begrudge me Olivia Baxter."

"My 'rich' parents cut me off when I decided to go to New York University instead of the University of West Virginia," Faith said. "They wanted me to go to school in state and marry Jefferson Winslow and be his dutiful wife, raising our kids in Dorothy and living in the biggest house while Jefferson took over the running of the coal company."

"I put myself through school," she told him. "I did what you did, Alex. I *worked*. There were times I was so tired, I couldn't work up the strength to complain about how tired I was. When I graduated, I worked my ass off at regional newspapers until I had enough clips to impress an *L.A. Times* recruiter I met at a job fair. I worked there for six months, and two years ago, I got a job at *Personality!* I've worked hard and paid quite a few dues, but the only way I'll truly be able to write my own ticket is to break a story with serious weight. Loving Alexander Brannon is in my past. Exposing Zander Baron could be the key to my future."

Pulling her hand from his, Faith grabbed her recorder and handbag and slipped out of the booth, leaving Zander helplessly watching her walk away.

Faith pushed open the door and stumbled into the sunlit morning, hoping that Alex would come after her. Putting on her RayBans to hide her puffy eyes, she slowed her stride to her car. So many times she had prayed to see him once more, and she had fantasized that she would. But in her fantasies, the meeting had taken place in Heaven or some other otherworldly realm, not in a back booth in one of L.A.'s famed dining establishments.

The location hadn't mattered, not nearly as much as her reaction to the meeting. Her body had responded to him as if starved for the sensations it had known with him in their youth. Fanning herself with one hand, she leaned back and faced reality—that her exposé might not be as easy as she had hoped it would be.

CHAPTER 4

Faith climbed Kayford Mountain to the secluded wooded area high above her parents' backyard. She had brought one candle with her. Faith wanted to make her birthday wish far from the curious stares of her family and friends, so now she was sitting on a thick, fragrant bed of pine needles and damp earth at the highest point in town, looking up at a sky full of twinkling stars waiting to hear her wish. Surely the heavens would grant her the one thing she wanted if her request had so little distance to travel.

As dusk fell, heavy rain clouds moved in to darken the purple-pink sky, giving it an ethereal beauty made more extreme by the rustic location she'd chosen to make her wish. With the wind picking up, the orange flame of her tiny pink candle had struggled to live long enough for Faith to accomplish her task. With her one desire filling her heart and a long draw of air expanding her lungs, she pursed her lips and blew, trading the life of the flame for that of her wish.

The wisp of smoke vanished into the wind, and Faith drew her knees to her chest, hugging them tight. Pinpoints of starlight tried to break through the cloud cover, and Faith thought the hectic sky her loveliest birthday gift. The wind picked up as though determined to drown out the music of the crickets and owls serenading her as she closed her eyes and tilted her head back, musing on her wish.

"Hey."

That single syllable startled and exhilarated her as she whirled around.

Alex had come up on her like a creature born to the mountain woods, magnificent in his faded blue jeans and threadbare T-shirt.

"It came true," she said breathily.

"What?" he asked.

"Hi."

"Hey," he repeated. "What are you doing up here?"

"Just watching the sunset. The sky is so pretty tonight. I've never seen it like this. All troubled and restless."

He sat close to her, lacing his fingers together with his elbows braced on his knees. "I never get tired of the view from up here," he said. "It's like a scene from a movie."

"Today's my birthday," she blurted, suddenly nervous.

He turned toward her, his eyes violet in the twilight. "Well, happy birthday, Faith."

"Thank you."

"Eighteen," he murmured. "Bet your folks gave you something real nice."

"Yeah, they did." Not particularly anxious to discuss her gift, she cleared her throat. "It's a combination birthday and graduation gift."

"The Camry is a good, solid car," he said, keeping his eyes on the tumultuous sky.

"How did you know they got me a Camry?"

He shrugged. "Everybody knows everybody's business in Booger Hollow. Of course, some things can be kept secret, if you're careful."

"I don't know how much longer we'll be able to keep our thing a secret," she sighed. "Darlene Cross keeps asking me where I've been 'disappearing' to after school lately."

"What did you tell her?"

"That if she didn't stay out of my business, I'd tell her boyfriend that she's got your old yearbook photo taped up in her gym locker and that she kisses it every day."

Alex chuckled dryly. "Cool."

Faith gave him a poke with her elbow.

"Would you really rat her out like that?"

"Only if she forces me to," Faith said. "I can keep a secret, but not at the expense of having my own leaked. How did you know I was up here?"

He picked up a cluster of fragrant white pine needles and passed their length between his thumb and forefinger. "I followed you."

Her parents and those of her friends always talked about Alex as though he were the boogeyman. But painting him as an ill-bred, uncouth vagabond who roamed the nights peeking into their daughters' bedrooms had the opposite effect of what they had intended. Rather than scaring the girls away from him, the warnings had fed their fascination with him, and Faith's fascination had led to friendship.

"I saw Jefferson Winslow pestering you after your dance class today," Alex said. "Thought I would have to sock him in the jaw if he didn't leave you alone."

"I can handle Jeffy Winslow," she responded, referring to him by the name she'd used since their first day in kindergarten. "Our folks married us off in the crib. Trouble is, I'd rather throw myself off this mountain than spend the rest of my life in Raleigh County married to a bratty Winslow."

"Me, too," Alex replied wistfully.

"You mean you don't want to marry a bratty Winslow either?" Faith teased.

Alex blessed her with a rare smile. She took his arm and rested her head on his shoulder.

"I'd rather die than spend the rest of my life in Dorothy," Alex sighed.

The yearning in his voice tugged at Faith's heart. She shivered, and she wasn't sure if it was because of Alex or the sudden chill in the wind.

"You can leave town anytime you feel like it," she said. "I still have another month of school, but come fall I'm starting at New York University. One more summer in Dorothy, and my life, my real life, really begins." She quietly cleared her throat. "You know, you could leave too, if you wanted."

"Where am I supposed to go, Faith?" he asked sadly.

"There are lots of things a resourceful guy could do in New York City."

"With what money? I got nothin', Faith. I couldn't even get hired at your daddy's mine. What makes you think I could get a decent job someplace else?"

"You could go to college," she suggested. "You're smart, you—"

"You just don't get it, kid," he said, shaking his head. "You don't understand how the world works."

"I understand plenty," Faith said, stubbornly crossing her arms over her chest. "And don't call me kid. You're only a year older than I am."

"I didn't have the grades for college," he said. "Honors American history didn't compensate for the way my grades fell toward the end of my Lincoln High career."

"Only because you were out sick so much." She took his left hand, her fingertips grazing the network of scars that represented the nature of his sick days. "I could talk to my dad," Faith offered. "If he met you, I know he'd give you a job."

He'd looked at her then, and his sadness brought tears to her eyes. Alex had touched her face just below her ear, and his gentle caress raised her to her knees, drawing her face closer to his.

The wind had gained in force, bending the trunks of the youngest trees and thrashing them with the branches of the bigger ones. Faith's hair lashed her face and Alex's hand as they moved closer together, aware of nothing other than each other.

"You're legally an adult now," Alex murmured. "A grown-up woman."

He brought his lips to hers, touching them with such tenderness she felt the tremble in them. Alex wasn't like the boys at school because there was so little boy left in him. Faith had been kissed before, but never like this. Never had a boy gently parted her lips with his tongue to touch hers, the resultant jolt of electricity leaving her breathless and limp as she melted into his arms.

She was loath to separate from him even to breathe, her mouth seeking his as his head shifted, his nose sweeping hers in passing. She smiled through their kiss, thrilled by the rasp of the stubble above his upper lip and the taste of his mouth.

She could have reveled in his kisses from that moment until forever if he hadn't torn away from her.

"We should go," he said.

The gravity of his tone returned her to the mountainside, and for the first time she noticed the rumbling sky. The sky, which had been as pretty as a present, was angry, black, and layered with storm clouds that seemed to weigh heavily on the treetops.

Alex took her hand, pulling her roughly to her feet. Faith moved into the protective circle of his arms, blown there by instinct or by the violent wind now forcing the trees to dance crazily. When the rain came, it fell all at once, as though the sharpened tips of the tallest evergreens had ripped open the cloud bellies.

Carefully picking their way down the mountain, Alex stayed in front of Faith, helping her maintain her footing even as torrents of rain made their path precarious. He lifted her over hollows and caught her when she stumbled over a large rock. The rain saturated their clothing instantly, leaving his T-shirt nearly invisible and plastered against the hard muscle of his arms and torso.

Her sweet pink blouse and blue jeans soaked through, Faith shivered.

Cold was the least of her worries when the ground began to shudder. "Alex?" she called over the howl of the wind. "What's that?"

His fearful expression sent terror through her. "The mountain."

His terse explanation made no sense until she looked behind them. Her first impression was that a tidal wave of hot cocoa was bearing down on them. But then she grasped what Alex had already figured out—the storm was washing away part of Kayford Mountain.

Alex's grip on her hand tightened, and he began running. His hold was the only thing that allowed her to keep up with him, but as the water overtook them, Alex drew her closer and braced their bodies against the thick trunk of a white pine.

Her face hidden in his chest, Faith was too frightened to do anything other than cling to him. The muddy wave carried debris past them, the trunk of a dead tree battering their white pine hard enough to shake Alex's hold on its lowermost branches. The cloudy brown water reached Faith's waist and was climbing steadily higher.

"We can't stay here," Alex sputtered, shaking filthy water from his long dark hair. "The water is going to take this tree down the mountainside."

Faith sobbed. She saw nothing of the idyllic mountain she had known all her life. The patchy groves of hardwood trees, the fields of sparse grass—all swallowed by the onrush of angry water.

"I know this mountain," he said, his brittle smile doing little to ease her fear. "We can't outrun the water, but we can hide from it."

He made a move to leave the safety of the tree, which had become increasingly unsure as each wave of water left it bending closer to the ground. Too scared to move, Faith clung to its branches.

"Will you trust me?" he shouted over the roar of the water and a booming crack of thunder.

She nodded, blinking tears and dirty water from her eyes. Her teeth chattering from fear and cold, she could barely squeeze out the words, "With my life."

Alex maintained his hold on the tree with one hand and used the other to shift Faith. "Climb on my back," he told her. "And when I let go of the tree—"

"Don't let go!" she cried. "We can wait here until the rain stops! My parents will be looking for me, and someone will find us."

He roughly took her chin and forced her to look at him. "The roots aren't going to hold this tree in place much longer." As if to illustrate his point, the white pine lurched, sweeping Alex off his feet. "None of your father's heavy machinery can do anything until after the water crests. Our best chance is to ride the runoff to the mudstone at the hollow. The rock will shelter us until the flooding stops."

"I can't," she whimpered. The pine made another wrenching shift, and Faith screamed.

In that instant, Alex simultaneously flipped her onto his back and let go of the tree. Faith pressed her face into his shoulder and held onto him with all her strength. The current was so strong, her legs floated behind her as the water threatened to rip her away from him. With her arms wrapped around Alex's neck so tightly, she wondered how he could breathe as he rode the murky wave toward the side of the mountain.

Debris crashed into him, and he struck something solid and hard hidden beneath the sloppy waves. Knocked off his direct course, he fought his way back toward the outcropping of mudstone by catching the branches of trees not yet uprooted by the flood.

Faith's muscles burned but she held onto Alex, silently trusting that his plan would work, that he would find a way to save them from the violently eroding mountain. "Hold your breath!" he shouted only a second before he sank beneath the surface.

Faith clamped her eyes shut and pressed her face hard to Alex's back, protecting it from the unidentified objects in the water that battered and scraped her body. Her lungs burned for want of air, and several times she feared she would be ripped from Alex. The muscles of his back and shoulders were rock hard as they worked within her grasp, and she wished that she could do something other than impede him with her stranglehold.

Hungry for air, her lungs pulsated painfully, but she forced her lips to stay pinched shut, her airways to remain closed. A more complete form of darkness began to overtake her when she felt her hands being pried apart under Alex's chin. Only vaguely aware of a tumbling sensation, the thud of her body against a hard, cold surface yanked her back to her senses. She drew deep breaths, coughing out the water that had sneaked in with the air.

Once her eyes cleared, she saw a curtain of brown water filled with rocks, branches and the other detritus of the mountain rushing past her. Wiping soggy locks of hair from her face, she looked around and saw that she was snug in a cave-like crevice in the mudstone. Just as Alex had said, the space was protected, the rock overhanging it acting as a ramp off which the floodwater ran into the hollow below.

Trembling violently, Faith realized what Alex either had not known or hadn't wanted to tell her—the shallow crevice was big enough for only one person.

"Alex!" she screamed, shifting carefully so as not to slide off the wet rock floor and into the hollow. Sitting as close to the edge as she dared, she scanned the water below, seeing only the misty backsplash of the polluted water pouring into the hollow. The water ran fast and hard. A tree fell into the hollow, and the force of the water striking it smashed it in half.

Clasping her hands to her mouth, Faith sobbed, the force of them shaking her bloodied and bruised body. "Alex," she cried, murmuring his name over and over until she had no voice left.

"Alex!" Faith gasped, jerking upright. Panting, she struggled to free herself from the bed sheet tangled around her legs and hips. She tumbled out of bed, went to the open window and took deep breaths of clean, cool air.

Her recurring dream was also her recurring nightmare, only this time she woke up angry instead of miserable.

Alex was alive and well and living as Zander Baron, and despite her anger, she was glad that her dream finally had an ending, even if it wasn't completely happy.

Standing in the breeze from the window, she wrung her hands, recalling the three-day search for bodies after the flood, a search that had yielded no sign of Alexander Brannon. His own parents had given him up for lost, and soon after had filed suit against the Lady Emiline Coal Company for the wrongful death of their son. Although legal, strip mining had so compromised the mountain that the heavy rain had produced a catastrophic flood. The Brannons had sought compensation far longer and harder than they'd sought their son's body. Even though Faith's mother was one of the few people in town who attended the memorial service organized by Red Irv, Faith had felt completely alone in mourning him.

Even now, while she felt an overwhelming sense of relief that Alex was alive, she couldn't share that news with anyone—not because she thought it would ruin his career, but because she knew his assessment of his importance to Dorothy was correct. Other than Faith, hardly anyone missed Alexander Brannon.

She paced her bedroom, desperate to talk about everything. Even though it was the middle of the night, she could call Magda, but Magda was first and foremost managing editor of *Personality!* Anything she confided had a very good chance of ending up in the pages of the magazine.

Daiyu was someone with whom Faith was friendly enough to call at two in the morning. But her story with Zander was too good, and Faith had no confidence that Daiyu would be able to keep the biggest secret that had ever come their way.

Faith dialed the first few digits of her parents' phone number, certain that her mother would pick up on the first ring, no matter the late hour. She hung up the phone before the call could connect. Her relationship with her mother had blossomed over the years, but she knew it would be a tremendous shock for her to learn that Alexander Brannon hadn't died in the flood.

The person she wanted to talk to was the very person she needed to talk about.

Alex.

Shivering in the chilly wind, she stepped away from the window, rubbing her bare arms to warm them. She wanted to kick herself for not getting Alex's phone number at Krasco's. It would be impossible to reach him directly.

Accepting that indirectly would have to do, she went into her cozy kitchenette and began burrowing through her handbag. She found her smartphone and called Brent Baxter.

"This better be good," he answered on the third ring, his voice gravelly with sleep.

"I need to talk to Alexander Brannon," Faith said. "Now."

"Who is this?" Brent demanded, suddenly sounding fully alert.

Faith admired the fact that he didn't pretend not to know who she was talking about. "Faith Wheeler. I met with Alex this morning, and I have a few more questions for him."

"Miss Wheeler, do you have any idea what time it is?"

"As a matter of fact, I do," Faith said sweetly. "It's about thirty-six hours before my deadline."

"Could I ask who your story is going to be about?"

She understood his meaning perfectly. "I haven't decided yet. That's why I need to talk to him."

"Miss Wheeler, I've come to understand that you and Zander—"

"Alex."

"You two have history, and I understand that things didn't end well back then. But I hope you aren't writing your story for revenge. Zan—I mean, Alex—deserves better than that. I'm prevailing upon you as his friend, not his agent. He's a good guy, and he's been through a lot. He doesn't deserve to be embarrassed in the media."

"I don't want revenge, and I don't want to see him hurt," Faith said. "But I have a job to do. I need his help to figure out the best way to accomplish that."

"Could I ask you a question, Miss Wheeler?"

She brought her feet up to the seat of her chair and scratched at the petal-pink polish on her toes. "Sure," she finally sighed.

"Were you in love with him?"

Stinging tears sprang to her eyes. Her heart pounding, she swiped them away. "Yes."

"Hmm. That makes things a bit more interesting."

"How so?"

"I think he loves you, too."

"He doesn't know me," Faith said. "Not anymore."

"I know him, and I am very concerned about what he's willing to sacrifice to make you happy. My mother has discovered so many people, and very few of them are who the public thinks they are. Some of our clients are so lost in Olivia Baxter's mythic reinventions, they really start to believe they're the people she has taught them to be. That raw, rough-edged mountain man I met five years ago is still very close to the surface of Zander Baron. I don't think you'll have to scratch very hard to get to Alex, and I won't let you ruin him, Miss Wheeler."

"You can't stop my story, Mr. Baxter," Faith countered.

"No, I can't," he conceded. "But I think I can postpone it."

"I don't like this," Daiyu complained, slumping against one of the rectangular columns in the lobby of the Beverly Wilshire Hotel. "It's too straightforward. I feel like a mall photographer."

"Quit complaining," Faith whispered fiercely from her position behind the column. "Harley Tatum's bachelor party is one of the most hush-hush get-togethers in town, and you and I are the only invited media. This will be a great story for us."

"For *you*," Daiyu sulked. "My photos are going to look like crap. I'm used to flying by the seat of my pants, not walking around in the light posing people like Olan Mills."

Faith rolled her eyes in exasperation. The Beverly Wilshire was one of the most storied establishments in Beverly Hills. Its Tuscan stone exterior and ornate Carrera marble façade were first made famous by *Beverly Hills Cop. Pretty Woman* later made the interior more famous—never mind that the interior shots of the latter movie had been filmed on soundstages.

The lobby of the real Beverly Wilshire looked nothing like the version in *Pretty Woman,* and Faith much preferred the muted champagnes and golds of the real hotel. Regal columns supported the high ceiling, and the entire space was a wonderful example of Italian Renaissance architecture.

In her punk/goth chains and ripped black denim, Daiyu looked as out of place in the glossy luxury of the lobby as the Clampett's jalopy at a Porsche dealership. With her camera hanging from her neck, strangers might have mistaken her for a tourist, but hotel employees and celebrities knew that Daiyu was one of the most talented photographers working in Los Angeles.

In an attempt to shorten the reins of one of his more notorious clients, Brent had organized Harley's bachelor party and had arranged for Faith and Daiyu to be added to the guest list. Brent's intervention was the only reason the desk manager tolerated the presence of *Personality!* personnel. Even so, he eyed them suspiciously.

"Is it going to be much longer?" Daiyu asked. "The early shift will be leaving the clubs soon, and I want to get some shots for my book."

Daiyu wasn't the typical paparazzo on the hunt for photos to sell to the highest bidder. Most of the images she captured were for *Personality!* stories, pictorials and fillers, but the best of her work was reserved for her book, a collection of artistic candids she had been working on for two years. From veteran stars like Sean Connery and Elizabeth Taylor to newcomers like Zander Baron, Daiyu aimed her lens at anyone she found beautiful, compelling, unusual, or all three.

"Harley Tatum better be sober," Daiyu groused. "I want him for my book, but not if he's drooling and playing with his toes."

"Could you try to show a little enthusiasm for this job?" Faith pleaded. Shifting her satchel on her shoulder, she craned to see around the artistic arrangements of fresh lilies on the table in the center of the lobby, to improve her view of the entrance. "Harley and his guests should be pulling up in their limo any minute now."

"*Now I know it was a waste of time, workin' so hard to make you mine,*" Daiyu sang, the notes breaking with an odd country twang as she gazed at the chandelier high above the flower table. "*Another guy comes and sings his song, you turned away, you done me wrong.*"

"Please," Faith winced. "Didn't we hear enough of that song after he won *Rising Star* last year?"

"I can't help it," Daiyu said. "I have a talent for instantly learning all the words to songs everyone hates."

Faith spied the nose of a Hummer limousine gliding to a stop before the sparkling glass doors of the hotel entrance. Loud male laughter soon filled the spacious lobby, and Faith recognized Harley Tatum's voice before she saw him and his cohorts. A hotel employee guided them toward the elevator, with Harley's boot heels announcing their procession across the highly polished marble floor.

"We're on," Faith said, leaving the sanctity of the pillar. Daiyu fell into step behind her as she caught up with Harley's party.

"Whoa!" Harley said, his blue eyes sparkling when he caught sight of Faith. "Brent went high-end for us." He took off his cowboy hat and, holding it over his heart, he bowed to Faith. "And how many diamonds are you rated?" he asked with a flip of his long, strawberry blond hair.

"She's not a call girl," Zander growled, moving to the front of the group. "She's a reporter." He took Faith by the arm, the gesture as much possessive as protective. "What are you doing here? This is a private party."

Faith shook out of his grasp. "Brent Baxter invited me to cover Harley's bachelor party for my magazine," she answered, smiling primly. "I have a deadline to meet, and I needed a story. A good one."

"So you're crashing the bachelor party because of me?" Zander asked.

"I'm here because of Harley Tatum," Faith explained. "When an up and coming country rocker's first CD goes platinum the same week he completes his second stint in rehab, proposes to his baby's mama and decides to get married, it makes the magazine. *Personality!* prefers to emphasize the positives in a celebrity's life. Harley's attempts to start over and build a decent life for himself will make a great feel-good cover story."

Zander clenched his jaw, which only emphasized its squareness.

"Would you rather I write the story I had originally planned?"

The lift of her eyebrow took him straight back to a secluded lookout spot on Kayford Mountain, and it disarmed him. The more he studied her, the more familiar his feelings for her became, and the harder he found it to leave her side.

"Olivia traded my story for Harley's," Zander said knowingly.

Faith and Zander held back while the other men and Daiyu entered the elevator. "Don't undersell yourself," she whispered. "It'll take more than Harley's stag night to compensate me for holding off on the scoop of the year."

"Just the year?" Zander asked, moving close enough to catch the scent of her hair. "Now who's underselling me?"

"You've only got one box-office hit on your filmography," Faith said, her heart thumping so hard she thought he might be able to see it bouncing against her low-cut blouse. "If your next two flicks do as well, then my scoop might warrant an upgrade. It's directly proportional, Zander. The brighter your star shines, the bigger your secret becomes." She sidestepped away from him and entered the elevator, where Harley's eyes went straight to her bosom. "I hope you can bear the weight of it."

≫⊜

"Holy crap."

Daiyu said what Faith was thinking as they moved through the eighth-floor suite where their private butler was taking drink orders for Harley and his guests.

"This place is bigger than my parents' house. Heaven probably doesn't have a living room this big," she sighed.

Faith brushed her fingers over the large, peculiar petals of a ginger flower protruding from an enormous floral display occupying the entire top of the telephone table nearest the door to the suite. The tropical arrangement complemented rather than overwhelmed the subdued beige and green décor.

The thick carpeting silencing the clomp of his boots, Harley exited the second of the two master bedrooms. "This ain't no party until some honey shows up, and ain't nobody here but us fellas." He eyeballed Faith and Daiyu, who quickly ducked behind Faith. "Of course, one pretty filly is better than no pretty fillies."

Harley made a beeline for Faith, but Zander intercepted him before he could get within arm's reach. "Why don't you grab a cranberry juice or something from the bar?" Zander suggested. "Brent said that he'd arranged for the entertainment. Let's just wait for it to get here."

Harley snatched off his straw cowboy hat and threw it to the floor. "Cranberry juice?" he exclaimed. "There ain't no dang alcohol here? Aw, man!"

"Dude, you've been out of rehab for about ten minutes," laughed one of Harley's friends, who was dressed similarly in high-end designer cowboy apparel. "It's the rest of us who ought to be complaining about a dry stag party."

"Who's that guy?" Daiyu asked, venturing out of Faith's shadow.

"He's a civilian," Zander said. "Justin or Dustin, or something. He's one of Harley's friends from Tennessee. He's not in the business."

"He's cute," Daiyu remarked. She made a half-hearted attempt to smooth down her hair, but the heavily shellacked spikes popped right back up. "Excuse me, Faith, Mr. Baron," she said. "I think it's time for my close-up."

Daiyu was a good foot shorter than Harley's friend, and they couldn't have been more different in appearance, but they seemed to hit it off. Daiyu said something, Justin or Dustin bowed his head closer to hear her, and then laughing, the pair started toward the balcony and the fully stocked—but non-alcoholic—bar.

"I don't know how she does it," Faith said, staring past Daiyu and fixing her gaze on the view of the Hollywood Hills. "She can get any guy she wants."

"And you can't?" Zander asked skeptically.

"No. I can't. Things start out okay, but then I just lose interest. I don't want to settle for someone who doesn't have that spark."

"What spark?"

"You know what spark," she said. "That thing that makes you eager and impatient and breathless knowing that you're going to see him or be with him. It's what brings everything else about him into full Technicolor. It's—"

"I know what you mean," he said. "I've been missing that spark, too."

"You seemed to like Kiki Langlois's spark," Faith said.

"Kiki . . . Hell, Faith, I dated her two years ago. Once. How do you know about her?"

"I work for *Personality!*," Faith said by way of explanation. "The research department dug up photos of you going back to your first public appearance with Brent Baxter."

"He's the one who set up the date with Kiki," Zander said. "He thought it would be good exposure for me."

"Exposure is right." Faith snorted. "She wore a top made of cellophane and latex. And she was hanging all over you."

"Kiki has a thing for brooding, blue-eyed men, or so she says."

"Do you have a thing for ex-supermodels?"

"My thing prefers ex-cheerleaders," he answered, his voice low.

Faith's mouth went dry, but she maintained her unruffled exterior. "It won't work, Zander."

"What?"

"Your charm. I'm not going to fall for it, so give it up."

"Look, I came over here to keep Harley and the rest of his boys from trying to turn you into their party favor." He took a step back, his hands raised in surrender. "I don't have an ulterior motive."

Faith was tempted to believe him even though he hadn't looked her in the eye when he denied having a hidden agenda. "I can handle myself just fine," she insisted. "I don't need rescuing anymore."

"I brought some entertainment to hold us over until the Fleiss girls show up," one of the guests said, opening a silver attaché case on the low table before the sofa. "I got *Good Will Humping, Bravehump, Raiders of the Lost Hump, White Men Can't Hump, Humpleberry Finn—*"

"I'm startin' to see a pattern here," laughed a man in a business suit. Faith recognized him as the co-founder and executive producer of a new studio called Swirl Productions.

"—*Great Sexpectations, Pulp Friction*—"

"Just pick one!" someone hollered.

"—*Frisky Business, Gonad the Barbarian, Guess Who Came at Dinner*—"

"Put on a dang DVD already!" Harley laughed.

One of the guests aimed a remote control at the fifty-inch plasma television and powered the set on. After slipping a disc into the DVD player, he resumed his seat on one of the ottomans. Harley and his friends cheered when the opening credits rolled.

Faith folded her arms over her chest and lifted her chin in a stubborn tilt Zander knew well. "If your agent thinks that this juvenile display of male foolishness is an equal trade for your story, he's got a whole other think coming."

Zander took her arm and walked her to the powder room off the living room. "Could you lower your voice?"

She yanked her arm free and set her hands on her hips. "Something newsworthy better happen soon, or I'm running with the piece I've already started working on."

Glowering, Zander started to argue with her, but loud, persistent knocking on the door to the suite distracted him. He was closer to the front door than the butler, so with Faith following him, he opened it.

"Hey," greeted a man dressed in a safari hunter's outfit. "Is this Harley Tatum's bachelor party?"

"Uh, yeah," Zander said, forcing back a smirk.

"Great," the man smiled. "I brought the entertainment."

Already indignant at the prospect of having to endure strippers, Faith vowed to pop Brent a good one in the eye if a pimp dressed as the Crocodile Hunter ushered in a bevy of girls dressed suggestively as animals.

Zander opened the door wider and stepped aside. The other guests approached the door, fairly drooling in anticipation as *Bravehump* hero Willie Phallus loudly called for freedom in the background.

The Safari Man entered the suite, greeting everyone he passed with a smile.

"Please tell me *you* aren't the entertainment," Harley said.

The Safari Man looked behind him, his smile fading upon seeing that he was alone. "Damn it, Candy," he muttered under his breath, marching back to the door.

He leaned into the corridor and impatiently gestured to someone out of view. "Would you please come on in here? You're on!" Turning back to the guests, he said, "I'm sorry about this, guys. I don't know what's going on. We've done the Wilshire so many times, I guess Candy is a little bored. But I promise, you'll get a good party."

Harley eagerly rubbed his hands together. "Well, bring on sweet Candy!" he crowed enthusiastically. "This is my last *hoo*-rah before I enter wedded bliss and the land of the same trim 'til divorce do we part. I got a sweet tooth and I can't wait to get my last piece of Candy! Ain't no nookie like single man—*monkey*?" he finished with a squeal when the safari man led an orangutan in an orange diaper into the suite.

CHAPTER 5

To preserve Harley's fresh sobriety, his friends took turns sneaking down to sidebar and The Blvd, which were housed in the hotel, for drinks. As his pals became rowdier, so did the party, and the orangutan was at the very heart of it. Harley seemed to enjoy the animal's presence more than he would have enjoyed that of traditional stag party entertainment.

"Hey, Safari Man, can you get him to do me?" Harley asked the trainer.

"Sure," Safari Man said. "Candy, do the cowboy."

Candy loped over to Harley and stood in front of him, his soft brown eyes moving over Harley.

"If this critter is male," Harley said, "why'd you name him Candy?"

"He wouldn't answer to any of the male names I tried to give him. He likes Candy. That was my ex-wife's name," Safari Man explained with a sheepish smile. "She couldn't handle our success once me and Candy started getting big bookings. She made me choose between her and Candy, so I picked Candy."

Faith and Zander slowly eased away from Safari Man, neither of them daring to imagine how Candy the orangutan's charms could have had outshone those of Candy the ex-wife.

Candy had finished his quiet study of Harley and returned to his position atop the cocktail table, which he was using as a stage. He stripped off the costly silk tie he had taken from the producer when imitating him and dropped it to the floor. Candy took Harley's hat and put it on his own head, and then with the distinctive wide grin of his species, he mimed the strumming of a guitar. When he opened his mouth and "sang" a few short, choppy, high-pitched notes, the men cheered and laughed raucously, Harley loudest of all.

Moving stealthily around the room and among the men crowded around Candy, Daiyu captured the merriment, taking shot after shot.

"Brent is a genius," Zander said.

Faith laughed as Candy tossed off the cowboy hat and then looked at Zander. He lowered his head and studied the room from his lowered brow line, his thumbs hooked into the waistband of his monkey pants. Candy stood perfectly erect, his big belly protruding. Faith could have sworn the orangutan was scowling.

"Holy crud, he's doin' Zander!" Harley howled. He laughed so hard the only sound he made was a tight, whistling wheeze. When he fell off his ottoman in tears, holding his middle, Candy broke his pose and resumed his regular sway-backed posture, grinning from ear to ear.

"He's really good," Faith laughed. "Man, he did you perfectly."

Zander grunted. "Let's see how funny Harley thinks this is when he can't find his wallet."

Zander directed Faith's eyes back to Candy. The orangutan was easing Harley's wallet from the back pocket of his jeans while he was still curled up in laughter.

Safari Man had retreated to the lavish buffet, and he was putting away cold shrimp as though he hadn't eaten in weeks.

"I really hope Daiyu got a picture of Candy making a monkey out of you," Faith chuckled. "I'm going to frame it and put it on my desk."

"Look at him now," Zander said, smiling smugly. "Still think he's funny?"

Faith turned to find Candy standing on Harley's abandoned ottoman. Her satchel was slung over Candy's slight shoulder.

"He's adorable," Faith said. "What's so—hey . . ."

She finally noticed that Candy had slathered his lips with the same lipstick she was wearing.

"Great," she grumbled. "Now I've got monkey cooties all over my new Viva Glam. That's fourteen dollars down the drain."

"Candy looks almost as good in red as you do, sugar!" Harley choked out through a fresh fit of laughter.

Although tempted, Faith managed not to kick him as he writhed on the floor, kicking his heels. She took her bag from Candy and began taking inventory of its contents. "I want to make sure he didn't steal my identity the way he stole Harley's," Faith explained.

"I wish I could be there when Harley explains his night with Candy to his fiancée, Zander said. "Even if she believes him, she won't believe him."

"He'll be able to offer next week's *Personality!* as proof," Faith said. "I'll get a great story out of this. Monkeys and Paris are always good sellers."

"Paris?"

"The city, not the celebutante," Faith clarified.

"Hey," Harley interrupted, "We're taking Candy to the Mediterranean pool. Y'all comin'?"

"This is getting better by the second," Faith said under her breath, following the group out of the suite.

Walking upright with a fluffy towel slung over his arm, Candy held Harley's hand. They had to travel through the lobby to get to the Mediterranean pool, and Harley seemed proud to escort Candy. Hotel visitors laughed, stared or clapped while the hotel staff moved along as though an orangutan strolling to the pool happened everyday.

But then a young woman recognized Harley. Whether she was a hotel guest or one of the star-watchers who lurked outside the hotel hoping to catch a celebrity, Faith never knew. In the ensuing chaos, that detail mattered little.

"Harley Tatum!" the woman screamed, her blonde hair flying as she ran at him. The rest of her greeting was an indecipherable howling that scared Candy so badly, he leaped onto Safari Man, nearly toppling him.

With moves like wide receiver Randy Moss, the blonde avoided hotel security personnel and managed to reach Harley, who caught her full weight when she launched herself at him.

"I love you, Harley! You're my most favorite singer ever!" she gushed.

Harley fell backwards, but Justin or Dustin and the studio executive caught him before he hit the floor. It took the two of them plus a security guard to pry the girl's arms from Harley's neck.

"I voted for you about a million times every night when you were on *Rising Star*, and all my friends voted for you, too!" the girl wept as she was dragged from the lobby and toward the exit. "I love you so much and your songs are the best! Can I get your autograph? Can I get a hug? Can I have a photo with you?"

"Uh oh," Harley said, voicing the thought they all shared upon seeing the girl, still in tears, speaking to a cluster of paparazzi and pointing into the lobby.

"We better get gone," Justin or Dustin said. "They're coming."

Daiyu offered a goofy smile when he took her hand.

Holding their cameras high and snapping photos as they came, photographers flooded into the lobby, hoping to snap as many shots as they could before hotel security drove them back to the street.

"Zander Baron's with him!" one of them called, and the tide of flashing cameras divided, one half swarming Harley and the other closing in around Zander.

"Oh, man, this is so awesome!" Harley grinned. His friends closed in around him, pressing him into Faith and Zander. Being so much shorter, Faith disappeared between the two men. Their group was soon swallowed by paparazzi, which the hotel staff was trying to remove.

"I don't mean to spoil your fun," Safari Man said, holding up a hand to shield his eyes from flashes, "but has anyone seen Candy?"

Beverly Hills cop Gerard Lewis parked his cruiser at an angle on Rodeo Drive to block traffic from the site where a white van with a handicapped hangtag had run aground on the center divider covering the old trolley tracks. He had been heading back to the station for the night when he saw the van speed away from the Rodeo Drive entrance to the Beverly Wilshire hotel, the doorman in hot pursuit, before promptly crashing.

Yawning, he approached the driver's side of the van. This would be the highlight of his night—ticketing a drunk and waiting for the tow truck to show up. "License and registration, please," he requested, stepping up to the driver's window.

Officer Lewis did a double take when a pair of long arms ten times hairier than Robin Williams's ended with two hands firmly gripping the steering wheel. His eyes followed the arms to the body they were attached to, and Candy the orangutan responded to the officer's wide-eyed shock with a huge grin full of big, blunt yellow teeth.

Officer Lewis reached for his gun.

"No!" Safari Man shouted in panic, skidding to a stop near the officer. "Don't shoot him! He's harmless!"

"And unarmed!" Faith added as she, Daiyu, Zander and Harley joined the Safari Man.

The rush of paparazzi from the hotel, along with Harley's sobbing fan, surrounded the van and began shooting from all sides, the camera flashes adding a strobe effect to the peculiar scene.

Officer Lewis, one hand still on his gun, radioed for backup and a tow.

"I'm so sorry, officer," Safari Man explained. "We were performing at the hotel, and then all these photographers came in, and Candy got scared and must have run off."

The officer glared at Safari Man. "Get him out of there," he said, jerking his head toward the driver's seat of the van.

"Shouldn't we wait until an ambulance gets here?" Safari Man asked. "Candy might be hurt."

"Get your monkey outta that vehicle!" Officer Lewis ordered through clenched teeth.

"Candy, come on boy," Safari Man said.

The ever-obedient Candy came flying out of the window feet first, and he used the officer's shoulders to swing himself gently to the street. He stood at attention beside the officer, smiling for the cameras.

"Where'd he get the van?" Faith whispered to Daiyu.

"Who knew he could drive?" Daiyu replied.

Officer Lewis took off his helmet and vigorously scratched his head. "I don't even know where to begin citing you for this. Failure to control your animal, unlicensed and uninsured driver at the wheel, damage to public property—"

"Aw, officer sir, he didn't mean no harm," Harley said. "Look at him. He's just a monkey."

"Orangutan," Safari Man promptly corrected.

Pointing his finger as though it were as lethal as his gun, Officer Lewis marched toward him. Aping the officer's posture and attitude, Candy followed. Some of the photographers started laughing too hard to take photos.

"Whatever it is, it has no business driving a vehicle! I'll need to see your identification and your animal permit." The officer held out his hand.

So did Candy.

Harley made a subtle slicing gesture, mutely telling Candy to quit the mimicry.

Safari Man handed his cards over to Officer Lewis.

"All of you, stay right there while I call this in," the officer said. He started back to his cruiser, and Candy followed, perfectly copying the swagger of the officer's shoulders.

Officer Lewis spun around to see what was so funny. Spotting Candy, he pointed at Safari Man. So did Candy. "Subdue this animal!" Officer Lewis yelled. Candy said the same thing, only in orangutan.

"That's enough, Candy," Safari Man told him. "Come on over here."

Sirens in the distance signaled the arrival of Officer Lewis' backup. Most of the photographers dispersed to avoid confrontations with the police.

"I guess it's officially a party," Faith muttered. "I'll get a great story out of this."

The sirens grew louder, and Candy grew agitated. The lights and noise of the newly arrived cruisers and fire engine scared him, and he leaped into Harley's arms.

"Aw, Candy, I ain't gonna let nothin' hurt you," he cooed.

Candy thanked him with a big, juicy kiss to the side of his head.

Daiyu took a series of quick shots.

"And there's our cover," Faith said proudly.

"Can we leave now?" Daiyu asked.

"Yeah, I think we've got enough for our happy-slappy puff cover."

They started back toward the Wilshire, passing the hotel's manager on his way to the accident site. They stopped when Zander trotted up behind them.

"You can't leave now," he said.

"Keep walking," Daiyu advised. "Let's get off the street."

Faith and Zander understood her meaning when they saw three reporters quickly approaching. They returned to the hotel, and after being cleared by security, they joined the rest of Harley's friends waiting in the lobby.

"Don't you have to stay until the end of the party?" Zander asked.

"I've got enough for a solid piece," Faith said. "I'll call the Beverly Hills police department in the morning to get the report on Candy and Safari Man. That's the only end I have to tie up."

"So I can scoot?" Daiyu asked. "Justin wants me to shoot him in private."

"Can't keep your cowboy waiting, can you?" Faith chuckled. "Thanks, Daiyu."

With a brisk salute, Daiyu turned and sprinted to her cowboy, who caught her around her waist.

"Well," Faith said, "I have a story to file." She gave Zander a brotherly punch in the arm. "See ya."

He grabbed the strap of her satchel as she turned to go. "You couldn't stay a little while longer?"

"I could." She crossed her arms. "But why would I?"

His hands deep in his pockets, Zander rocked on his heels. "Um . . . maybe you should hang around and keep an eye on your friend." He threw a thumb in Daiyu's direction. "You should never leave a man behind."

"That 'man' is twenty-six years old and has a black belt in shodokan karate. Daiyu can handle herself. But you'll look out for her, won't you? You're the big hero, remember?"

Zander recoiled as if stung, his reaction taking her back to that rainy day on Kayford Mountain.

"Alex, I'm sorry," Faith said, reaching for his hand. "I didn't mean that the way it came out," she explained in a rush. "I was referring to the hero you play in your movie, not—"

She stopped abruptly and looked away. Even now with him alive and well before her, she couldn't bring herself to discuss that day out loud.

Zander tightened his grip on her hand just to make sure she wouldn't try to take it back. "I knew you were okay," he said quietly, moving closer. "I couldn't have left without making sure you had been found."

"That wasn't enough, Alex." She stared into his eyes, trying to force understanding into the depths of their beauty. "You didn't just leave Dorothy. You left *me*. I thought . . ."

His fingers grazed her jawline, starting a tremble in her lower lip. "What?" he asked gently. "You thought what?"

"I thought we came from the same hive. We understood each other when no one else did. I thought that we . . . were a *we*."

"We were just two frustrated, lonely kids back then," Zander said. "Things change."

"Yes, they do," Faith agreed. "Now we're two frustrated, lonely adults with some unfinished business."

"Look, out me or don't, but quit waving it over my head."

"I'm not talking about a story," she said. She took a quick, deep breath, steeling herself for her next words. "I still have feelings for you. And until I know what to do with them, I won't know what to do with your story. And what's more, I think you have feelings for me, too."

Avoiding her eyes, he said, "Faith, you're talking about something that happened a long time ago. You can't expect that I still—"

"Then why are you still holding my hand?"

He looked down but made no move to release her hand.

"Kiss me."

He grunted in surprise, his gaze going straight to her lovely lips.

"Kiss me, and if you can honestly say that you feel nothing for me, then I'll drop your story."

"A kiss for your silence," he said. "Sounds like a good trade."

He lowered his head to kiss her, but she pulled back. "Only if the kiss doesn't mean anything to you," she emphasized.

115

"And if it does?"

"Then I want full disclosure. I want to know everything you've done since the day you left Dorothy."

"What do you plan to do with that information? Assuming your hypothesis is correct and your kiss makes me sing like a canary."

"That's still up in the air," she said. "I still have a job to do, and a scoop is a scoop. The story is going to get out, Alex, and I might as well be the person to write it. The more information I have, the better job I'll do. It'll be good for both of us."

"Then I guess we'd better get on with settling this." Taking her by the waist, he drew her against him. He gently smoothed her hair away from her face, and instantly he realized how much he missed the curls he had so adored back in Dorothy. With her skin warming his palms and her hands relaxed against his chest, he knew that he had been tricked, not by Faith, but by his own heart. For so many years, he'd told himself that she was better off without him, that she was too good for him. He now understood one simple fact: He had to have Faith.

Her image now and the one he'd carried in his memory for so long smoothly merged. He wouldn't have thought it possible for her to have grown more beautiful. There had been days when he'd been working at the auto shop, and as darkness fell, the lights in the studio above McGill's Pharmacy would burn into the night. Mesmerized, he would watch Faith extend her arms and legs into positions both graceful and impossible, and he wouldn't blink for fear of missing even the most subtle curve of a finger.

That vision of her had been burned into his brain. Now, with her smile both wary and eager, her eyes deep and dark and holding curiosities he could only imagine, she was as lovely and every bit as powerful as she had been all those years ago. He closed the distance between her lips and his.

Faith's hands tightened, her spine relaxed, and her body bowed into Zander's. His hands clenched handfuls of her blouse as the delicate brush of lips evolved into deeper exploration, a sharing of textures, a complete re-education.

Her fingers moved into the hair at his nape, the silkiness she found there so familiar even if the cut and color were not. The heat of his mouth warmed her all over, and in trying to get even closer to him, she pushed him into one of the columns.

Everything below Zander's waist hardened as he braced himself against the column and Faith wrapped herself around him. He raised his chin, giving her access to his neck, and she took full advantage of it. As his hands moved over her backside, Zander imagined her wrapped in the petal-pink leotards she'd worn when she danced.

Her body was fuller, but just as firm and supple as it had been that last time he'd kissed her. She was more confident in how to use it, her movements eliciting reactions that made him ache and shiver.

"Faith," he exhaled into her neck, marking her flesh with searing kisses that invited her to touch him more intimately.

She ran a hand along his inner thigh, stopping just short of the hard knot behind the fly of his jeans. Zander whimpered when she drew back altogether, her lips giving his lower one a slight tug in the process.

"Well?" she asked, pressing the back of her hand to her kiss-swollen lips. "Did you feel that?"

Still slumped against the column, he untucked his shirt and let it fall past his hips to cover his answer. Faith's smile was so smug, so satisfied and so sinfully delicious, Zander could only bang his head against the column in frustrated surrender.

"So I guess I'll have my people contact your people to set up an interview," she said brightly.

"Do that," he said. "I lost."

"Did you?" Faith replied, lifting a finely arched eyebrow.

With that, she backed a few steps away before turning and heading for the exit.

Magda's desktop was empty but for her candy dish, her phone and a grainy eight-by-ten glossy of a couple kissing against a column in the lobby of the Beverly Wilshire Hotel. Chomping on a length of watermelon taffy that gave the office the sent of a kindergarten classroom, Magda got right down to business.

"Give me one good reason why I shouldn't fire you right now," she said.

"Because I'm one of your best writers," Faith said.

"Not good enough. Try again."

"Because we're friends," Faith suggested.

"I never let friendship interfere with business. Next."

"Because you can't see the face of the woman Zander Baron is kissing," Faith said wearily, rubbing her forehead. What she really wanted to do was kick herself. Paparazzi had been all over the hotel, and even though she and Zander had been pretty far back in the lobby, there was little a well-aimed telephoto lens would have missed. She'd been concerned with one thing only—finding out if Brent was right about Zander's feelings. Her own agenda had trumped that of the magazine's, and she'd broken one of the cardinal rules of reporting. She'd lost her objectivity.

"Bingo, kiddo." Magda sat back in her chair and began unwrapping a fresh rope of taffy, this one strawberry. "I liked the *Monkeying Around with Harley Tatum* piece. Daiyu's photo is going on the cover. I don't know how that man managed it, but he looks handsome *and* charming with that gorilla in his arms."

"Orangutan," Faith said.

"Whatever." As if throwing down a gauntlet, Magda tossed the remainder of her taffy onto her desk. "We need to talk, Scoop. I can't have one of my reporters running around with the new It Kid. It compromises the integrity of the magazine. It took me years to re-shape *Personality!*'s image from a run-of-the-mill tabloid specializing in catching married celebs climbing out of their mistress' windows to a legitimate rival to *People*, and you being shot making out with Zander Baron—"

"It won't happen again," Faith said.

"How's the Baron piece coming along?"

"I've hit a kink."

"A kink. A kink is not good. Describe it, and I'll tell you how to untangle it."

Faith sat on the arm of one of the chairs facing Magda's desk. She had always appreciated Magda's cool efficiency and relentless professionalism. Her unique ability to be domineering yet endearing, had earned the loyalty and trust of her staff, her readers and the celebrities whose lives she used to fill the pages of *Personality!*

There was no problem she couldn't handle. Temperamental stars, demanding agents, obnoxious publicists, reporters and photographers who filed their stories late—all child's play for Magda, who at thirty-three was *Personality!*'s youngest managing editor ever.

"Have you ever gone into something expecting it to be one thing, and you come out on the other side and it's something totally different?" Faith asked.

"Guess what I hate more than cellulite?" Magda responded.

"What?" Faith asked.

"Riddles. Spit it out, Faith. What's the deal with the Baron story?"

Faith's amusement withered. "Remember when I first proposed doing a piece on Zander Baron?"

"Yes," Magda said, stretching the syllable out to indicate her mounting impatience. "I told you to go for it. You're a talented writer, an excellent interviewer and you've never let me down when it comes to finding creative ways to get a story." She glanced at the photo. "I don't exactly sanction this particular approach to an interview, but I don't know . . ." She laced her fingers behind her head and reclined in her chair. "Baron's a looker. I might have done the same thing, given the chance. I figured the Baron story would be a slam-dunk for you."

"It is." Faith stood and paced in a small circle, holding her head in both hands. The flared sleeves of her pale pink tunic slid up to her elbows. "It was."

Magda's nose for news caught a scent. She perked up and straightened in her chair. "You uncovered something good, didn't you?" She pressed a button on her phone, activating the intercom. "No calls, Butchy, thanks," she said into the speaker, then disconnected. She leaned to one side to see past Faith.

"What are you doing?" Faith asked.

"Looking for shadows under the door," Magda whispered. "Butchy has taken to eavesdropping."

Faith looked and saw a pair of blunted shadows at the seam where the bottom of the door almost met the carpeting.

"Butchy's the cutest receptionist I've ever had, but he's one nosy bastard," Magda said. "He's always trying to get an angle on where to send his head shots and resumés. This is the last time I hire a model turned actor turned administrative assistant."

After the shadows disappeared, Magda said, "Okay, we're in the Butchy-free zone now. So what did you get on him? Is it major?"

"To him."

Magda rested her elbows on her desk and rocked forward. "He killed someone, didn't he?"

Faith swallowed hard, unexpected emotion forming a hard lump in her throat. "Kind of."

"Who?" Magda asked hungrily. "His mom? His dad? An old girlfriend? I always thought he had the look of a fugitive. Give me the goods, doll!"

Her heart heavy with somber remembrance, Faith averted her eyes as she answered. "His mother died in what was called a household accident about eight years ago, but the consensus was that his dad gave her one beating too many. His father died of cirrhosis a couple of years after that. He'd been dead in his trailer for a week before he was found."

Magda's excitement died. "Jeez, Faith," she gasped. "The kid's got more family drama than Hamlet. It kind of contradicts the 4-1-1 Baxter and Baxter have been peddling all these years."

"It certainly does," Faith agreed somberly.

"Yet I still detect a trace of Eau de Scandal," Magda said. "Tell."

"I'm not sure I can."

Taken aback, Magda's expression cooled. "This isn't a congressional hearing, kiddo. I'm not going to subpoena you or hold you in contempt if you don't tell me his big secret. But as your managing editor, I can reassign you. I can give the Baron piece to another writer. I already know that I don't have one who'll show the same sensitivity and concern for Baron. His story is a career-making piece. Have you lost sight of that?"

Faith displayed the West Virginia backbone that had gotten her this far in her career. "Do what you have to, but I won't give my research to another writer."

"I wouldn't expect you to," Magda said gently. "For right now, just answer me this: Why does the Zander Baron story have you so alloverish?"

A short laugh burst from Faith, which defused some of the tension. Faith admired anew the tightrope Magda walked between friend and boss. "I know him. We grew up in the same place."

"How is that possible, Faith? You're from some mining town in West Virginny. Zander was raised in Wyoming."

Color flooded Faith's cheeks. "Well, Dorothy was the name of the town, but Zander and I lived in an area called Booger Hollow."

Magda's jaw ticked. "Suave, sexy, mysterious Zander Baron is a Booger Hollow boy from WV? Is that what you're hiding?"

"I'm not hiding it," Faith protested. "He is."

"Well, hell, if the boys in Booger Hollow look like Z.B., then I'm calling my realtor," Magda said.

"They don't," Faith assured. "Zander was truly one of a kind. In high school, all the girls were crazy about him."

"You, too?"

Faith studied her thumbnails. "He was so . . ."

"Mysterious," Magda said.

"And . . ."

"Dark," Magda purred.

"Yes. And he was so handsome it hurt to look at him. He was the only boy who looked like a man."

"No wonder Olivia Baxter snared him. Do you know where she comes in?"

"He literally ran into her, or she ran into him, when he came out here. I'm not exactly sure when he ended up in L.A., but he disappeared from Dorothy when he was nineteen."

"Disappeared?"

"There was a flood," Faith explained, her voice tremulous. "It was bad. Sixty people were injured, and the guy you know as Zander Baron died."

"Disappeared," Magda said.

"Left," Faith conceded. "I took it very personally. We, uh . . ." Suddenly feeling very self conscious, she cleared her throat.

"Yes?" Magda prompted.

"He was special to me. I thought I was special to him, too."

"And this brings us to the kink," Magda murmured. "He abandoned you, Faith. You don't owe him a thing now."

"I know. But I'm not sure I have it in me to betray him."

"I'm not unsympathetic to the position you're in. As a friend, I'd tell you that you need to meet with this man and find some closure. Real closure, not hormonally-charged tonsil hockey in the lobby of the Wilshire. But as your managing editor, I'd have to be insane to pass up a chance at a cover story revealing the secret origin of Zander Baron.

"May I assume that you wrote for the *Booger Hollow Gazette* in your spare time?" Magda teased, easing the tension.

"It was the *Lincoln High Observer*, and no, I didn't write for it," Faith said. "My father thought reporting would take too much time away from my schoolwork. He wouldn't let me participate in too many extracurriculars in school. I was a cheerleader, but my parents also had me in ballet, piano, French and drawing classes outside school."

"You little mountain deb, you," Magda laughed. "And all this time, I thought you were a self-made, cosmopolitan woman of the world."

"I am self-made," Faith said defiantly. "I applied to schools they approved of, but I wanted to go into journalism. They wouldn't pay for school unless I switched to art history, business or education. I didn't want to spend four years in college only to go right back to Booger Hollow, get married, and stare at the framed sheepskin on the wall. I wanted to be a reporter because I thought it would give me the chance to travel and meet different people. My father thought I'd toe the line if he cut me off, so I had to make my own way."

"At eighteen?"

"I knew that they would help me, if I ever really needed it," Faith admitted. "They were waiting for me to crack and crawl back to them begging for help. I didn't cave. I waited tables at a pizza joint, I made change at an all-night Laundromat, I cleaned the rat cages in the biology department—when I wasn't in class or studying, I took any job I could to cover my tuition and rent. Between work and a couple of merit-based partial scholarships, I got through school."

"I never knew that you were so tough, cookie," Madga said with an admiring smile.

"I chose to be on my own," Faith said. "Zander didn't. He didn't have the kind of parents he deserved."

"Any foster care involved?"

"He might have been better off if the state had intervened. He managed to make a life for himself that no one back in Dorothy would ever believe."

"It's a great story, Faith. If the public knew about it, his stock would skyrocket. America loves an underdog who works hard and becomes a top dog."

"America might love it, but Zander wouldn't."

"Are you kidding?" Magda scoffed. "For the past three years, the kid has worked like a Spartan. He's in the middle of a film, and he starts another one as soon as it wraps. The industry can't get enough of him, and the public is starting to follow suit. The up-and-comer cover we did in January with Baron's photo generated more mail than any other cover in the past sixteen months. That issue outsold all our celebrity death and near-death issues, and that *never* happens. Magazines like ours are escapist entertainment. The public will devour a story about one of the least among them becoming one of the greatest among the Hollywood elite. He's the J.K. Rowling of Hollywood hunks. He came out of nowhere, from nowhere—no offense—and is within reach of superstardom, and you're saying he won't jump at that? Is he insane?"

"No," Faith answered. "He's very proud."

"For God's sake, Faith, every actor in Hollywood has a fat ego."

"Pride isn't the same as ego, not for Zander," Faith said. "He left Dorothy with nothing and nowhere to go. He's rebuilt himself, and I don't think it's our right to unravel his life to sell magazines . . ." She shook her head.

"What is it, Faith? You don't think he'll do something drastic, do you?"

"I think he would disappear again."

Magda took a moment to study Faith's face, and Faith knew that she was deciding her next move. When Magda sighed and slumped back in her chair, Faith felt more hopeful about the story.

"Do you think anyone else from Booger Valley recognized Zander?" Magda asked.

"Booger Hollow. I doubt it. He looks so different now. People never paid much attention to him back then, anyway, other than to make fun of him. Everyone thought he died in the big flood ten years ago. People back home haven't recognized him, because you don't always see what's right in front of you."

Magda winced. "This story keeps getting better and better, and it's killing me to have to sit on it." She retrieved her taffy, pulled off a cigarette-sized length of it, and propped the end between her lips. "I might have to start smoking again."

"If anyone else from Booger Hollow had recognized him, they would have spilled the beans by now," Faith said. "It's hard to keep secrets these days."

"Well, we're going to keep one," Magda decided. "At least for a little while longer. Zander knows that you've got his complete X-file. Let's play it cool and see how Mama and Baby Baxter respond. My guess is that they'll take the story to one of our competitors, or they'll put their trust in us."

"Why would they do either of those things?" Faith asked.

"Well, Zander would make a fortune if he sold his story to one of the other rags. And the Baxters would get the pleasure of pissing you off for uncovering their secret," Magda explained. "I'm banking on the latter."

"Why?"

Magda picked up the photo and studied it. "This photo ran on the Internet, *TMZ*, *Access Hollywood* and MTV News, but no one could name the mystery woman Zander's making out with. This is the first photo I've ever seen of him caught in a frisky moment. He's usually exceptionally discreet. Honestly, Faith, I wasn't sure it *was* you until you confirmed my hunch when I called you in. If I'm reading this photo right, I don't think Baron would betray you. If he gives himself up to anyone, it'll be you."

"Thanks, Magda," Faith said, grateful for the reprieve.

"Don't thank me yet," Magda said. "For now, the story is yours, and I know you'll handle it with tact and sensitivity. You are the best person to write it, but I want this story before some other rag gets it. You and I both know how news travels in this town. Sooner rather than later, someone else will figure him out, same as you did. He'll be exposed—that's a given." Magda sharply arrowed her green-eyed gaze at Faith and added, "It may as well be by someone who loves him. Still." She handed Faith a tissue from the flat box in her desk drawer. "That's the kink, isn't it?"

"Yep," Faith smiled feebly, dabbing at the corner of her eye. "That's the kink."

CHAPTER 6

"Is she there?" Zander asked. He leaned against the stone wall while Brent disconnected his call and tucked his cellphone into the pocket of his reversible Marc Ecko track jacket.

"She's at the free weight station," Brent said. "Ariadne says she's been there for about an hour and that she's just finishing up her workout. She has a massage scheduled in twenty minutes, so that gives us a little time."

"Us?"

"This is a team effort. If it looks like you're getting in too deep—or not deep enough—I'll run interference and get you back on track."

"I can handle Faith," Zander insisted.

"Given your performance at the Wilshire, that's exactly what Mom is hoping to avoid," Brent said with a wry grin.

Zander bit back the insult he wanted to spit at Brent. He and his mother had reason for concern. Not since the end of World War II, when a sailor laid a smooch on a nurse in Times Square, had a photo of a kiss so captivated the public. The barely viewable photo of Zander and his "mystery lover" had graced the covers of numerous magazines in the two weeks since the kiss. Incredibly, no one had leaked Faith's name to the media, and the coverage of

Zander kissing an anonymous woman sent his Q factor into the stratosphere.

While the Baxters wanted to capitalize on this publicity windfall, it had to be done with finesse and cunning to avoid damaging the image they had carefully constructed for Zander. It would be a delicate dance with intricate steps, the most important of which was gaining Faith's allegiance.

Zander had eagerly accepted his assigned role: to keep Faith faithful.

Step one would begin the moment he entered Venus Adonis, one of the most exclusive fitness centers in Beverly Hills. Located near the corner of Wilshire and N. La Cienega Boulevards, the club had an elite Hollywood clientele. A pair of stony-faced doormen were dressed in leather and beaten bronze costumes that made them look like Spartan warriors, and until they moved to open the door, Zander thought they were well-crafted props left over from *300*.

"Mr. Baron, Mr. Baxter, welcome to Venus Adonis," welcomed the perky blonde receptionist standing behind a waist-high Lucite counter.

"Hi, Ariadne," Brent said. He held his splayed fingers a few inches above the fingerprint recognition console Ariadne had swiveled to face him. "Thanks for the heads-up on Brenda Starr. I've been trying to get a lock on her for the past four days."

"No problem whatsoever, Mr. B.," Ariadne said. Flashing her dimples, she leaned forward, the bodice of her mini-toga barely containing its jaunty contents. "Anything for my favorite agent."

Zander quietly snorted, well aware that Ariadne's assistance had come at a price. Brent had arranged for her to attend an invite-only audition for a pilot being developed by a cable station.

"Make sure you're on time tomorrow morning," Brent advised. "Punctuality counts almost as much as talent in this business."

Ariadne giggled her assurances and waved them into the center.

From the outside, the design of the building blended with its neighbors, a series of neutral-colored high rises and one-story specialty boutiques. The interior was something else entirely.

Ancient Greece intertwined with twenty-first century tackiness and technology. The lobby featured a floor-to-ceiling sculpture, pale as alabaster, of Atlas—whose face bore a suspicious resemblance to Gerard Butler—with a stylized globe propped upon its shoulders. Flexible lighting cables that slowly moved through a pastel rainbow were woven through the tarnished copper wire and crudely rendered bronze plates forming the continents of the globe.

Opposite Atlas was a matching sculpture of Venus rising from a chemically generated cloud of fog with blue-green backlighting meant to represent the seafoam from which the daughter of Zeus had risen. Venus' long auburn hair moved against a breeze generated by a source that could be heard but not seen, and Zander smiled appreciatively when he realized that the alabaster goddess of love had been given the face of actress Leila Arcieri.

Looking over his shoulder, Zander addressed the receptionist. "Where's Adonis?"

Laughing, she pointed at the male statue and replied, "Don't tell me you missed him, Mr. Baron."

"Atlas holds up the world," Zander said. "Adonis was just a pretty face."

"Is that right?" Ariadne said. "You should go on *Jeopardy!*"

"I'm already in jeopardy," Zander muttered.

"Come on, genius," Brent said. "You're wasting your mojo on the wrong woman."

The two statues flanked a wide archway, through which Zander and Brent moved to reach a short flight of low, wide stadium stairs leading to the Atrium. Weight-lifting and conditioning machines, free weights, elliptical trainers, bikes and other equipment designed to torture one's physique into optimum health were situated beneath a cathedral ceiling reminiscent of the Parthenon.

The white and chrome color scheme was broken up by washed-out blues, greens and pinks, but the place still seemed too antiseptic for Zander's taste. In his faded gray sweatpants and worn black T-shirt, Zander thought he looked like he was there to repair equipment, not to work out on it.

Zander found himself in one of the most surreal scenes he'd ever experienced in California. Almost everyone in the gym wore a phone headset, or had a smartphone pressed to an ear or clipped to a waistband, and there wasn't an ounce of extra body fat anywhere, not even on the toga-wrapped staff wandering through the

Atrium offering wheat grass, carrot juice or ginseng cocktails along with a Venus Adonis specialty—chilled, lemon-scented, oxygenated sweat towels.

"This is ridiculous," Zander snickered after spotting a particularly scandal-prone celebutante at a wall-length mirror. More famous for her surgically-enhanced physical attributes and long, dark hair than a particular talent or contribution to society, her idea of exercise seemed to be studying her profile and asking those nearest her if her concave belly looked fat.

"Very few people come here to actually work out," Brent told him. "They come here to be seen. There's a three-year waiting list for memberships and a two-year waiting list for employment."

"People actually line up to put on a toga and cater to the spoiled and spray-tanned?" Zander asked.

"A lot of industry folk work out here," Brent said. "Ariadne replaced a girl who got a part in Jensen Lee's new movie. He saw her at the front desk, liked her and cast her in his flick."

"It's so easy for some folks, huh," Zander remarked.

"It's easy to get that first chance," Brent told him. "You gotta have talent to keep yourself working. That's the difference between you and most of the other overnight sensations. You're here to stay, as long as we can get a stay of exposure from Miss Wheeler."

"I guess I'd better get on with this," Zander said. "Wish me luck."

"Like you need luck," Brent scoffed.

Zander passed a gaggle of Lakers cheerleaders dressed in baby tees and short-shorts, and a familiar young actor working with a buff trainer who gave Zander a long, admiring wink.

Smiling uncomfortably, Zander gave the trainer a brisk, two-fingered salute, earning a squeal from the man.

Faith sat astride a padded, gray weight bench, watching herself in the mirror as she used a ten-pound chrome dumbbell to perform a set of bicep curls. She caught Zander's reflection, and her eyes narrowed as they tracked his progress toward her.

"Need a spotter?" he asked, stopping beside her.

"What do you want?" she replied.

"Nothing," he shrugged. "I saw you over here and I thought I'd come over and see if you needed a partner."

"I do quite well on my own," she said curtly. She pursed her lips and shot a jet of air at the lock of hair that kept flopping onto her sweaty brow.

"You sweat a lot," Zander remarked. "Should I call for a towel?"

"I think Calliope and Clio are making the rounds," Faith said. "They're racing over here, probably to get to you."

Zander watched them in the mirror. The toga-clad blondes seemed to be in a power-walk race as they made tracks to the free-weight station, each bearing a silver platter of folded towels.

"Are you here to *do* something with those muscles of yours, or are you one of those?" Faith snapped.

"Those what?"

"The people who come here in full makeup and their fanciest exercise apparel just to pretend to work out, when what they really want is to make contact with a director or a producer."

"There's no harm in that," Zander said.

"See that guy over there, the one in the silvery-gray Speedo unitard?" Faith gave a discreet nod in the man's direction.

Zander looked and then recoiled at the sight of the man's rotund belly testing the limits of the space-age spandex. "He looks like a pregnant porpoise."

"That pregnant porpoise just started casting for a big-screen version of *Johnny Sokko and His Flying Robot*," Faith said in a low voice. "That's why he's got six hand-maidens and two male servants burying him in lecithin shooters and spot massages."

Noticing Zander staring, the casting director waved and smiled broadly.

"He recognizes you," Faith taunted. "Why don't you go over there? Maybe you'll get your big break."

Zander threw a leg over the weight bench nearest Faith's. He drew back, startled, when a male attendant stepped up and stood at rigid attention. Twice as wide as Zander, his oiled muscles looked like balloons lodged under his skin. His head and his neck appeared to be a single unit, and from the back, Zander thought his head looked like a bullet. A bullet crowned with a laurel wreath.

"Your pleasure, sir?" the attendant asked, dropping to one knee and bowing his head.

"Are you fu—" Zander started.

"It's okay, Ajax," Faith interrupted. "We can get the weights ourselves."

Ajax pressed his right fist to his heart. "As you wish, mistress."

Zander chuckled. Faith jabbed his shoulder. "Stop, you'll hurt his feelings."

"This place is ridiculous," Zander groaned, looking at the ceiling, which had been painted to suggest a distant view of a cloud-shrouded Mount Olympus.

"If it's so ridiculous, why do you have a membership? Wait, let me guess—Olivia Baxter sends you here for the 24k-gold facials to keep you pretty for the cameras." She transferred her dumbbell to her left hand, and braced her left elbow against her inner left knee. Slowly, precisely, she began curling the weight.

"Nice guns," Zander said, watching the powerful movement of the sleek bicep under Faith's skin. "I'm not a member. Brent is. I'd have to mortgage my house to pay the dues here, although his mother swears by the caviar facials she gets once a month." Zander grabbed two twenty-five-pound dumbbells. "Unlike some people, I work too hard for my money to throw it away on a gym with a staff that looks like a dinner theater version of *Caligula*. A bad version at that."

Faith glared at him. "For your information, *Personality!* holds the membership to this place, not me. We get a lot of stories by lurking around here. And I work very hard for a living. At least what I do requires brains."

"*Monkeying Around with Harley Tatum*," Zander said, making light of the headline of her latest cover story. "Yeah, that's real nuclear science."

Faith swung both legs to the side of her bench nearest Zander and whispered in his ear. "Trust me when I say my next cover story will be much, much more enlightening."

He caught the light, slightly sweet musk of her sweaty body when she stood and walked away, and combined with the sultry rasp of her voice and her breath in his ear, Zander suddenly felt lightheaded. Still clutching his dumbbells, he followed her, stopping short as she mounted an adductor machine. A low ache settled deep in his belly as he stared at her shapely dancer's legs braced in the machine, which kept them wide apart.

Faith brought her legs together slowly, sending a sixty-pound weight stack rising on its cables. Her white shorts were very short, and Zander watched the flexion of her thigh muscles. He idly wondered if he was drooling, swiping the back of his hand across his mouth—just in case.

"Come to insult me some more?" Faith asked. "If so, hurry up and get it over with. I have a massage in a few minutes."

"I want to know why it's so easy for you to splash my private business all over the cover of a magazine," Zander said, forcing his gaze away from her legs.

Unfortunately, it went straight to her bosom, which expanded against her white spandex camisole with each deep inhalation.

She let the weights clang back into place and dismounted. "Dead men don't have secrets, or hadn't you heard?" she grinned, her face mere inches from his. "And since you seem to have forgotten, I think I proved a long time ago that I can keep a secret."

"Don't I know it."

"What's that supposed to mean?"

"It means I remember perfectly well how good you are at keeping a secret. You hid me easily enough when we were kids, yet you're red-hot to out me now."

"You know we had to meet in secret!" she whispered angrily. "If my father had known I was sneaking off to see you, he would have shipped me off to boarding school!"

Zander counterattacked. "Of course. It would have just been too horrible for Justus Wheeler to know that a monosyllabic hillbilly was defiling his precious, virginal daugh—*OOF!*"

Faith's punch caught him just above his navel, driving the air, and a loud grunt, right out of him. "Don't turn this into something it isn't!" she said. "My father would have sent me away for dating anybody he hadn't handpicked himself. I had friends, a big house and nice clothes, but I was just as much a prisoner in Booger Hollow as you were!"

"A prisoner of privilege," Zander said, standing his ground. "Poor you."

Fuming, Faith stomped off toward one of the corridors branching off the Atrium. Just inside the tall, wide, arching entrance to the Bodyworks Center, she stopped at another reception desk and accepted a gauzy white robe and a pair of white slippers from a smiling young woman. Faith glared back at Zander before disappearing around a corner.

"How's it going?" Brent asked, coming up behind Zander. "Is she warming up to you?"

"Oh, yeah," Zander said lightly. "She's steaming."

"Should we call it a day then?"

"No," Zander said, his resolve hardening. "This is going to be settled one way or the other, right now."

A smile and a BAXTER MANAGEMENT business card was all it took to distract the countergirl manning the desk at the entrance to the Bodyworks Center. While the young woman ogled the card, Brent peered at the twin menus mounted above her head, detailing the massage and yoga services offered beyond the bluish-white walls behind the check-in counter.

Brent selected an item from the massage menu. "Tell me more about the, uh, Gua Sha. What exactly is that?"

The woman turned to look, and the moment her back was to him, Brent waved Zander into the center.

"Oh, you'll love it," the receptionist gushed. "Our Gua Sha master will apply olive oil and herbs to your skin to promote blood flow, open your pores and cleanse your skin. She'll use a flat tool to scrape your skin, which will facilitate the pain-relieving properties of the treatment. Now, where are you having pain?"

"I'm pretty good right now, actually," Brent said smoothly, one eye on the countergirl, the other on Zander, who moved deeper into Bodyworks. "Do you have anything that involves four or six-hand massage? I've really got a lot to handle."

The girl giggled, and Zander rolled his eyes. He grudgingly admired Brent's skill at altering his charm from smarmy to winning, depending on his goal. The young receptionist gobbled up every oily compliment oozing from Brent's mouth, allowing Zander the time to stroll the corridor, peeking through the porthole windows in each door.

The high ceilings and oversized doors gave Zander the feeling that he had entered an alien environment, one in which people paid obscene sums of money to have their orifices probed.

That very thing was underway behind a door labeled Colon Hydrotherapy. The opaque glass of the porthole, thankfully, didn't permit a clear look at the figure lying on his or her side on a table, but the movements of the white-smocked technician standing at the figure's backside were unmistakable.

Zander passed the Balinese Massage room, from which wafted the scent of coconut oil. The door to the Sound Therapy room opened as Zander stepped in front of it, and he collided with a technician bearing an armful of equipment. Tuning forks, rattles, a skin-covered drum and a bronze bowl hit the carpeted floor.

"Sorry about that," Zander said, stooping to help pick up the articles.

"All is forgiven," the young man said cheerily, pressing his palms together in a friendly bow. He had a pronounced Indian accent, and a bright smile appeared between his reddish-brown cheeks. "It'll take more than a little bump to harm a Tibetan singing bowl. Are you my six o'clock? I'm just finishing up with my previous client, but—"

"No, I'm actually looking for someone," Zander said. "She's, um, having a . . ." *A facial? A massage? A tooter routing?* Zander struggled to recall something from the menus he'd only glanced at earlier.

"She's having a treatment," he finally finished. "With some oil, and—"

"The Raindrop Massage?" the sound therapist suggested.

Zander snapped his fingers. "That's it! Right. Raindrop. Could you point me to the Raindrop room?"

"Straight down the corridor, make a right, and it's the fourth door on your left, sir," the therapist answered.

"Thanks," Zander said, starting off.

"Be blessed," the therapist called before going in the other direction.

Once he rounded the corner, Zander picked up speed. The Bodyworks Center was much bigger than he had imagined. If the Raindrop room wasn't the right one, he had at least two dozen more portholes to peep through.

The fourth door on the left was closed, but pressing his ear to it, Zander made out muffled voices.

". . . will do that to you, although it's usually a bacterial or viral cause behind this sort of problem with the spine," a pleasant female voice was saying. "This is only your first treatment, but I guarantee it's a good way to start undoing all the damage your ballet and cheerleading did to your back. Would you mind terribly if I popped out for a bit to replenish my thyme oil?"

"Please, go right ahead," Faith responded.

"You just lie here and relax, and I'll be right back, okay?"

Zander darted away from the door, falling into step behind a man in a terrycloth bathrobe who had just exited the neighboring Chi Nei Tsang room. The fellow's eyes were glazed, as though his experience had been pure bliss.

Hurrying to retrieve her oil, the Raindrop room attendant outpaced Zander and the man in the bathrobe. Zander took a couple of steps backward before turning completely and slipping into the Raindrop room.

Faith was lying on her stomach atop a table draped with gauzy white cloth, her eyes closed, her head resting upon her crossed arms. The table was slightly inclined, giving Zander a view of her body, which was nude but for a whisper-sheer white cloth covering her backside. His body responded with such intensity and immediacy, he almost groaned in pain.

The track lighting edging the ceiling had been dimmed, and the skylight admitted only the purple-pink shadows of the approaching sunset. White candles of varying thickness and height lent warmth and illumination to the room, the shadows of their flickering tips bringing the stone walls to life.

A wheeled silver cart at Faith's hip contained several glass bottles with different levels of colored fluid. The carpeting muffling his footsteps, Zander stepped up to the table, took up a squat, rounded bottle, and quietly slipped out the stopper. He identified the contents with one sniff: peppermint.

Smiling impishly, he went to the door and turned the simple thumb lock. Returning to Faith's side, he opened each of the bottles on the cart. He recognized several scents—oregano, basil, lavender, peppermint, lemon, orange and rose—but most he didn't. He separated the unfamiliar scents from those he knew before unstopping all of the citrus and spice oils. Raising a bottle in each hand, he took his cue from the room's title and sprinkled droplets of oil along Faith's spine.

She inhaled softly, her bottom reflexively popping an inch or two upward. "That feels really nice," she sighed.

"It gets better," Zander said.

Faith spun around and sat up so fast, she nearly rolled off the table. Grabbing the fabric covering her hips, she pulled it up to her chest, concealing her nudity without concealing it at all.

Too surprised and angry to speak, she sat there, her chest and shoulders heaving. "You—Are—I—" she stammered before finding her voice. "If I wasn't naked, I'd beat your brains out!" she hollered.

"Shh!" Zander urged, setting down the bottles. "Do you want that lady to catch us?"

"That lady is the one who's *supposed* to be here, not you!"

A bump on the door interrupted them. "Mistress Faith, the door is locked," came a woman's voice from the corridor.

"It's okay," Zander said confidently, preemptively drowning out anything Faith would have said. "I'll take care of this one."

"No, you won't!" Faith hissed.

"Mistress Faith, what's going on in there?" the woman persisted.

"I just want to talk to you," Zander whispered. "Please."

The technician tried to force open the door, but with each passing second, Faith knew that she would give in to him. Looking into his eyes, she could deny him nothing.

"It's okay," she called. "Someone else has already started my treatment."

"I've got the thyme oil right here," the woman insisted weakly. "I could just slip it right in there."

"We're good, thanks," Zander firmly, effectively dismissed the woman.

"All right, then, as you wish," the woman said sadly, her voice fading as she moved from the door.

"What do you want?" Faith asked. She gripped the cloth at her bosom tighter, hoping that would still the tremor in her hand.

She wasn't ashamed of her body or shy about Zander looking at her. In a city full of women who strived to see their clavicles and hip bones jutting through their skin as a mark of beauty, Faith took pride in what Magda described as her "fleshiness"—her full breasts and hips, the plushness of her thighs, and the supple rounds of her bottom.

The set of Zander's jaw, the bright heat in his eyes and the prominence at the front of his sweatpants told Faith that he, too, appreciated her fleshiness.

"Well?" she prompted when he kept staring instead of answering her question.

"What's the matter with your back?" he asked.

"At the moment, it's got orange and lemon oil running down it," she said.

"Seriously," he said.

"If you must know, I have a bit of lower back pain from time to time. From dancing."

"And cheerleading."

"Eavesdropper."

"Why come here? Shouldn't you go to a doctor?"

"My doctor recommended regular massages," she said.

"Roll over."

"No," she said peevishly, the left side of her upper lip hooked in a tiny moue of distaste. "Get outta here."

"Would you just roll over?" he prodded gently, covering the hand at her bosom with his own. "I'm pretty good at backrubs. I injured my back filming *Burn*, and I learned a few things when I was in physical therapy."

"Humphf," she snorted doubtfully.

Zander grabbed the edge of the cloth she lay on and gave it a sharp tug, flipping Faith onto her stomach. His hands went to her lower back, his thumbs gliding along either side of her spine.

"You—*ummm*!" Her protest morphed into a primitive purr of pleasure as Zander leaned into the motion, ironing out the knots in her back muscles.

"Is this too hard?" he asked.

"You tell me," Faith giggled.

Zander self-consciously took a small step back. "Not funny. You have no idea what you do to me."

"You brought this on yourself. I didn't invite you in here."

"You're enjoying this, aren't you?"

"Yep."

Zander's jaw hardened, almost as much as another part of him had. His hands tensed as he manipulated the muscles of her back, rubbing oil into a glossy sheen on her skin. He licked his lips, the softness of her skin whetting his appetite as thoroughly as the heady scent of the oil. Faith remained motionless, eyes closed. To his chagrin, Zander thought he heard soft snoring.

The injustice of the situation he'd created was irksome. While she lay there, seemingly indifferent to his touch, he was on the verge of begging her to coat her palm with oil and use it to bring a happy ending to the pressure building low in his loins.

He had sought her out with ulterior motives: gain her silence by winning her affection. But the truth of the matter had worked its way into his consciousness just as he worked the oil into Faith's flesh. He wanted her, plain and simple, secret or no secret. Even more, he wanted her to want him just as much.

"We need to talk about what happened at the Wilshire," he told her. "Because of the deal we made over that kiss."

"What kiss?"

Annoyed, he ran his hands over her buttocks, his thumbs lightly delving into the separation between them on their way to her right upper thigh.

Faith pressed her mouth into her left bicep to stifle a moan.

"Do you expect me to believe that you forgot about it?" he asked.

She made a conscious attempt to steady her breathing before replying. "You're just a guy who owes me a story. You're a career milestone, and just another fraud actor with a prefabricated past."

"Is that so?"

"That's so."

"What if I refuse to give you your interview?" He dripped oil onto her left buttock and watched it trickle east and disappear.

Goosebumps rose along Faith's skin, following the work of Zander's hands and thumbs as they oiled her. He left her incapable of speech after widening her thighs and dripping more oil onto her, making sure it traveled into the valley hidden against the table.

"Coming from Zander Baron, that wouldn't surprise me," Faith managed, her voice thick, husky. "Alex Brannon would stick to his word. Alex Brannon would—"

He showed her what Alex Brannon would do. Bending forward, he took her earlobe between his lips.

He suckled it, drawing on it sharply and nipping it until Faith started to turn onto her back. His well-oiled hands glided over her skin, shaping her breasts to give him prime access to her nipples. Her back arched and she helped him climb onto the table. Straddling her, his hands full of her, he clapped his mouth to hers, kissing her deeply as she clutched handfuls of his T-shirt.

Kneeling over her, her legs between his, he took his time studying her. So many nights he'd lain awake in his leaky corner of the Brannon trailer with nothing but fantasies of Faith giving him the courage and will to face the next morning. He had imagined what she would look like naked, but his brain had never fashioned anything as lovely as what he was now seeing.

Her skin . . .

It was her loveliest feature, the thing that had first captivated him. The candlelight painted chocolate shadows that defined the roasted honey curves and planes of her body. The cinnamon peaks of her breasts reacted to his gaze, prettily puckering tight and leaving his mouth dry. His eyes traced her midline from her sternum, over her defined abdominal muscles, and down to the narrow ribbon of neatly trimmed floss between her legs.

Faith was still very much the girl he'd known back home, but her "bacon strip" was distinctly Californian. He absently took his lower lip in his mouth, mutely conveying his desire to lick her, to discover if her skin and floss were as delicious as they looked, to feel her melting in his mouth.

"Who are you?" she murmured, sitting up just enough to take his face in her hands.

In the subdued light, his hair looked darker, much closer to the shade it had been the last time she'd seen him in Dorothy. In some ways, he looked younger now than he had then, most likely because he no longer dealt with the daily stress of just surviving in Booger Hollow. He was well fed and had a warm bed to sleep in at night. That hard, edgy look of hunger and despair was gone.

She had always seen past the frustrations and emotions that had prematurely etched lines in his face. Now, as he brought his mouth to hers, he resembled the Alex Brannon she had always seen with her heart.

The intervening years between their first kiss on the mountain and this one fell away along with her inhibitions. Burying her fingers in the thick, honey-gold silk of his hair, Faith welcomed his hands and his lips, her body responding in ways she never would have known at eighteen.

Through his clothing, she felt the hardness and heat of him. The hands that had been so calloused from working in an auto body shop were only slightly less so now, and his caresses left her craving more intimate contact. Her thighs fell apart in silent invitation, and Zander responded by cupping her nearly bare mound.

Her backside and head pressed into the padded table while her torso rose to meet Zander's mouth. His lips closed around her nipple, drawing it to a sharper point as the longest finger of his right hand sought the softest, most sensitive spot behind her bacon strip. Zander's long, leisured strokes generated lubrication slicker than oil, and he massaged it into the firm pink pearl under the heel of his palm.

Faith's mouth opened wide, her eyes closed and her abdomen rose and fell dramatically as Zander's finger explored further, dipping inside her as he continued his intimate massage.

The gentle pinch of his lips and the soft nibble of his teeth at her breasts worked in concert with the motion of his right hand. He knew he'd found the spot he was looking for when she issued a ragged groan and clutched at him, one of her hands clamping around his wrist. Not to stop him, but to urge him on.

Hunching over her, the muscles of his right arm hard, he used his left hand to push her right breast closer to her left, enabling him to lap both her nipples at once. One long, hungry draw sent her into hip-bucking pleasure that left her thighs quivering and her slick tunnel constricting around his finger.

Zander withdrew and hopped off the end of the table. In one strong motion, he took Faith by her hips, tugged her bottom to the edge of the table, and raised her pelvis. He sank between her thighs and sampled her sweet earthiness, lifting her just enough to make sure that his tongue explored every part of her slippery seam. Faith gasped in shock and delight. No man had ever explored her so fully, so boldly, subjecting her to sensations that continued to escalate. When Zander covered her again to kiss her, his mouth tasted of the oil he had applied to her along with her own unique flavor.

She had never given herself so freely, so openly to a stranger.

But then, the man in her arms wasn't a stranger. He paraded the streets as Zander Baron, but his touch was that of Alex Brannon, the man her heart had known, had kept alive.

He smoothed her hair from her face and used his thumbs to wipe perspiration off her brow while waiting for her breathing to return to normal. "I missed you," he whispered, his simple confession giving her soul the same pleasure he'd given her body.

"I mourned you," she responded.

He had the decency to look guilty, which made it easier for Faith to release the remnants of her anger.

"I can't write a story about you," she said.

"I'll give you the interview," he told her. "I was just being an ass—"

"I can't write it," she repeated, running her fingers along his cheek. "Not after this. It wouldn't be right."

"No one would know about this," Zander assured her.

"Someone always finds out." She smiled. "Brent probably knows already. That's why you came here, isn't it? To seduce me? To tempt me into keeping Zander Baron's big stupid secret?"

He phrased his answer carefully. "I came here because you were here. Because I haven't stopped thinking about you from the second I saw you at the press conference."

"*Personality!* will assign your story to someone else. Sooner or later, the truth about you is going to come out.

Don't you think it would be better if the story came from *you*? Hiding behind Zander Baron won't keep—"

"I'm not hiding," he said brusquely.

"What do you call it, then?"

"I'm working under a stage name," he lamely explained, looking at a spot between her eyes rather than into them. "A lot of people have done it. Paul Hewson, William Broad, Gordon Sumner . . ."

"Bono, Billy Idol and Sting changed their names for their art, not to hide from their past lives." She shifted from beneath him. Pressing close together, they lay on their sides, one of her legs between his.

"It's just a name," he insisted gently. "What difference does it make?"

"It makes all the difference," she said. "There were times when we were kids when I thought I'd die if I didn't get out of Booger Hollow. But once I left, I actually started to miss the place. It wasn't perfect, it still isn't, but it's my hometown. It's where I'm from, and it helped make me who I am today. I'm proud of where I'm from, and I'm damn proud of how far from that I've come. You should be proud, too, Alex. You don't have to hide who you are behind Zander Baron."

"I'm still the same guy who fell in love with you when—"

"Neither of us is the same," she cut in. "Obviously, we still have certain feelings for each other, but we don't know each other the way we used to."

"We can change that," he said.

"Yeah? How?"

He responded with a lazy, sexy half smile that was all Alex Brannon, and it took Faith back to a secluded mountain lookout beneath the sun-kissed, cloudless skies of Booger Hollow, West Virginia, where she had found her first love.

CHAPTER 7

Zander's cell phone rang just as he exited his trailer. His artfully distressed wifebeater, part of his wardrobe for his role in *Everyday Achilles* as a struggling single father at war with drug dealers, offered little protection from the chilly wind etching new patterns in the desert sand.

The scene he was about to film was set in July. Temperatures in Death Valley climbed as high as 120 degrees Fahrenheit in the summer, so early spring was a much friendlier time to shoot. Computer graphics engineers would add the heat elements later, but for right now, Zander was chilled.

He warmed considerably, however, after he answered the phone.

"How did it go yesterday?" Brent offered instead of a hello.

"You should have waited around," Zander said, following the bundled electric cables leading to the filming location.

"You were in there with her for over an hour," Brent said. "I had things to do."

"She's dropping the piece," Zander told him. "She thinks she put herself in a compromising position—"

"That's the best kind," Brent said.

"It wasn't like that. Not exactly."

"However it was, thank God, you got her to back off. The poor thing probably didn't know what hit her," Brent laughed lightly.

"She knew," Zander said. "She returned fire, and her weapons are better than mine."

"I'm just glad that sword isn't hanging over your head anymore. Mind if I ask what you said to her?"

"I invited her to dinner tomorrow night."

A beat of silence. Then, "You didn't."

"Yeah, I did."

"Where are you taking her?"

"Fawnskin."

Brent groaned. "Zander, I can't see anything positive coming from getting yourself in deeper with this woman. She's backing off, for now, but the more she gets from you, the more likely everything you say and do will become material for *Pers*—"

Brent was still complaining when Zander disconnected the phone, handed it to a production assistant for safekeeping, and went to his mark prepared to take on a drug kingpin.

Zander had offered to arrange a car for her, but Faith decided to drive herself to Fawnskin, California, a pretty little resort town in San Bernardino County. She wanted her own vehicle at her disposal, just in case she needed to make a quick getaway.

She liked long drives, and the ninety-mile trip was relaxing. As she drove the picturesque route, she recalled the way her father often stood on their back patio in Booger Hollow, surveying his five-acre spread at the base of Kayford Mountain. "God made West Virginia," he would proclaim, breathing deeply of the fresh mountain air.

On His day off, Faith thought now, basking in the glorious vistas before her as her sensible compact gobbled up the miles between Pomona and San Bernardino. She loved the mountains back home and in the west, but California also offered hundreds of miles of coastland and desert plains to explore. The first time she had hiked Muir Woods and stood breathless at the base of a giant redwood that had taken root when the Romans reigned, she knew that she was home, that California was the place for her. The state overwhelmed her with its natural beauty, its diverse population and all the levels of excitement it offered, from star sightings at the Los Angeles Farmer's Market to the occasional earthquake.

When Big Bear Lake came into view, Faith knew she was getting close to Zander's house. She had never been to Fawnskin, yet a sense of muted excitement and eagerness energized her. It was the deep familiarity she felt every time she'd gone back to Dorothy after leaving for college. As much as she'd disliked Dorothy in high school, she'd come to love it as an adult, because it was where her parents were, because it was home. Alex's presence in Fawnskin gave the small mountain that same feeling.

The beauty of the sunlight toasting the silvery-blue surface of the lake added to the excitement she tried hard to restrain. In the weeks since seeing Alex at the press conference, all she had wanted to do was spend more time with him. She had traded his story for the chance to revisit their history, but Faith believed she had done the right thing. She hoped Alex would do the right thing, too, not for a story or for her, but for himself.

She turned off Rim of the World Scenic Byway onto Seminole Drive. The blind driveway at the intersection of Seminole and North Shore Drive was the one she sought. Her heart began throwing itself against the wall of her chest as she carefully guided her car up the winding, tree-lined path to a two-story A-frame nestled in a shady grove of towering fir and poplar trees.

The dominant feature of the house was the A-frame, its tall, wide windows and French doors offering incredible views of Big Bear Lake and the mountains beyond it. Faith pulled her car as far to the left side of the driveway as she could, parking in the shade of a black cottonwood tree behind a silver sports car that looked like something from a sci-fi flick. Before she had taken the key from the ignition, the front door of the house opened and Zander ambled out in his bare feet, jeans and a T-shirt.

Faith couldn't tell if he was glad to see her or if he had reservations about an invitation delivered in the heat of a thrilling moment. She grabbed her satchel and cardigan from the passenger seat and stepped out of the car. Zander took her left elbow, tugged her to him, and gave her a sweet kiss on her forehead.

"You made it," he said, relief evident in his tone and posture.

"It was an easy drive," she said. "And your directions were excellent." He took her satchel while she draped her cardigan over her arm. "It's so beautiful here."

"It's a long way from that damn trailer in Booger Hollow, that's for sure," he mumbled.

"Your house is gorgeous, Alex," Faith said. "It looks as though the mountain gave birth to it."

"It's Ponderosa pine, inside and out," he said proudly. "And it's all mine. It was the first thing I bought after I signed my multi-picture deal with Swirl Productions."

"I thought you lived in L.A. or Bel Air," Faith said.

"I have an apartment in L.A., but I only use it when I'm filming," he explained. "I spend my off time here."

"Away from all the hustle and bustle. No wonder it's so hard to get shots of you out and about."

"If you want to be seen and photographed in L.A., everyone knows which spots to go to," Zander said. "All those punks you see shielding their faces from the paparazzi know what they're gonna get when they shop on Rodeo Drive or have dinner at Mr. Chow's. I avoid those places."

"Because you don't want to be recognized," Faith said.

"Well, it worked until you came along." He slid an arm around her waist when the front door opened before them.

"Miss Wheeler," Brent said, coming outside. "How are you?"

"Fine." Faith cut an annoyed glance at Zander.

"Brent was just leaving," Zander said firmly.

"Of course," Brent agreed. "I can take a hint."

"If you could take a hint, you would have waited until Monday to give me the screenplays you wanted me to read instead of driving all the way out here this morning," Zander chided.

"I'm just looking out for my favorite client," Brent replied.

"You wanted to make sure that I came alone," Faith said.

"You've got me all wrong, Miss Wheeler," Brent said, backing toward the silver, bullet-shaped car. "I wanted to see if you would actually come at all."

Faith's hand reflexively tightened around Zander's.

"Drive safely," Zander advised, hoping to avoid a confrontation between Faith and Brent. "And slow down."

"What kind of car is that?" Faith asked, taking a few steps toward it.

"A Fleming Viper." Brent put on his Oliver Goldsmith sunglasses and struck the classic Speed Racer pose at the side of his car. Dressed in a cashmere turtleneck and worsted wool trousers, all in black, the talent agent resembled a secret agent circa *The Man From U.N.C.L.E.* "The company only made forty of them. It hits sixty from stop in 3.2 seconds with a top speed of 205 miles per hour. It's got a 6.0 liter V-12 engine. That's a 650 horsepower—"

"Yet it took you almost three hours to get here," Zander cut in.

"I didn't want to get ticketed," Brent said. "Again. See you kids later. Stay out of trouble."

Brent got into his car, eased it down the driveway and gave a short wave before turning out of sight.

"That car must have cost a fortune," Faith said.

"About 700 G's," Zander said.

"I'd never spend that kind of money on a car."

"Neither would Brent. He's got the Fleming Viper on loan for three days from the set of one of his clients. And I can see that you're not into investing in cars." Zander patted the sun-faded red roof of Faith's Camry. "I'm kind of impressed that you're still driving this thing."

"It'll be eleven years in June," Faith smiled. "You said it yourself, Alex. The Camry is a good car. It had its first oil change at Brody's. I still have the little sticker Mr. Brody put on it, reminding me to get the oil changed every three thousand miles."

Alex peeped at the odometer. "Seventy thousand miles? That's it? Even so seems you would have upgraded by now."

"Look, entertainment reporting is more glamorous than lucrative," Faith said. "That car Brent drove off in is worth about eighteen times what I earn in a year. I made more money at the *L.A. Times* than I do at *Personality!* I traded the national byline for a few bucks. It's worth it. I mostly drove this car from Dorothy to New York City when I was at school. You don't really need a car to get around in NYC. Unlike L.A. As long as this thing keeps passing California emissions tests, I'll keep driving it. Besides . . . I love this car. My car and my furniture have traveled from job to job with me, like faithful old friends."

He shook his head. "You're too sentimental."

"You're not sentimental enough."

Zander let the remark pass without comment. "Come on inside and see the rest of the place."

Zander got the door for her, and he closed it once she had entered the foyer, which opened into a great room with a twenty-four-foot vaulted ceiling. A deep fireplace centered within a roughly hewn stone framework enhanced the room's stylishly rustic charm.

She followed Zander to the kitchen, which seemed small, but was completely modernized and opened into the dining section of the great room.

Proudly, Zander took her through the three large spare bedrooms, a storage room and a bathroom on the upper floor. Two bedrooms had views of the mountains, the third looked out on Zander's two-bedroom guest house. Faith was impressed by the skylights and solar panels that had been installed throughout the house to provide light, heat and clean energy.

A two-story sunroom and the master bedroom were on the main floor. One large rectangular skylight above the deep, wide whirlpool tub brightened the master bath. The bathroom had no personal touches other than black bath and hand towels neatly hung over silver warming bars and a bowl of navel oranges propped between the twin basins sunk into the grey marble counter.

She salivated when Zander led her into an adjoining walk-in closet, which was bigger than her entire apartment. When they entered Zander's bedroom, he seemed bent on rushing her through it.

"Hold on," Faith said, planting her feet.

Zander shifted from foot to foot and cracked his knuckles, his unease becoming evident as Faith studied the one piece of art she'd seen in his home. Titled "Anna," the Thierry Ona print pleasantly assaulted Faith's eyes. A dancer in a blood red dress performed a jeté against a golden sun framed in burnt orange. The dancer's brown limbs were long and thin, her head and face amorphous. Centered on the wall directly opposite the head of the bed, the print was the first thing Zander saw when he woke up and the last thing before he fell asleep.

"I like it," Faith said, trying not to read too much into the presence and positioning of the print, though it stood at odds with the long-haired, sullen, outcast biker she had known.

"Brent saw it once and said it looked gay."

"Have you noticed the way Brent dresses? He's not exactly a paragon of heterosexual taste."

"Could we move this tour along now?"

Not quite understanding why Zander was so uncomfortable, Faith let him off the hook. For the time being.

She liked the simple, masculine beauty of Zander's home. His furnishings were sparse and uniformly practical in every room. The only adornment Faith noticed upon their return to the great room were three square wooden bowls filled with pecans, natural pistachios and walnuts situated on the darkly stained cocktail table in front of the sofa.

Faith had been most impressed by the studio tucked between the upstairs bedrooms. One wall was mirrored, the adjacent wall offering a heart-stopping view of the lake and mountains. Stained panels of solid Ponderosa pine covered the two remaining walls. A corner shelving unit housed a sound system, a flat-screen television, a wooden bowl heaped with bananas and apples, and neat rows of bottled water.

Faith instantly fell in love with the bright warmth of the room. Tossing her cardigan into a corner, she centered herself in a patch of sunlight in the middle of the room. Faith did what came naturally whenever she found herself standing before a large mirror. She struck first position.

Zander, his thumbs hooked in the belt loops of his jeans, watched Faith's transformation with slack-jawed adoration. She straightened her spine and tucked in her pelvis, lifted her chin, and squared her shoulders. The heels of her white slip-on Keds touching, she turned her feet outward in a straight line. Her arms formed graceful arcs, her hands, palms up, elegantly positioned at her upper thighs.

With her hair twisted into a loose knot, her white scoop-neck T-shirt gave Zander an unencumbered view of her slender neck and collarbones. She moved from first position to second, third, fourth and fifth, her feet and arms shifting smoothly, lyrically. Her body seemed to tell a story as she brought her arms close to her chest, delicately folding them, and slowly bent forward, raising her left leg until she was in a full arabesque.

"Thank God for cotton lycra blends," she murmured, swinging her left leg forward and lifting her arms to generate the momentum to raise herself on demi-pointe. "I haven't done this in years. Partner me, Alex."

She held a hand out to him, and for a moment, he couldn't move. In her white shirt and jeans, this Faith kept blurring with the younger version he'd so longed for back in Dorothy. That she would be standing in a room in his own house, with her welcoming him into the poetic beauty of her dance, was a dream made real.

"Are you okay?" she asked, wearily dropping out of her pose. "You look funny."

"I'm fine." Scratching his head, he closed the distance between them. "I don't dance, you know."

"So what do you do in this room?" She rested her forearms on his shoulders. "Just stare at your pretty self in the mirrors?"

"I practice."

"You practice staring at yourself?" She grinned.

He led her to a door concealed in the wall facing the windows. He pressed it slightly inward, and it popped open to reveal the closest thing Faith had ever seen to a medieval armory outside of a museum.

"Are these real?" She ran her fingers along the flat of a broadsword.

"Real enough," Zander said. "I don't want the fighting in my movies to look fake."

"It is." Faith picked up a set of ebony nunchucks. She swung them, and would have whacked herself in the head if Zander hadn't caught the free end.

"But it doesn't have to look like it. My fights and stunts are well choreographed, but it's up to me and the other actor or stuntman to make them convincing."

"The fight between you and the bad guy in *Burn* looked convincing," Faith said as Zander returned the nunchucks to their hook and closed the door to the storage room.

"Probably because Archer Eddings and I didn't get along during filming," Zander said. "He's a prick."

"I've heard that," Faith said. "He's got an ego on him. Word is, he wanted the part that you got."

"Yeah, and he let me know it every chance he got. He'd watch the dailies and try to tell the director how I should be performing. Are you hungry?"

"Sure," Faith said. "What are we having?"

With a sly grin, he gripped her shoulders and turned her to face the lake. "I won't know until we catch it," he murmured in her ear.

～✑～

Zander had been teasing her about catching their dinner in the lake. A gorgeous fillet of salmon rubbed with lemon, garlic and minced fresh basil would spend a few minutes on the indoor grill, carefully tended by Zander, while Faith stood in front of the open pantry.

She had volunteered to retrieve the raspberry vinegar Zander wanted to use in his homemade salad dressing. She had opened the pantry only to be confronted by a wall of food. Sugar-laden breakfast cereals lined the uppermost shelves, cases of soda in every flavor were stacked like cinder blocks on the floor and in between stood products representative of a supermarket Who's Who.

"I thought you lived here alone," Faith said.

"I do," Zander said over the sizzle of the salmon he'd just put on the grill. "I've been thinking of getting a dog, but I don't really spend enough time here to properly take—"

"You've got lots of housemates." Faith read off their names. "Betty Crocker. She looks like a fun gal. Uncle Ben. I hear he makes a good bowl of rice. Mrs. Butterworth. I don't know about her, she looks like the jealous type. I'll bet her head spins every time Aunt Jemima sits next to Orville Redenbacher."

"I like to keep a well-stocked panty," Zander explained. "You never know when people will come by."

"When was your last party?"

Zander dropped his eyes and concentrated on slicing a shallot. "Never had one."

"Are you having one soon?" Faith again looked at the contents of the pantry.

"What's with the questions?"

"I worked at a food co-op in college. Your pantry is better stocked than the co-op ever was." Taking the raspberry vinegar from the area it shared with five other kinds of vinegar, Faith brought it to Zander.

"I thought only black people drank grape soda," she commented, handing him the vinegar.

"You want one?" Zander grinned. "I bought it special for you."

He dodged the light punch Faith threw at him and unscrewed the cap of the vinegar. He poured a couple of tablespoons of it into a small plastic canister with a plunger built into the lid. "Mind giving this a few pumps, to mix the dressing?" he asked, pushing the canister over the surface of the fireslate counter they were sharing.

The aromas of fresh oregano, basil and garlic mingled with the fruity scents of cold-pressed olive oil and vinegar as Faith set the contents of the canister spinning. "This smells good enough to drink straight," she remarked.

"Personally, I'd rather have wine," Zander said. "I've got a few nice whites in the basement, if you feel like picking one."

"Work me to death, why don't you," Faith smiled, rolling her eyes. "Which way to the basement?"

Zander pointed to a door off the rear of the kitchen. Flipping the light switch just inside the stairwell, she stepped lightly onto the pine steps. The staircase was steep, but the varnished steps were wide and so well made that they kept their silence under Faith's weight.

The basement was carpeted and chillier than the main floor, but it wasn't the cool air that gave Faith unpleasant goosebumps when she reached the last step.

The basement ran the length of the house. The furnace and hot water heater were tucked in a corner opposite a room with pine walls and a glass door. The rest of the space was occupied by five-tier, stainless steel shelving units. One section was filled with canned goods, another with boxed goods, still another with cases of bottled water. Plastic bins, the same shade of penal grey as the cinder block walls, contained bags of potatoes, onions, apples and oranges. Faith squatted to peep into the nearest bin and she saw an assortment of fresh carrots, beets, squash and cabbage.

"Did you get lost?"

Startled, Faith popped up to her full height and spun to face Zander. Before she could shape her expression into something less revealing, the merry light in Zander's eyes flickered out.

"What's the matter?" he asked warily.

Faith turned, once more scanning the fully stocked shelves and bins. The one question she wanted to ask died on her lips as its answer blossomed in her mind.

I can't afford to pay you more money, but I can let you have two meals per eight-hour shift.

As easily as she recalled his voice, Faith closed her eyes and pictured Red Irv, his sweaty bald head gleaming pink in the cold, blue-white light of the fluorescent bars of his diner. From her usual seat in a rear booth, she'd had an unobstructed view of the dishwashing station in the cluttered little kitchen.

She had just started her senior year at Lincoln High, the same school from which Alexander Brannon had graduated a year earlier. Knowing that she would no longer be able to eyeball him at school every day, she'd started going to Red Irv's after her ballet class, ostensibly to grab dinner and study. The thing she studied most was Alex as he went about his work.

Red Irv opened his diner every day at five A.M. dressed in blinding white—chef's jacket, trousers and floor-length apron. He resembled a giant marshmallow. But by the close of dinner service, his cooking whites

169

were so smudged with food and grease that he ended his workdays looking like Poppin' Fresh's indigent brother.

Faith had been checking and re-checking her calculus homework, deliberately dawdling until Red Irv's closed so she could leave when Alex did. She was the only patron left in the place, but Red Irv and Alex seemed to have forgotten about her as they spoke in loud voices from the kitchen.

"I don't need your charity," Alex had said, his voice dark with defiance.

"Then you're the only Brannon who doesn't, because your daddy begs his coffee and eggs off me every morning, and your ma comes in every Saturday night asking for scraps for her dog," Red Irv responded, his blunt, Irish-accented words delivered with his meaty fists set at the place where his massive gut hung over the ties of his apron.

Alex's reply was so quiet, Faith struggled to hear him. "My mother doesn't have a dog."

"Don't I know it," Red Irv boomed. "Look, Alex. You're a good kid, a real good kid. You deserve better than what you got. I ain't tryin' to prickle your pride, but you gotta eat. I don't want you pickin' leftovers off my customers' plates after you bus tables. I can't give you a raise, and even if you had the money to pay me for meals, I wouldn't take it from you, not with your daddy fleecin' you every week. Two meals per eight-hour shift. Deal?"

Faith hadn't seen Alex, not with Red Irv's big stomach filling the doorway. Her face had grown hot in the way humiliation and embarrassment had of roasting one's flesh from the inside. Alex's quiet pride, honed by the harassment and ostracism he routinely received from the town, saved him now in the face of Red Irv's offer.

"It's a deal, but only if you let me do the windows twice a week," Alex said confidently. "Save you some money on the service you normally use."

Red Irv smiled gratefully. "The bastard has doubled his prices in the past two years, so I'll take you up on that offer, Alex. Thank you."

Red Irv had stretched out a hand, and Faith assumed that he and Alex were shaking on it. She jerked her head back to her math book when the two men started out of the kitchen. Alex had wiped down three tables and Red Irv had completed counting out his cash drawer before either noticed her.

"Faith!" Red Irv called boisterously. "I thought you left. How're you gettin' home, honey?"

Alex had studiously rubbed circles into the nearest table, his white towel flapping over the edges.

"I'm walking, I guess. I'd better get going, before it gets too dark."

"Alex, call it a night and get the lady home safe," Red Irv directed.

"It's okay," Faith had said, standing to shove her text and notebooks into her backpack. "I'll be fine."

"I'd feel more comfortable if you had an escort," Red Irv insisted. "Go on, Alex, get outta here. I'll get the floors and lock up."

Without a word or a look at Faith, Alex had gone back into the kitchen, emerging a few seconds later having traded his dirty apron for a weathered leather jacket. Giving Red Irv a nod good-bye, he'd gone to the door and waited for Faith.

"Where's your bike?" she'd asked, nearly running to keep up with Alex's long, quick strides.

"At Brody's," he'd snapped. "It needs a new battery."

"Batteries are easy to replace, aren't they?"

He had stopped and shoved his fists deep in the pockets of his jacket. "I can't afford food. What makes you think I can afford a battery for my bike?"

His gaze was chillier than his voice, and a shiver moved through Faith.

He started walking again and Faith trotted alongside him. He wouldn't look at her, and he said nothing else to her. He didn't slow his pace until they were well beyond the center of town.

"You're not fooling me, you know," he said softly.

"What are you talking about?"

He stopped, confronting her twenty yards from the entrance to her cul-de-sac. "You're not the first chick in this town to hang around Red Irv's because you've got a hankerin' for white trash."

"Red Irv isn't white trash!"

"I meant me, goofball."

"I'm not a goofball." Faith stubbornly raised her chin. "And you aren't trash."

Her assertion seemed to nudge the chip on his shoulder. "Everyone else in town seems to think so."

"I've lived here my whole life, and I've been called a lot of things, but you're the first person to ever call me a goofball," Faith said.

He rolled his eyes and groaned. "I was talking about what people think of me."

"Well, I don't think that about you."

They spent an awkward moment of silence as night deepened around them. On the other side of the WELCOME TO KAYFORD ESTATES sign, golden light burned from the windows of the four- and five-bedroom houses. Alex watched a family of four sitting in their dining room, the man at the head of the table reading a newspaper while a woman Alex assumed to be his wife poured his coffee. His son and daughter seemed to be having an animated debate to which both parents seemed deaf.

Back the way they had come, far on the other side of town, Alex's home sat nestled at the end of a dead-end road, the only light provided by a cracked street lamp. He clamped his jaw and breathed heavily through his nose, steeling himself for the long walk to a home that felt more like a prison.

"You're supposed to be walking me home," Faith said. "Red Irv said."

"He's not my boss once I leave the diner. This is far enough. Your porch light is on, and I can watch you walk the rest of the way from here."

"Okay, then . . . thanks for walking me most of the way home." Faith took a few steps, but then turned to face him again. "You could walk me to the front door, you know. My folks won't kill you."

"Are you sure about that?" he called.

It wasn't until later, after they'd begun meeting in secret on the mountain, that Alex told her he had followed her, at a distance, every night she'd walked home from Red Irv's. Dorothy was a friendly small town, but it was just big enough to attract an element that occasionally liked to stir up trouble. In following her home, Alex had wanted to ensure that no harm ever came to Faith.

They had never discussed what Faith had overheard at Red Irv's, but after seeing his pantry and basement, Faith realized that Alex had yet to outgrow his fear of again going hungry.

He walked stiffly to the wine cellar and threw open the door. Wincing in anticipation of hearing glass shatter against the wall, Faith sighed in relief when she noticed that the door was on a pressure hinge, which saved it from Zander's temper. She entered the room before it closed and found Zander standing in front of a long, chest-high wooden rack. Each diamond-shaped cubbyhole contained a bottle of wine, but Zander seemed to stare beyond them. Faith assumed that his mind was where hers had just been.

Her gentle touch on his arm started his words. "I used to wake up every morning feeling as if I were serving time for a crime I didn't commit. There were days when . . ." His words caught in his throat as hot emotion swelled inside him.

"Those days are gone now," she soothed, gathering him in an embrace meant to show him that she could share the burden of his pain. She did, always had. When she had seen Orrin Brannon slap him outside Red Irv's because he'd failed to turn over his paycheck fast enough, when he'd sponged up his heavily medicated mother from the curb in front of Buzzy's Tavern, and when his former classmates came home from college and sat in the diner ordering Alex around as though he were their personal slave, Faith had wanted to scream and shout, to do all the kicking and punching that he couldn't.

She hadn't known how to comfort him then. Her little jokes, smartass comments and horrible nicknames for his tormenters seemed to amuse him, but the moment they parted ways, his melancholy returned. She now had other skills at her disposal, and she readily employed them to return him from the place and time he had worked so hard to keep in the past.

She took his hands and brought them closer to her face. Surgery and medication had softened the appearance of the scars she had learned beneath the tall evergreens on Kayford Mountain, but the stories of their origins still weighed on Faith's heart. She pressed her lips to them, hoping that her kisses would show him that she cherished everything about Alexander Brannon.

He curled his hand over hers, pressing kisses to her loosely folded fingers. Inching backwards, he put some space between them to avoid getting too carried away.

"I've got a pinot noir rosé that should match well with dinner," he said, pulling the bottle from its cubby hole. "It can carry its own against the strong flavor and fat of salmon." He selected another bottle and dusted the label before displaying if for her. "Or if you'd prefer a white, this sauvignon blanc has notes you'll find intriguing."

Respecting his wish to tread on less personal ground, Faith hooked her thumbs through her belt loops and asked, "When did you learn so much about wine?"

"When Olivia Baxter decided that Brent and I needed a bit of refinement," he grinned. "She put us in dance classes, a cooking class—"

"The ABCDs of the modern renaissance man," Faith chuckled. "Acting, booze, cooking and dance. You're fully armed to seduce, on screen and off."

"That's the nice thing about acting," Zander said. With two bottles of wine tucked under one arm, he held the door open for Faith. "I can be anything I want."

"Or anyone," Faith muttered as she passed him.

CHAPTER 8

Faith had accepted Zander's invitation to go for a hike to work off the salmon, couscous and wine they had gorged on for dinner. The thin trunks of close, young poplars provided excellent handholds for her to pull herself higher and easily keep pace with Zander. Her Keds were ill-suited for the trek, but the trail Zander had chosen was free of fallen branches and large stones and was thickly cushioned with desiccated pine needles. A few steps ahead of her, Zander breathed heavily, his lungs working harder the higher he climbed. When he stopped, Faith drew up beside him, smiling even as she panted for breath.

"Okay," Zander said. "Turn around."

Taking her by the shoulders, he gently spun her. What little breath Faith had left caught in her chest at the sight of the San Bernardino mountains with Big Bear Lake at their feet. Serenity washed over Faith, and she relaxed against him.

"This is disgusting," Faith beamed, taking a deep breath of cool air scented with freshly disturbed earth, pine sap, and damp cedar bark. "It's so beautiful, but it's a different kind of beauty from back home."

Zander shrugged. "Mountains are mountains."

Faith grunted.

"What?" Zander asked.

She turned her head, catching his gaze. "It's purely accidental that you bought a house in one of the prettiest mountain ranges in California," she remarked with a skeptical pinch of her lips.

"Sure. Half the state is mountains. They're hard to avoid."

Faith kept further speculations to herself, particularly her suspicion that Zander lived in the mountains because they reminded him of home.

"People back home say if you flattened West Virginia, it would be bigger than Texas," she told him. "West Virginia is more vertical than horizontal."

"You're just a walking Mountain State encyclopedia, aren't you?"

"I'm just trying to suggest that if you like mountains, West Virginia is the place to be. Fawnskin reminds me a lot of Booger Hollow. It's just got a sexier name."

He would have openly balked at her suggestion that he return to West Virginia if her remark hadn't been accompanied by a smile so lovely that their mountain view dimmed in comparison.

"The only thing I would have ever gone back there for is right here," he said.

The sun sank further behind the mountains, taking the last of its warmth with it. But Zander's words, and the finality with which he spoke them, warmed Faith all the way through.

"Why didn't you?"

Zander hoped it was a trick of the sunset stealing a bit of the light from her dark eyes.

"Why didn't I what?" He took a few steps away from her and leaned against a mature fir tree.

"Why didn't you ever come back? For me."

"Faith," he groaned, wincing. "I've told you already—"

"I know, you hate Booger Hollow, but that's not good enough." She went up to him, standing toe to toe. "You didn't hate *me*."

"What's done is done," he uttered in exasperation.

"I thought I was going to die," she persisted.

"I wouldn't have let anything happen to you," he said.

"You're the reason I thought I'd die!"

"That's not how I remember it," he mumbled.

"I don't mean then." A tremor crept into her voice. "After. When I believed you were dead. They never found your body, obviously, so I didn't even have a grave to visit. You just disappeared. I couldn't eat, I couldn't sleep."

"Yet you recovered in time to start classes at NYU in the fall," he said blithely.

Faith pinched him. Hard.

"What the—" Zander protested, grabbing at the aggrieved flesh on his upper arm.

"I had to get away from Booger Hollow! It was the only way I could stop thinking about you all the time! When I came home for Christmas that year, I hurt so much that I—"

A soft, silent raindrop cut her off.

Faith swallowed hard, her ire giving way to a flare of panic.

Zander curved an arm around her shoulders and began guiding her back down the mountain. "We'll make it back before the storm hits," he assured her. "This mountain hasn't been mined to death. The rain doesn't have the effect here that it does in Booger Hollow."

Their descent was faster than the climb, but Zander's timing was off. The wind picked up, bringing heavy, dark clouds that emptied their contents all at once, drenching them by the time they dashed through Zander's front door. Breathing heavily, Faith slammed the heavy door closed behind them, slumping against it as though the wind and rain were attempting a home invasion.

Whether from fear, cold or a combination of the two, Zander couldn't tell which rattled drops of rain from the tip of Faith's nose as she leaned on the door, her forehead pressed to it.

"I'm sorry," she gasped. "I just . . ."

"I know." Zander thought of a hundred ways to comfort her, but a gentle touch to the back of her head was the one he settled on.

The rain had completely restyled her. Rain saturated the fibers of her sweater, weighing it down so that it clung to her breasts and arms while hanging loose at her hips. Before Zander's eyes, her hair was springing back into the curls he'd so loved when they were teens. The curls that had tickled his chin the last time he'd seen her, the first time he'd kissed her.

"It does that when it gets wet," Faith said without looking at him, in response to the faint tug at one of her curls.

Zander let it spiral around the tip of his finger. The texture of her hair was the softest substance he'd ever known, something between silk and air. His nostrils flared slightly as he took a long whiff of it, the scent so familiar and welcome that it infused him with the blissful rush of a narcotic.

"I always liked your curls," he said. "When I saw you at the press conference, I didn't recognize you right away because your hair was straight. But when I got a good look at your eyes . . ."

"The eyes always reveal who you are." She turned to face him, once again composed now that she was safe from the storm. "Who are you?" she asked, intently searching his eyes for the answer. "I know you, but you're a complete stranger."

"I'm someone who got caught in an early spring rain and now I'm freezing. I need to change."

You've done enough of that already. With that disquieting thought, Faith watched him retreat to his bedroom.

Faith stood at the windowed wall, mesmerized by the artistry of the storm in the growing darkness. Thunder echoed through the mountains, prefacing silver-white flashes of lightning that fractured the heavens, which healed themselves instantly. Peculiar grey-bright light illuminated heavy clouds the same shade of purple-black as a two-day old bruise. Rain angrily spattered the surface of the lake, sizzling on contact.

Two inches of polarized, bulletproof glass separated her from the fury of the storm, but Faith still trembled.

She was far from phobic about storms, but they still made her uncomfortable. This one in particular brought back memories she had repressed for a long time. She crossed her arms over her chest, tightly hugging herself.

So focused on the storm, Faith was unaware of Zander's presence when he came to the studio. Two wine glasses in one hand, a bottle of wine in the other, and a black T-shirt draped over his left shoulder, he stood in the wide doorway, stopped dead in his tracks by her reflection in the glass.

His arms dropped heavily to his sides, the weight of sudden emotion filling his chest. He had changed, selected the T-shirt for Faith and, thinking that it would help warm her up, he'd gotten the wine. His tasks hadn't taken more than a few minutes, but it was all the time needed, upon seeing her again, to free the feelings he had kept deep within himself since leaving Dorothy.

Love and desire were too feeble to name what he was feeling for Faith as he studied her in the warm golden glow of the muted track lighting.

The lively chestnut, auburn and sienna curls and the delicious brown skin that had drawn him to her in Dorothy continued to do so, only now his longing had grown stronger. Either because of the years they had spent apart or his renewed intimacy with her, his feelings, achingly potent, poisoned his ability to think and behave rationally. He took a few steps into the studio, and he realized that everything he had done in the past ten years hadn't been for himself, to escape his past or to escape Dorothy.

It had all been for her.

For Faith.

For her approval, her respect. For her love.

"Take off your clothes."

Faith whirled around with a start. His command, the croak of his voice as he issued it, the intensity in his eyes and the hard set of his jaw left her shivering, and not from the chill of her wet clothing.

He seemed taller, broader, certainly more imposing as he came toward her, presumably to enforce what had seemed like a practical directive. There was nothing menacing in his demeanor, which encouraged her to dare a step in his direction. And to obey him.

Zander had no delusions that what had initially been a practical concern was now something far different. Her clothes were surely uncomfortable, but once her soggy top was in a heap on the floor, he acknowledged the bare truth: After years of dreaming and wanting, he wouldn't wait another minute to have her.

Faith unsnapped and unzipped her pants as she moved to the center of the room. Keeping her eyes on Zander's in his reflection, hips shifting right, left and right again, she peeled off her jeans and stepped out of the pool of white.

Standing against the rear wall, Zander appreciated her dexterity in unhooking her pretty bra. The ivory garment glowed against the darkness of her skin, and Zander momentarily envied the way the damp lace briefly clung to her flesh before she drew it away from her body.

Out of habit, Faith's hands went to her breasts, lightly massaging them now that they were free of constraint. Zander remained motionless, but he made a sound, something between a grunt and a groan. Her back to him, Faith bent over to slide off her sheer cotton panties.

His hand tightened around the neck of the wine bottle as his gaze moved over her. Individually, her attributes were lovely, but collectively her beauty overwhelmed him. Responding to her touch, his gaze or both, her nipples tightened, the plum-dark buds inviting him to lick his lower lip.

Further down, below her toned stomach and abdomen, he noticed the absence of the strip of floss with which he'd familiarized himself at Venus Adonis; the only curls on view now were the ones on her head.

Zander let the wine bottle thunk to the floor, and Faith's entire body responded when he came at her. He took her by the waist, roughly tugging her in to kiss her. Faith's arms went around his neck, her fingers into his hair. Zander's fingertips dug into the meat of her right thigh as he pulled her even closer, bringing her leg around his hip.

His kisses, as tumultuous and fierce as the storm still raging outside, wandered over her face, laying claim to her eyes, her lips, her chin, her lips, her cheeks and her lips once more before sampling the soft skin of her throat and the hollow of her neck. Following a path delineated by her abdominal muscles, he kissed her wherever his lips happened to land, moving lower until he rested on one knee. Clutching the firm rounds of her backside with both hands, his tongue traced the crease joining her right thigh to her pelvis as he guided her right leg over his shoulder.

His domineering tone and posture gone, he succumbed to his hunger for her. The taste of her sweet sweat met the tip of his tongue as it sought the precious pearl nestled within her bare folds. Faith's knees weakened, the moist heat of Zander's mouth and the forceful probing of his tongue sending her to a place of mindless need.

His left hand supported her, clamping her bottom almost painfully while the fingers of his right hand opened her to more fully enjoy the tasty target peeking from its delicate hood. Grasping handfuls of his hair, Faith gasped in time to the intense, minute measured pumps of her hips, which met the actions of his tongue and teeth. Firm yet gentle, insistent yet leisured, Zander generated sensations that both weakened and strengthened her.

Zander's right knee folded under him when Faith's legs gave out, and her weight drove her off balance. Curling his arms around her thighs, he sank onto his back, refusing to separate his mouth from her. Faith's forearms caught the brunt of her weight, sparing her knees painful contact with the hardwood floor.

She wouldn't have noticed a couple of cracked patellas, not with Zander's fingertips softly moving through the valley between her buttocks, coaxing her legs wider.

Reaching and pulling, lapping and suckling, Zander kept her prisoner to his greed, even tightening his grip when she tried to straighten her arms in push-up position to give him more breathing room.

An upward stroke of his nose followed by the pinch of his lips trapped her breath in her lungs. Faith's hands clenched, her limbs stiffened, her backside flexed as her hips rode Zander's head into the flooring. Her air left her in a loud, gasping cry of relief and pleasure, which climbed even higher when Zander coated two fingers with her liquid silk and added them to the work of his mouth. Slumping helplessly over him, Faith allowed him to roll her onto her back. Unwilling to give her a respite, he moved his fingers precisely, slightly curling them upward while drawing them forward and back an inch at a time.

Faith took her breasts in her hands, her back arching, her knees nearly drawn up to her shoulders. Her incoherent sounds of pleasure eventually formed words, and she begged Zander to join her.

To Faith, there was nothing better than anticipation. Too often, waiting for a thing was more titillating, more exhilarating, than the actual receipt of the thing she wanted.

Not this time. Zander was touching places she never knew she had, taking her to levels of physical delight that she had only fantasized about. When Zander slid along her body to bring his face even with hers, she met him with a smile before cradling his head.

"I want this," she told him, wrapping her legs around him. "I've wanted you for so long."

His jaw hardened and his eyes searched hers for a moment. The past and the present seemed one as he wrestled with desire and responsibility. There was no tension in her body, at least none born of apprehension. But there was plenty of tension in his. He wanted her in a way he hadn't dared imagine back in Dorothy.

Her body was ready for him. He'd seen to it. His was ready for her, too, judging from the pressure and pain behind his zipper.

Framing her right breast in his hand, he brought his mouth to it, bedeviling it with the same skill he'd shown between her legs. "I won't hold back," he mumbled between teasing tugs and kisses. "I don't think I could, even if I wanted to."

She nodded, her breathing coming harder.

He raised his head. "Are you sure?"

She answered by way of a kiss that sent fire straight to the ache in his groin. Scooping her into his arms as he got to his feet, he raced downstairs to his bed. Faith spread herself languorously, moaning in contentment. "I could live in this bed," she purred.

"I'd like the company," Zander said.

The Savoir bed had been a housewarming gift from Brent. The hand-built, horsehair-stuffed mattress had extra padding, and had been built to specification with Zander's height, weight and lower-back problems in mind. The bed was one of Zander's favorite places to spend time when he was alone, and now he couldn't wait to share it with Faith.

She belonged there.

The flat gray-blue of the stormy sky left the room in cool shadow. Zander pressed a wall switch, and soft golden light warmed the room. Faith nestled deeper into the bed, the heat of Zander's gaze insulating her from the bleak chill of the storm.

Faith inhaled deeply as Zander slipped off his shirt and stepped out of his jeans.

"Wait," Faith said abruptly, stopping his progress toward her.

He had appeared topless in *Burn*, and he had been beautiful. Too beautiful.

Zander's torso looked as if it had been carved from flesh and bone with the skill of a Renaissance master, and Faith suspected that *Burn*'s digital arts team had erased the imperfections she now saw. Burn scars from his years working at Red Irv's striped his left forearm, and slash marks and jagged, raised scars of unknown origin dotted his torso. His right hand self-consciously went to a thick band of mottled scar tissue under his left collarbone, although he kept his eyes on Faith's.

He had been walking her home from Red Irv's the night his father had stormed out of Buzzy's Tavern after losing a week's pay betting on Mountaineers baseball. Catching sight of his son, Orrin Brannon had called him aside, demanding money. Accustomed to taking his frustrations out on his boy, Orrin responded to Zander's empty pockets by striking him with his half-empty beer bottle. The bottle broke against Zander's collarbone, and the jagged edge ripped through his black T-shirt and the underlying flesh.

Zander had shoved his father hard into Buzzy's brick front, so hard that Orrin never lifted a hand against him again. But Orrin's last act of violence had been his worst, leaving Zander with a four-inch gash over his heart. The combination of night and Zander's black T-shirt had camouflaged the blood flowing freely from the wound, and he had assured Faith that the dampness she saw was splattered beer.

He had seen her safely home before returning to the diner in time to give Red Irv a good scare. If he hadn't been in such pain, he would've enjoyed Red Irv's look of horror at the way the fluorescent lights and blood loss had turned his complexion bluish-gray. Red Irv, a former butcher, had smelled the blood on Zander before he'd seen it, and he'd locked up the diner to take him to the Raleigh County Medical Center. An eager young physician's assistant had given Zander a row of neat stitches, a tetanus shot and a prescription for an antibiotic.

He had never told Faith how seriously he had been hurt, but she knew now. All of his secrets were now exposed as she opened her arms and beckoned him into her embrace.

Her lips sought his scars, blessing them. There were so many, and he needed them. They were all that made him look truly mortal, and all the more beautiful. Her attention pacified his emotional scars, and helped him ignore the physical ones, and he wrapped her up in him. His left thumb teased and stroked her right nipple, his mouth found her parted lips while his right middle finger glided into her to work her once more.

Granted freer access to him, Faith slipped a hand between them and took hold of the rigid velvet pressing into her abdomen. Her heart thumped hard and she made a high-pitched grunt of surprise when she loosely wrapped her hand around it.

"How many double-As does this thing take?" she asked.

Zander raised his head, a modest smile between his crimson cheeks. "You're not . . . you've . . . I assume you've been with—"

"I'm not a virgin, Alex," she said. "I had a life in the time I thought you were dead."

He nuzzled her cheek, two fingers stroking the slick, hot flesh between her thighs. Faith closed her eyes and drew a deep breath through her nose, moaning in pleasure as he massaged and gently stretched her, readying her.

"I won't hurt you," he assured her. "I promise."

Faith wasn't so sure. His length and weight were daunting, and combined with the fact that it had been months since her last relationship, she was even more grateful for the time and skill Zander spent preparing her. He suckled her earlobe, the heel of his palm kneading her sweating pellet; he flicked his tongue over her nipples in turn, his fingers delving deeper, widening her.

With maddening patience, he brought her close to the edge of release and then pulled back, until she was ready to weep.

Zander quickly snatched a condom from the top drawer of his night table. In his eagerness to put it on, he poked his thumb through the lip of it. His hands trembling now, he retrieved another one, carefully slipped it on, then covered Faith with his body.

All of him felt hard and strained against her, from his elbows, which framed her head, to his feet, which had separated hers. There was nothing he could say that she hadn't already read in his eyes, and with a whispery kiss to her forehead, he raised his hips and angled himself into her.

Faith curled her pelvis upward to meet him, her back and neck arching, her mouth opening in silent protest at his initial, shallow invasion. Her chest and abdomen rose and fell with the deep breaths she took to help acclimate herself to his entry. Zander worked just as hard to stop himself from driving as far into her as he could.

Beads of sweat appeared on his forehead and upper lip, his biceps quivered from the strain of taking their union so slowly. Sympathetic to his discomfort and craving the fulfillment of her own pleasure, Faith locked her legs around his middle and used her feet to urge him forward.

All at once all of him filled her, and for a second she clutched at his arms as if she could push herself from beneath him. A tear trickled from her right eye and Zander kissed it away as he stroked her hair from her face.

"I'm sorry," he murmured, holding completely still but for the kisses he dotted on her face and ears. "I'm so sorry, babe."

"I'm fine," she assured him, nodding. "Really."

Zander pressed the tip of his fingertip to a tear welling in the corner of her left eye. "Then why are you crying?"

Explanations eluded Faith, for all her talent with words. So many wishes, so many prayers had led to this moment. His fullness within her, his weight upon her, his arms around her, his gaze locked with hers, Faith slowly exhaled, and she felt as if he were melting into her, that they had finally, truly and completely reunited.

She took his face in one hand and kissed him, answering him the only way she could. Cradling her head, Zander's sweat-dampened hair cloaked their faces as he began a slow, steady rhythm meant to erase her discomfort and ready her for the very best he had to give.

Faith began smiling through their kisses when he shifted his hips a bit, just enough to alter the points of slippery friction between them. A low growl of sexual delight crawled from Faith's throat, and with renewed gusto she moved her hips to greet each thrust of Zander's.

She opened herself to him completely, her abdomen tightening as she crunched forward to take his backside in her hands. The powerful working of his buttocks gave her an additional thrill as she urged him on, craving a deeper union.

Her touch triggered reactions in Zander that enslaved him to his desire for her. He grabbed her wrists in turn, throwing her arms over her head. He sat back on his heels, tugging her by her hips to keep her with him. With her beauty fully exposed before him, he used his right thumb to expose the candy-pink nub winking at him with each thrust into her. Faith cried out, her torso flexing as her climax gripped her. She clamped hard around Zander, and he could hold himself back no longer.

His fingertips digging into the meat of her hips and buttocks, he held her in place as he drove into her, each pulse of his hips satisfying years of longing yet making him want her all the more.

Like stones dropped into a deep, still pool, Faith's pleasure seemed to ripple from the point where they were joined, the sensations growing stronger, evolving in nuance and intensity as they radiated outward. She gripped her head and bit her lower lip, convinced that she would die from pleasure as she rode the intoxicating convulsions to their completion.

A light sheen of perspiration covered her face and torso. Her hair was a wild tangle upon his pillows. The jiggle of her breasts put him in the mind of two healthy dollops of chocolate mousse tipped with dark chocolate kisses. But it was the movement of her tongue over the plump of her lower lip that sent him far beyond any carnal bliss he'd ever known. He emptied himself inside her with such force, it momentarily frightened him into thinking that he'd shot off the condom. Frozen in a rictus of sheer pleasure, he couldn't let go of her or pull away from her to check its status.

Once he could move, he collapsed over her, gently pinning her wrists over her head to give himself the freedom to tenderly kiss her every place his lips could reach. Greedy now, Faith moved her hips in subtle figure eights to passively take more of what he'd spent himself trying to give.

Still holding her wrists, Zander generously contributed to her solo efforts by dedicating his teeth, tongue and lips to her breasts. A tiny snap at her right nipple, a long draw on the left, and Faith was again voicing her pleasure, her noises a complement to the waning music of the storm.

She pulled her wrists from his grasp but only to take one of his hands and to cup his face. "That was cool," she laughed quietly.

Zander eased out of the bed and went to the window. He opened it a few inches, allowing a rush of cool air to circulate through the room. The breeze raised goosebumps on his arms and chest and stirred the sweet, musky perfume of their lovemaking—which raised another part of Zander's flesh.

Before he rejoined Faith under the covers, he unfolded the black fleece blanket that he kept at the foot of the bed, spreading it over her before burrowing beneath it to join her. "Will you stay?" he muttered into her knuckles, kissing each of her fingers.

Faith's giddiness waned. He had always been the more humorless of the two of them, but the gravity of his tone sobered her. There was so much time to make up for, and she didn't want to waste a second of getting on with it.

"Yes," she responded simply. "I—"

He caught the rest of her acceptance in a kiss. Smiling into it, Faith again opened herself completely to him, sure in the knowledge that the young man she had loved so dearly had never stopped loving her.

CHAPTER 9

"The last time I was at Buzzy's, the only food he was serving was three-year-old beef jerky," Faith said around a mouthful of her grilled portobello mushroom and mozzarella sandwich. She licked a smear of balsamic marinade from her thumb before setting the sandwich back on her plate. "I didn't know tavern food could be so good. Is the focaccia made here?"

Zander speared a chunk of his fourteen-ounce ribeye and swiped it through his "dirty" mashed potatoes before popping it into his mouth. He answered Faith with a nod, and wiped his mouth with a big red-and-white gingham napkin as he chewed and swallowed. "The owner's wife and sons bake all the breads fresh," he explained. "You never know what's going to be on the menu."

"I like this place," Faith said.

Faith had passed the yellow-painted brickfront businesses that housed He's Not Here on her way to Zander's, but she never would have noticed the second-floor establishment if Zander hadn't brought her to it. The front door of the bar was in back of a laundromat, at the top of two flights of weathered pine stairs that turned out to be far sturdier than they looked. The interior was dark, made more so since it was well past sunset, and it took a while for Faith's eyes to adjust once Zander ushered her inside.

Most of the smallish, circular tables with their gingham coverings were empty, but it was a Sunday night. Only a few people seemed to recognize Zander, turning and whispering to their companions as they watched Zander lead Faith to a table set apart from the others, very near the low dais that doubled as a stage.

The décor was standard—neon signs for Coors, Anheuser-Busch, Heineken and Rolling Rock; shot glasses, refrigerator magnets, postcards and other items celebrating the tourist appeal of Big Bear Lake and the neighboring mountain ski resorts; a jukebox that was likely more decorative than functional; a long bar with three stations, only one of which was manned. Darkly stained pine rafters high overhead provided a faint scent that mingled with that of spilled beer and the too-familiar aromas of deep-fried and grilled foods.

Faith couldn't help thinking that one of the reasons Zander liked He's Not Here was because the smell of the place was so similar to Red Irv's, although the menu was very different and distinctly Californian with its wide vegetarian selections featuring local produce and its extensive selection of West Coast wines.

Zander had ordered two glasses of the house white, a 2002 Oregon Reserve pinot gris from King's Estate that Faith did her best not to gulp.

"Good call," she declared, licking a drop of wine from the lip of her goblet. "There's an unusual taste. It's citrusy, but there's something else I can't identify."

"Quince," Zander said, finishing the last of his steak.

Propping her right elbow on the table, Faith rested her chin in her hand. "The golden apple of Hesperides that Paris was supposed to give to the most beautiful goddess among Hera, Athena and Aphrodite was actually a quince."

"Paris chose Aphrodite," Zander said. "Good move."

"She promised him the most beautiful woman in the world if he chose her."

"Helen," Zander said. "Never mind that she was already married to a Greek king. Menelaus."

"You did a report on *The Iliad* back in high school, didn't you?" Faith grinned widely, gleefully recalling Zander's first appearance on stage. "It was for Mr. Crockett's Western civilization class. You guys did an assembly one morning and acted out part of the Trojan War. You were Hector, and that asshole Leland Birch was Achilles, which didn't make sense to any of us because Achilles was supposed to be half god and Leland was barely half human." She snickered, oblivious to Zander's discomfort. "The whole audience cracked up when Leland was supposed to drag your corpse around the walls of Troy, but he wasn't strong enough to drag you in that crazy foot-powered chariot you guys made. It was so funny watching his feet spinning while he tried to pull you along in your toga and your motorcycle boots. Oh, my God, that was such a good assembly," Faith laughed.

"Wanna try the quince tart for dessert?" Zander asked, hoping to quickly quiet and distract her.

"Sure," she responded, her laughter fading. "Are you in a hurry to leave?"

"Don't you have to leave early for Los Angeles tomorrow morning?"

"Yes, but I'm having fun, and I want to hear the band. My editor will understand if I'm a little late."

Zander grinned into his empty plate, pleased that Faith enjoyed the quirky charm of his favorite hangout.

"He's Not Here," Faith said, reading the words burned into the exposed beam over the bar. "I love that name. It must be hysterical when a patron's wife calls and someone answers, 'He's not here.'"

"I lived here for about a year before I even knew this place existed," Zander said. "I never would have found it if I hadn't run into Grover Dylan at the Harley-Davidson outlet in Loma Linda."

Faith chomped into a thick-cut French fry. "Who's Grover Dylan?"

"He's the lead guitarist for the house band. They're playing tonight."

Faith turned the napkin dispenser so that the entertainment calendar for the month faced her. "Knuckle Deep?" she giggled, reading the act scheduled to perform.

Zander chuckled. "Yeah. Grover's a character."

"So he's into bikes and you're a regular at his home bar," Faith said. "Why, he sounds like an actual friend, Alex."

His eyes darted around. The two couples nearest them were engaged in lively conversations and enjoying their meals too much to have overheard what Faith had said. Even so, Zander leaned farther over the cozy round table and said, "There's no Alex here. Okay?"

"Sorry," Faith said coolly, sitting back in her chair.

This was the first awkward moment between them all weekend, and Zander acted quickly to defuse it. "Wanna meet Grover?"

"Sure," she snapped. "I'd love to meet your friend, *Zander*." She grimaced, hating the sound of his new name, his stage name. "*Zander*, I'd like to order another glass of wine, please, Zan—"

"Damn it, Faith," he broke in sternly.

After a moment of guilty silence, she apologized. "It's hard for me to get used to that name," she explained quietly, leaning across the table. "I don't know you as that person. Everything we gave each other last night and this morning pushed that person even further away from me. I love who you really are. I wish—"

"Hey, man!" Zander said suddenly, slightly standing to greet a tall, slim man with long blond hair. "How ya been, Grover?"

"Not bad, not bad," Grover replied. In one fluid motion, he grabbed a heavy chair from a nearby table, spun it, and sat backward in it at their table. "How're things by you, kid?" His arms crossed on the back of the chair, his bright blue eyes slid over Faith, his full lips lazily pulling into a smile that reminded Faith every bit of the Grinch's as he plotted the theft of Whoville's Christmas. "Looks pretty good from here."

Faith resisted the urge to roll her eyes. Grover looked exactly as she expected of the lead singer of a band called

Knuckle Deep. He wore the requisite faded blue jeans with threadbare Radiohead T-shirt. His tanned skin and sun-gold locks were evidence of the amount of time he spent in the California sun, which made his eyes appear vibrant, electric. He wasn't as cinematically handsome as Zander, but Grover was more than pleasing to look at, with his full lips and strong, square jaw and chin. His most attractive qualities were the same elements of mystique and deep-seated vulnerability that had first attracted her to Alex.

With his tablemates sizing up each other, Zander cleared his throat to catch their attention. "Faith Wheeler," he said, taking her hand, "Grover Dylan."

Grover slipped Faith's hand from Zander's, brought her fingers to his lips and barely pressed a kiss to the back of them. "You look familiar, Faith."

"I just have one of those faces," Faith said.

"She's a *Personality!* reporter," Zander told Grover. "You've probably seen her photo in the magazine with her features."

"See ya." Grover stood and started away.

Zander went after him, pulling him back to the table by one arm. "She's cool, man," he assured Grover.

"I don't bite," Faith assured him.

Liar, Zander mouthed over Grover's shoulder.

Once Grover and Zander resettled in their seats, Faith made an effort to learn more about Grover. "Zander tells me that you're the lead guitarist for Knuckle Deep. How old were you when you first picked up a guitar?"

Grover lazily picked at Faith's leftover fries, nibbling the crunchy ends. "I was in the second grade, so I guess about seven or eight."

"How did you come up with the name Knuckle Deep for your band?"

"I think I'll let Zander fill you in on that one," Grover chuckled. "Maybe he could show you."

"What kind of bike do you ride?"

Grover cut a sharp glance at Zander. "Not as big as Zander's," he said pointedly.

"We came here on Zander's bike," Faith said. "When he opened his garage and I saw that Confederated Hellcat—"

"Confederate," Grover said.

"Huh?" Faith grunted.

"My bike is a Confederate Hellcat," Zander said with an indulgent smile.

"It's the love of his life," Grover said.

"Is that so?" Faith asked.

"It's a sexy ride," Grover said. "And rare. The company barely makes a hundred of them a year. Those Alabama boys gave that bike a three-inch frame, a flipped transmission so your ride doesn't drag to the left. It's got the comfort of a luxury cruiser and the handling of a sport bike. It's wicked stable, too. Lots of things you can do on a Hellcat."

"Um," Faith started with a nervous chuckle, "would you fellas excuse me? I've got to hit the head."

Grover quickly hopped into her unoccupied chair once Faith was out of earshot. He made quick work of what might have gone back to Zander's in a doggy bag.

"Dude, I can get you dinner, if you're that hungry," Zander offered.

"She's different," Grover said, taking a big bite of Faith's leftover sandwich.

"Different how?" Zander asked.

"I wouldn't have thought she was your type."

"Because she's black?"

Grover screwed his face into a look of disdain. "No, because she's a reporter."

"Yeah, well, that's something we've been working to overcome."

"I don't really know what your type is because this is the first time I've ever seen you with a woman," Grover remarked.

"You've seen me on television with dates."

"Yeah, but you weren't *with* those broads. Not like you're with this woman."

Zander scrubbed his hands over his face, finishing by smoothing his hair from his face. "It shows, does it?"

"All over the place," Grover laughed lightly. Glancing at her empty plate, he said, "She's a vegetarian."

"She said she stopped eating meat in college because she couldn't afford it."

"She's sweet."

"When we were growing up, she was the only person who was ever kind to me."

This was the most personal admission Zander had ever made to Grover. Zander elaborated no further, and Grover didn't pursue the subject.

"That's not what I mean," Grover grinned mischievously. "Every vegetarian I've ever dated has been sweet. Everywhere."

Zander's eyes glazed over. He seemed to stare at the amber star twinkling on the lip of his wine glass, but he was seeing Faith as she'd been earlier that morning, smiling and arched in bliss beneath him. He took a deep breath, imagining her taste. Whether it was because she was a vegetarian, Zander couldn't say, but Faith unquestionably was delicious.

"There's nothing like a sweet *sweet* woman," Grover said.

Zander got up. "I'm gonna grab another bottle of wine," he said, speaking over his shoulder to Grover as he headed for the bar. "Be right back."

Shaking his head, Grover started nibbling the parsley garnish that had adorned Faith's plate. "Like I said," he muttered to himself. "There's nothing like a sweet woman."

Faith jumped, startled at the sudden sight of Zander when she exited the bathroom.

"We need another bottle of wine," he told her, taking her by the wrist and pulling her out of the short corridor where the doors to the Coyotes and Kittens rooms—men's and women's—faced one another.

"Our table is that way," Faith said, jerking a thumb in the opposite direction as Zander hastily led her past the dining room.

"The wine is down here."

Zander pulled her into another short corridor that marked the entrance to a steep, narrow staircase. Faith's throat went dry as they descended into darkness. Despite her firm belief that Zander would never lead her into harm, Faith's organic fear of cellars reared. Every nightmarish scenario she had ever come across in her reporting career crept from the corners of her mind: secret cellars equipped with S&M equipment that would make the Marquis de Sade cringe; rats skittering along exposed beams, thick dusty cobwebs interfering little with their progress; spiders the size of a toddler's fist responsible for said webs; and worst of all, the cold, dank clutter of someone else's moldy, mildewy underground storage area.

At the bottom step, Zander pulled a fine cord that gave life to two rows of low-wattage bulbs hanging from the low ceiling. Faith had a scant moment to take in the neatly ordered giant-sized boxes, cans and bottles of pasta, beans and dressings before she found herself pushed against huge pillows of flour and sugar stacked shoulder high.

The cellar was dry and tidy, and Faith found an odd sense of comfort in the scents of the dried oregano, rosemary, thyme and sage hanging above them in fine mesh bags. She found greater comfort in Zander's hands as they moved under her shirt and along her skin.

"Do you want me to take off my clothes?" Faith asked, reading the open hunger in his eyes.

"I'll do it," Zander said, his mouth at her ear.

Faith took the solid muscles of his upper arms in a hard, almost desperate grip. Whatever he would do to her, she wanted him to do it. Now.

She had washed her white jeans and underclothes at Zander's, but she'd borrowed one of his white button-downs. The garment was two times too big for her, so when Zander undressed her from the waist down, the shirt tail fell well past her hips.

She wore no bra, so when he unbuttoned the shirt, he was met by a sight he never tired of, two globes of dark perfection that immediately started his juices running.

Faith leaned back on the baking supplies, eagerly presenting herself to him. Zander brought his lips to hers, while his fingers found the other pair between her thighs. Faith moaned into his kiss, rising on her toes to tilt her hips, making her most secret opening fully accessible.

In that perfect place between gentle and rough, Zander mined her heat until he struck the vein that brought forth the sweetness he had learned to crave. He primed her, coating his fingers then bringing them to her lips. Haltingly, she accepted his offer, reveling in her taste as he sealed it to her lips with a kiss. His fingers again dipped into her, probing deeper, matching the work of his mouth against hers.

Groaning, Faith clutched tight handfuls of his shirt, tugging it from his blue jeans. But when she went for the hard ridge angling away from his zipper, he swatted her hands away. Her second attempt to touch him was met with a decisive wrenching of her hands above her head, where Zander impatiently forced her to hold onto the lip of a metal shelf lined with a rainbow of bulk spices.

He threw her shirt open completely, then spent a short moment staring at her. Greed glittered in his gaze as his eyes moved from her face to the tight tips of her breasts, over the expanse of her abdomen, which clenched and unclenched from the force of her breathing, to the bare juncture of her thighs where she gleamed with her own diamond-colored fluid, and down the length of her legs.

Startling her for the second time, Zander grabbed her about the waist and turned her, making sure she resumed her hold on the shelf. He raised her shirt, his hands moving to the front of her pelvis as he did so. They met at the wetness between her legs, and Faith's backside pressed into his groin. She imagined that she felt him lengthen against her, and since he didn't stop her, she ground her buttocks against him.

Zander answered her actions with a new one of his own. He dropped to one knee and parted the firm rounds of flesh that had so taunted him. With a gasp of surprise, Faith buried her face in her left shoulder when Zander's tongue traced her from front to back and hungrily nipped at the puckered place that, other than her doctor, no one had seen since she'd been in diapers.

The exquisite indecency of Zander's act and the intense sensations it generated left Faith whimpering and begging him for complete release. But far too much, Zander enjoyed the taste of her.

Not completely merciless, Zander held tight to her left hip, steadying her, so he could work his right hand between her legs. His thumb entered her with enough vigor to wrench a cry of pleasure from her, but when he hooked his index finger and used the thumb side of it to knead her sweating pearl, Faith replied in a wordless language of mindless need.

His thumb sought the most sensitive spot within her, massaging it in concert with the motion of his index finger, creating a concentrated pinch that left Faith's thighs quivering, her head thrown back and her fingers numb against the unyielding metal of the shelf. His hand left her hip to expose the wink in her gluteal cleft, and Faith hollered for mercy when he applied his tongue to it.

She writhed against him, wanting more, demanding more. Her need became Zander's, and he quickly freed himself and plunged into her dripping center. Willfully disobeying him, Faith released the shelf to brace her left hand on the topmost sack. She reached between her legs with her right to discover another sack.

Clamping his jaw and shutting his eyes as tightly as possible, Zander submitted to his body's betrayal. The contents of Faith's right hand leaped higher, the contents of her sweet tunnel pulsated with his release, adding his heat to hers.

His thighs and bum hardened, his fingernails dug crescents in the skin of her hips, and he took deep, loud breaths through gritted teeth. The force of his climax left him dizzy and clinging to Faith for balance even as she continued to work his oversensitive flesh. He allowed her to pump every last twitch, every drop of satisfaction from him, and he assisted her by taking her breasts in his hands while he suckled her right earlobe.

Faith reached the summit of her pleasure, her body snapping against Zander with enough pressure to make him grunt in her ear. One long, hard constriction that flung her head back was followed by a series of shorter pulses, each one signaled by a moan that reminded Zander of the chorus from a song.

Zander held her to his chest, his hands constantly moving over her. He knew he should let her go, but he couldn't. He had never experienced a more perfect single moment, and he wanted it to last.

Perhaps sensing his need, Faith didn't try to disengage from him. His chin on her left shoulder, she turned her head to kiss him and nuzzle his nose with hers. She rested her hands over his, which were clasped at her waist.

"I don't think I'm scared of cellars anymore," Faith laughed lightly.

"I didn't know you were."

"There are a lot of things you don't know about me, Alex." Catching herself, she hastily added, "Zander. I'm sorry. I didn't mean to—"

"It's okay when we're alone." He kissed her forehead to iron out her wrinkles of concern.

"It's your name," Faith said. She swallowed back the rest of what she wanted to say: *It should be okay* all *the time.* "We should get back upstairs before someone else comes down to get a bottle of wine."

Zander agreed, but made no move to dress and leave until he'd kissed her thoroughly. Even then, Faith had to take his hand to lead him back upstairs and into the now full dining room.

"This place is heaven, man," Grover said, rocking on the back legs of his chair. "You got mountains, a lake—"

"A reservoir lake," Zander interjected.

"You got fishing in the summer, skiing in the winter, and pretty ladies all year round," Grover went on. "I love livin' here."

"Where are you from originally?" Faith asked.

"The Southeast."

"Have you always been a musician?"

"It's just a hobby."

Faith pressed on. "You don't do it for a living?"

"No."

"So what do you do for a living?"

"You're just full of questions," Grover said, an amused grin dancing across his face.

"You're a scientist, right?"

Grover's face froze for a tell-tale second.

"Your fingernails gave you away," Faith explained. "Every scientist I've ever met bites his fingernails down to the quicks."

"I'm a biochemist," Grover said. "My focus is on nutrition and creating safe, natural alternatives to chemical-based food additives."

"Sounds noble," Faith remarked.

"I try." Grover turned at the sound of his bandmates taking to the stage. "Think I oughta scoot. Time for me to bang out a note or two for these kind folks."

"It was nice talking to you, Mr. Dylan," Faith said.

" 'Mister'," he repeated with a chuckle. "I ain't that old, kiddo."

"How old are you?"

"She sure asks a lot of questions," Grover said to Zander, who gave the comment a dismissive roll of his eyes.

Grover made his way to the center of the dais, where two guitars—one electric, one acoustic—were propped up near the mike stand.

"He's a fascinating person," Faith said. "Very enigmatic."

"Yeah," Zander said. "He never asks questions. That's why I like him."

In replaying their conversation, Faith realized that Grover never once asked her anything. But something else occurred to her. "That's why you want a dog."

"Huh?"

"Dogs don't ask questions, either. You want companionship without letting anyone in close."

"I let you in," he said a bit defensively.

"Not all the way."

The discordant notes of Grover tuning his acoustic guitar sounded through the bar, and sitting so close to the speakers, Faith winced at the noise.

"I'm in the mood for something low-key tonight," Grover mumbled into the mike stand. "I hope you like this."

"C'mon, let's go," Zander said, standing and offering a hand to Faith.

"I want to hear him play," Faith protested.

Zander took her by her hand, pulled her from the chair and swung her into his arms on the area of scuffed hardwood designated as the dance floor. Grover began to play the acoustic guitar unaccompanied, and at first, Faith didn't recognize the evocative arrangement of a song popularized by Roberta Flack.

With Zander's hands at her hips, pulling her in close, she loosely draped her arms around his neck. Grover's rendition of "The First Time Ever I Saw Your Face" harkened back to the original, the 1957 folk song Ewan MacColl wrote for his wife. Just as Roberta Flack had with her soulful rendition, Grover had taken the song and remade it into something that truly belonged to him.

"He's got a great voice," Faith marveled. "I wonder if Magda would send *Personality!*'s music reviewer to hear him."

"Grover likes his privacy," Zander said, moving Faith a few feet to one side to make room for two more couples entering the dance floor. "He plays for fun, not for fame."

"He's so good," Faith persisted.

"Then just listen to him and enjoy him. Don't think about promoting him."

Faith did as asked, threading her fingers through the hair at Zander's nape. His hands pressed her closer as they moved over her back and bum, his eyes never leaving hers. Faith took pride in her ability to use words to communicate her thoughts and feelings exactly, and Zander took just as great pride in his talent for bringing the words of others to life. Yet they readily allowed Grover's passionate performance to reveal every emotion they shared as they danced in each other's arms. If a decade apart was all it took to lead to this moment, neither of them regretted a second of it.

The final notes had been sung and the other couples were returning to their tables while the drummer and bass player for Knuckle Deep took their positions for their next song. Faith and Zander remained in place, with Zander stroking Faith's curls from her face.

"I think we should get another bottle of wine," Zander suggested.

"I'd like to try that Australian shiraz I saw in your wine cellar yesterday," Faith said.

Grover, still at the mike, had strapped on his classic Les Paul, amped it up and was starting an original Knuckle Deep song meant to liven a staid Sunday night at He's Not Here. Making eye contact with Grover as he and Faith paid their bill, Zander nodded his thanks for Grover's opening song. It had been an incredible gift, and surely Grover's way of telling him something that he already knew: that Faith was a treasure.

The ride back to Zander's house was difficult.

It was very different from his first and last ride with her on his ancient, dilapidated Harley-Davidson. He'd certainly enjoyed having a teenaged Faith clinging to him on the ride home from the Calliope Grill, but it was far more exciting now, with Faith's lush and meaty woman's body wrapped around him.

She had clung to him in excited fright back when they were kids, her fists knotted in his belly, her arms stiff, her cheek pressed to his shoulder, her thighs rigid as they gripped his hips.

Her strong legs framed him and her hands were locked just below his waist. There was no tension in her body now, but there was plenty in his, especially with her hands fooling about so far below his waist. He had never been in danger of losing control of the bike, given the excellent handling and responsiveness of the Hellcat between his legs, but the one behind him was sorely testing him, especially once her right hand slipped into his jeans.

She stroked him, her fingertips light despite the constriction of his jeans once he filled the front of them. The brush of a feathery fingertip over his tip made him speed up, to get her home before he had no choice but to pull over and take her astride the bike.

Thankfully, the ride home was short, and he parked his bike in his driveway upon arriving. "It's distractions like that that get people killed on the road," he chastised as he removed his helmet and then hung it by its strap over one of his handlebars.

He didn't give Faith a chance to defend herself. She was still fluffing her curls after freeing them from her helmet when Zander twisted and took her by her shoulders, dragging her across his lap. Her helmet bounced to the smooth black pavement of the driveway as Zander kissed her, one hand reaching into her jacket to mold her breast to the shape of his hand.

"Having you only makes me want you more," Zander whispered against her lips. "What have you done to me, Faith?"

Caressing his cheek with a finger, she broke their kiss to say, "Nothing yet."

"I don't understand."

Lying in his arms, she stared past him, into the inky depths of the star-studded sky. "You see so many stars out here with so little ambient light. It's gorgeous."

Zander took her chin to return her gaze to his. "Don't change the subject. What did you mean just now with that 'nothing yet' comment?"

"You don't seem to like it when I touch you," she said on a sad sigh.

He laughed out loud. "Faith, I can't get enough of you. I—"

"You touch me," she explained. "You don't let me touch you. Not the same way. Your abdomen jumped when I touched you on the way back here."

"You caught me by surprise," he said. "Come on."

"What are you afraid of?"

"Not you." He abruptly stood her on her feet and dismounted the bike.

"Yes, you are," Faith accused. She wasn't about to be cowed, not now, and not about this. "Why won't you let me in?"

"I have." Zander started for the front door, his discomfort, both physical and emotional, evident in his stiff gait. "I've never been closer to anyone than I am to you."

"Then let me in all the way," Faith requested earnestly. "It's been too long and we're too old. I gave you my whole heart a long time ago. I want nothing less in return."

Zander unlocked the door. Faith jumped when he explosively kicked it open and went inside.

Hesitantly, she followed him, peering carefully inside the door before she entered and looked for Zander. He was standing in front of his dead fireplace, his face as hard and dark as the cold stone before him. "I don't know what the hell happened between the time we left the bar and now. One minute you're grabbing my package and the next you're accusing me of not letting you touch me. You can't have it both ways, Faith."

Without a word, she walked right up to him. She rose on her toes to kiss him, cupping him as she did so. Zander's hand clamped around her wrist, drawing it away.

"I rest my case," Faith said. "And now I'm going home."

She was at the door before Zander forced himself to call out to her. "Faith!"

"What?" she snapped without turning around.

"I don't want you to go," he humbly admitted. "Please."

She went back to him. Standing toe to toe, her face aimed up at his, she challenged him. "Then let me touch you. The way you touch me."

He threw his hands up in mock surrender and sat heavily on his sofa. "Fine. Whatever," he said, his right thumb and forefinger worrying his right earlobe. "I'm yours, baby. Do your worst."

CHAPTER 10

Faith took her time.

She asked Zander to make a fire, which he did. She asked him for the shiraz, which he retrieved, along with two glasses.

Her final request, that he take a seat on the sofa before the fire, was obeyed, albeit hesitantly.

Faith came at him slowly, carefully, rather the way she would have approached an injured wild animal. In some respects, that's exactly what Zander was. Faith was no expert, but she had her own idea as to why Zander always took such control of their intimate moments, and she wanted to prove it one way or the other.

She joined him on the sofa, sitting astride his lap to unbutton his shirt. He settled deeper into it and rested his arms along the back of it. His casual demeanor seemed strained; a flash of defiance in his eyes belied his apparent willingness to give Faith control.

Faith soldiered on.

She opened his shirt wide, baring his chest. She hunched forward to take one of the tiny tips capping his broad pectorals between her teeth. Her tongue swirled around it, sampling the smooth disk of flesh at its base before she nipped at it, pinching it with her teeth just hard enough to make him squirm in his seat and clench his fists.

He rose, solid and heavy, beneath her. She undid his jeans and tugged them down past his knees, leisurely studying his legs while she pulled off his athletic shoes and socks.

"You have man hair," she commented softly. "I really like that."

"What's 'man hair?' "

"Too many models and actors wax things that should be hairy," Faith said, glancing at his neat, honey-wheat nest. "Pruning the jungle is good, complete deforestation—not good."

Zander absently stroked himself. "Exactly how many naked trouser snakes have you seen?"

Carefully watching the movement of his hand, Faith pulled his jeans free of his legs. "I'll bet I've seen fewer bare batons than you've seen bacon strips and naked dugouts." She stood and undressed, watching him watch her as she did so. His fingers closed around his baton, his motions growing more animated as more of her body was exposed. Once all of her clothes had joined his jeans on the floor, she parted his knees wide and kneeled between them.

"Who was it?" he asked.

"Who was what?"

"Your first."

"My first what," she purred.

"You know what. Was it Jeffrey Winslow?"

"Jeffy Winslow was never really interested in me. He came to visit me at NYU once, and loved the city so much that he moved there. Everyone back home thinks he works in theater, and he does. He performs in tribute revue called Tina, Diana & Friends."

Zander's abs bounced in a light chuckle. "Who does Jeffy play?"

"Lola Folana."

"Your first time was with Lola Folana?"

"Do you really want to talk about this now?" She smoothly replaced his hand with hers, copying his technique. Chancing a glance at his face, she was pleased to see the battle waging there. His mouth would stiffen then relax, his lips parted. His eyes drowsed shut after he peered at her with something akin to wariness in them. His jaw clenched and relaxed, until finally his head fell back and his hips scooted forward in a mute invitation for her to go further.

Her fingers loosely laced around him, she stroked him, twisting her hands upward, meeting them with her lips at his tip. His abdomen jumped and he emitted a tiny grunt of surprise and satisfaction when his swollen cap glided against the hot, wet cushion of her tongue.

"Ahh, God . . . Faith," he groaned when she guided him deeper, his girth almost overfilling her mouth.

His legs opened wider and his hands went to her shoulders. His grip was too firm, and Faith thought he would push her away. She took him deeper, coordinating her breathing with the up and down movements of her head along the stiff length of his flesh while she busied her hands anew with the firm, warm weights at its base.

Zander's hands glided over the silky skin of her neck and shoulders, his fingers moved into the curls just behind her ears. He cupped her head but did nothing to interfere with her work between his legs, and sooner than he anticipated, he found himself near his breaking point, at that place where pleasure was almost painful. Acting automatically, he held onto handfuls of her curls and thrust forward again and again. Faith took all that she could, answering his deepest thrusts with a swallowing technique that created a vacuum the likes of which he had never experienced.

Faith was keenly aware of his readiness when she felt his twins crowding upward. She pried his hands from her hair, pulled her head from his lap and quickly mounted him, shuddering in pleasure as she fully enrobed him. Beneath Zander's hands, her thigh muscles worked as she raised and lowered herself upon him, arching her back and curling her hips forward to generate friction just as pleasing to her as it was to Zander.

Cradling his head to her bosom, she fed him her left nipple. Hungrily, he took it, instantly triggering a response that locked her around him, the constrictions of her intimate chamber initiating Zander's release.

His nails cut into Faith's skin, his abdominal muscles bunched and hardened, his toes curled. His head flew forward, the cords and veins in his neck standing out as he shouted his surrender. He gave her everything she had wanted, and a little extra, and she thanked him with tender kisses and caresses meant to bring him even closer to her.

Shaking in Faith's arms, Zander held her so tightly, he compressed her shoulder blades and interfered with her breathing. Faith returned his embrace, her arms wrapped around his head, her hands stroking his hair. He had given her the confirmation she had needed.

"I love you, Alex."

Faith's whispered words, the heat of them at his ear, started his heart pounding so hard he was certain she could feel it beating against her breast. He adjusted his hold on her, loosening it so he could see her face.

"You don't have to say it," she tenderly assured him. "I know you love me. You show it every second I'm with you. I wanted to know if you could accept it."

"I don't have a problem taking—"

She pressed her fingers to his lips. "Taking isn't the same thing as accepting. You know that."

He sat up straighter with her, allowing her to wrap her legs around his middle, allowing him to seal her body to his. He'd been with a lot of women, too many. Some for survival, some for base relief. But none of them had touched him, not like Faith. Her touch, back in Dorothy and now, were the only times he had been touched by someone who loved him.

The realization weakened him as it washed through him, and it took all of his remaining strength to hold onto Faith, his Faith, who knew all along what he had only just discovered.

Having never received healthy doses of affection, he'd never learned how to accept love. His parents had ignored him when they weren't abusing or stealing from him. He'd learned to take intimacy as it had been offered, but as Faith told him—that wasn't the same as accepting it.

He'd accepted it tonight, when Faith showed him the most important thing he'd never learned when he was young: that he was worth loving.

Faith hoped it was the last step he needed to take to accept everything else, especially the fact that he was Alexander Brannon, her Alex, the love of her life.

⁂

"I did the Farmer's Market this weekend," Daiyu said in response to Faith's inquiry regarding her weekend. "What'd you do? Or should I say 'who?'"

Faith swiveled from side to side in her chair, her legs outstretched. Her feet bumped a side of her cozy cubicle with each turn. "I spent some time near Big Bear Lake."

"With Zan—"

"Yes," Faith spoke over her. "We had a really good time."

Peering at Faith over the tops of her narrow black glasses, Daiyu folded her arms over her chest, carefully, so as to avoid puncturing herself with any of the jagged cloisonné anime characters pinned to the straps of her stretchy black paperbag overalls.

Faith stopped swiveling. "What's that look for?"

Daiyu shrugged a shoulder. "What look? I don't have a look."

"I thought I saw a look, but if there was no look . . ."

"There was no look," Daiyu sweetly assured her.

"Would you two knock it off?" directed a male voice from the neighboring cubicle. "You guys sound like a female Jerry Seinfeld and George Costanza."

"Are you on deadline, Vivian?" Daiyu called without leaving her perch on one edge of Faith's cluttered desk.

"Yes," he growled. "And I'm not even sure the piece is gonna run."

"Why's that?" Faith asked.

"No photo, no go," came Vivian's slow, deep drawl, which always put Faith in the mind of John Wayne.

Daiyu and Faith knew exactly what that meant. *Personality!* was a photo-driven magazine. Stories without suitable pictures didn't run, plain and simple.

"Who do you need?" Daiyu asked.

"Doesn't matter," Vivian said. "You ain't got him."

"Try me," Daiyu challenged.

Vivian's ancient leather and oak office chair creaked as he lifted his weight from it to lean over the cork divider. With his straight white teeth exposed in a neighborly grin, his jet-black hair neatly combed with a precise side part and his tanned forearms bared in a dark green polo shirt, Vivian looked more like a professional golf commentator than *Personality!*'s most senior entertainment news reporter. For fifteen years, Vivian had written a column titled *After Hours*, reporting on the antics famous folk got up to at some of the trendiest nightspots in Los Angeles. Vivian had stumbled into the gossip beat, after being assigned to the department by a former *Personality!* editor who hadn't known that he was a man.

"I've got a bit on Joaquin Phoenix."

"What flavor?" Faith asked. Joaquin Phoenix was one of her favorite actors, and Vivian's *After Hours* vignettes typically came in three flavors: Dumbsel-in-Distress,

Knight-in-Whining-Armor and the much rarer My Hero!

"Phoenix bought himself a My Hero blurb last night when he stopped to help a Dumbsel-in-Distress outside Catch, that new place on Sunset. The guy's a class act," Vivian went on. "He was leaving a restaurant, saw the girl being manhandled by some big dope and intervened."

"Any punches thrown?" Faith asked, tantalized by the image of "her" Joaquin going medieval on a bully.

"He didn't have to," Vivian chuckled. "Phoenix has one of those faces. You don't know if he's going to ask you the time or go for your throat with his teeth bared."

"He's *my* hero," Faith cooed.

"But the guy is a vampire," Vivian said. "Three photographers thought they got him last night, but he turns transparent on film."

"I got him," Daiyu said confidently. "He must have just been leaving the scene outside Catch. He looked all moody and windblown."

"He always looks like that," Vivian said.

"You want the pics or not?" Daiyu asked.

"What's it gonna cost me?" Vivian asked, his blue eyes sparkling.

"A post-awards ceremony shindig to be determined at a later date," Daiyu said. "Anything but the Daytime Emmys and the Country Music Awards."

"Done." Vivian shoved a hand at her.

"I'll e-mail the shots to production right now," Daiyu said, cementing the deal with a handshake.

"You're amazing, kiddo," Vivian said with a wink before sinking back into his chair, which answered with a loud creak.

"Who did you get at the Farmer's Market?" Faith asked, making room to allow Daiyu to slip a zip disk into Faith's computer.

"Pretty much everybody, but nobody good," Daiyu answered, making quick work of e-mailing the Phoenix shots to production. "You know who I'd really like to shoot?"

"Nope. Who?"

"You."

"Me?"

"You." Daiyu peered over the top of her glasses as she slipped her zip disk back into the case hanging from the silver chain around her neck. "And Zander Baron."

"I can see why you'd want to shoot Zander, but why on earth would you want to shoot me?"

"Here's the thing," Daiyu said, "you're pretty, he's prettier—"

"Thanks," Faith deadpanned.

"But the two of you together . . . it's magic. It's real. It's gorgeous."

Vivian reappeared over the cubicle wall. "You're dating Zander Baron?"

"No," Daiyu and Faith answered as one.

"This is so good," Vivian chuckled, settling once more on his side of the wall. "Scoops never just fall into my lap like this."

"What I wouldn't give for real walls," Faith muttered.

She smoothed her short, leather skirt around her hips as she exited her workspace, Daiyu right behind her. They wove their way through the maze of cubicles, hopped into an elevator, and took it to the lobby. They left the building and went straight to the one place they knew they could speak openly without being overheard.

"Could you at least turn on the air conditioning?" Daiyu asked as she settled into the passenger seat of Faith's old Camry.

"It's not hot," Faith protested.

"It's not hot *outside*," Daiyu disagreed, propping her booted feet on the dashboard. "It's plenty hot fastened up in this car."

Faith started the engine and turned on the air conditioner. A blast of chilled air rushed in with a loud, rattling wheeze.

"Do cars get emphysema?" Daiyu wondered aloud.

Faith got right to the reason for their escape from the news floor. "Why do you want to photograph me with Zander Baron?"

"Why are you trying to hide that you're seeing him?" Daiyu countered.

"It's an invasion of privacy," Faith contended. "I don't want people in my business."

"Invading people's privacy is our job. It's what we do for a living, it's what *Personality!* is. Why should we be exempt?"

"Who's 'we?'" Faith scoffed. "I don't see you taking pictures of you and your cowboy and plastering them all over the place."

"Justin is a civilian. Zander's in the biz. His photos are a bigger commodity."

"I'll ask him if he'll sit for you, but I can't be seen in a photo with him."

"I can't help being intrigued by your adamant refusal to sit for a pic with your man friend," Daiyu said suspiciously. "If I were a reporter, I'd probably dig a lot deeper into that."

"Leave it alone, Daiyu. Please."

"Look, it's not for the mag," Daiyu said. "It's for my book. Ever since I saw you and Baron makin' out at the Wilshire, I've wanted to shoot you two. You guys have something that oozes."

"We do not," Faith said emphatically, grimacing.

"I don't mean in a gross way. It's artistic. It's . . . emotional." Daiyu turned to face Faith. "You know that photo of John Lennon and Yoko Ono, the one where he's naked and clinging to her like a monkey on the trunk of a palm tree?"

"I always thought of it as more like a kid clinging to a parent," Faith said.

"Then you know what I'm talking about. That photo is iconic because of the emotion it captured. Some people love it, others are creeped out by it. The point is that it makes you feel something. I think I can create something just as timeless and beautiful with you and Zander."

"I appreciate the compliment, Daiyu, and I know how talented you are. If anyone could capture whatever it is that Zander Baron and I ooze, it's you. I just don't think it would be a good idea, at least not right now."

"I can wait."

"Okay, then."

Faith drummed the steering wheel, her hands further worrying the existing worn patches at ten and two o'clock.

"Since this thing is fired up, why don't you give me a lift to In-N-Out Burger," Daiyu suggested.

"I could go for an early lunch," Faith agreed, easing the car into first gear.

Daiyu gave Faith a full account of her weekend photo hunting, but Faith's mind remained elsewhere. As much as she would have liked to have a photo of herself with Zander, shot by someone as talented as Daiyu, no less, she knew that it would be that much easier for someone back home to make the connection that she already had between Alex Brannon and Zander Baron. As much as she wanted Alex back, she wouldn't force him out. The decision to reveal himself had to be his or it wouldn't mean anything to either of them.

※

Faith had almost given up on him when he called to tell her that he had just found a parking spot and was walking back to her building. Standing at her living room window, she scoured the sidewalk far below for him. It was late, and while her neighborhood wasn't the worst, neither was it the best, and the last thing she wanted was for him to fall victim to a mugging on his first visit to her apartment.

"Are you wearing a Dodgers baseball cap and a plaid shirt?" Faith asked, spotting a figure clutching a cell phone to his ear, his free hand in his pocket.

"Yeah, I'm in disguise," he laughed.

"Some disguise," Faith snickered. "You look like you were born here in east Los Angeles."

"Good. That's what I was going for."

Faith buzzed him in the second he set foot on the front step of her building. He bypassed the slow-moving elevator to sprint up four flights of stairs to get to her.

Wearing only a sheer white nightshirt and white bikini briefs, Faith welcomed him to her little apartment with a big kiss.

"It's been so long," she murmured, running her hands along his arms.

"Too long," he chuckled. "What, about thirty-six hours?"

"It seems longer. Fawnskin seems like a whole different time and place compared to now."

"You could always relocate, you know."

Faith's first impulse would have been to fly into her bedroom, pack whatever would fit into her largest suitcase and hop into her old car for a one-way trip to Fawnskin. But common sense prevailed, and she responded to his suggestion with a playful question.

"What would I do out there in the middle of nowhere while you were on location?" she asked. "I can't sing and play like Grover, and I don't think I'm cut out for waitressing at He's Not Here."

Faith's furnishings were clean and comfortable, and possessed a shabby elegance that Zander appreciated. He sincerely respected and admired the fact that she proudly lived within her means rather than dipping into the deep pockets of her parents to live in the style she'd enjoyed as a kid back in Booger Hollow.

"Fawnskin's got a great, colorful history," Zander told her. "There's hundreds of good stories you could write. The town's Gold Rush history alone could keep you busy for—"

"I don't want to be a human interest or entertainment writer for the rest of my life," Faith said, cutting him off. "I want to write impact pieces that matter."

"What's an impact piece?"

Faith retrieved a thick manilla folder from the low beachhouse desk that seemed to double as a dining room table. She led Zander to her overstuffed sofa, sitting beside him with her legs across his lap. He caressed their silken lengths from hip to ankle as she showed him the contents of the folder.

"This is a story about an allergen detection device developed by Westcott Technologies in Maryland," Faith said, handing him an article she'd torn from a scientific journal Zander had never heard of. "The head researcher is the founder of the company. He had a son with a severe allergy to peanuts, and the kid died after sampling food at a chili cook-off. One of the cooks didn't want her secret thickening agent known, so she didn't declare peanut butter on her ingredient list. The kid went into anaphylactic shock. He was in a coma for a week before his parents took him off life support."

"This is depressing," Zander said. "And this is the kind of thing you want to write?"

Faith showed him the next story. "*This* is the kind of thing I want to write. The Westcott story is only a small piece of this bigger story."

His interest piqued, Zander scanned the pages of the second article. "Cady Winters-Bailey," he said, reading the author's name. "I remember this scandal. It broke right before I started filming *Burn* with her sister, Kyla Randall. The story gave me the creeps."

"Doesn't it, though?" Faith said. "It just confirmed something that most of us have suspected all along."

"That computer companies can access our hard drives through the software they sell us?"

"Exactly. Emmitt Grayson, the CEO and founder of U.S. IntelTech software, just happened to get caught, thanks to two of his employees. Chiara Winters and John Mahoney used Westcott Technologies as bait to catch Grayson spying on the companies that bought his software programs. The story is incredible. I wish I'd been the one to expose it. Cady Winters-Bailey was nominated for so many awards for this story. Can you imagine? Having your own sister involved in exposing corporate espionage and living to talk about it?"

"You want to write meaty, hard-hitting news stories so you can cover your walls with trophies and plaques?"

"No," she snapped, closing the folder. "I want to write stories that make a difference in people's lives." She flipped the folder onto her coffee table. "No offense, but writing about a rehabbed singer's bachelor party and a mysterious actor's latest movie release isn't exactly earth-shattering. Or challenging. Or—"

"Okay, I wasn't offended at first, but I am now." He stopped her embellishments by grabbing her backside and tugging her fully onto his lap. "I'm the first to admit that acting is one of the most pointless, useless, purposeless, fruitless . . . Are you going to stop me at any point here?"

"So far, I agree with everything you've said." Faith smiled.

"But the only thing more pointless, useless and purposeless than acting," Zander said, a wicked twinkle in his eye matching his roguish smile, "is reporting on acting."

Faith swung her right hand but Zander caught it, forcing her fingers to wrap around his. Darting his head forward, he caught her mouth in a kiss. Faith, still smarting from his insult, nipped his lip sharply enough to draw a bead of blood that streaked his perfect Pepsodent teeth.

The coppery salt taste of his own blood stoked Zander's fires, and he clasped Faith's wrists in one hand, pinning them to the small of her back. He brought her chest forward, returning her assault by taking his teeth to her breasts. The fine, silky cotton of her filmy nightshirt did little to buffer the scrape of his teeth against the tiny darts poking against it. Mindful of their sensitivity, Zander took them in turn with only slightly less aggression than she had used on his lip.

She had flat-ironed her curls, and her newly straightened hair brushed against his hand when her head fell back in submission. Holding her in place with one hand, Zander used the other to grasp her breasts one at a time, positioning them to best please himself.

Faith responded, grinding her aching center against his denim-covered hardness. The movement of her abdomen against his, the power of her thighs framing his hips, her throaty gasps of pleasure—Zander never would have guessed that such a recipe would propel him to a climax so powerful, he tore the fabric of her shirt with his teeth.

Not completely satisfied, Faith sought to reach her goal as well. She wriggled from his grasp in his moment of temporary weakness and backed onto the coffee table. Reading her need in her eyes, Zander yanked off her panties with such eagerness, the right seam ripped. A streak of warm moisture along her inner thigh marked the path of Zander's entry, and Faith groaned low and hard when he plunged into her, awkwardly balancing himself on the low table. His rigidness probed her softness; his fleshiness slapped her firmness. Rapid recovery had never been an issue for him, but with Faith, it was instant. His body fit so well within her that he felt like a piece of machinery custom-crafted for her pleasure as her hips bucked in the throes of her release.

CHAPTER 11

Faith sat in the first-row aisle seat of the Troy Theater in Fawnskin, where Zander was making his first stage appearance outside of his stellar performance as Hector in a Lincoln high school production of *The Iliad*.

The invitation-only, black-tie event was a fundraiser for the theater, which was undergoing a $2 million restoration. Only half the house was fit for audience members, and the bare hardwood stage had no curtains, lighting or mechanical effects equipment.

The play, "Garden of Evils," had been written by a Fawnskin resident who had been happy to donate her material after learning that Zander Baron and his *Burn* co-star Kyla Randall were playing the lead roles of Victor McIlwrath and Desiree Calor.

Faith had invited Daiyu along to shoot the event for Vivian's *After Hours* column, and Daiyu had dressed for the occasion in a bright red bodystocking shrouded with a black bag dress. Not to be outdone by Daiyu's garishness, Faith went the opposite direction, aiming for sexy, smooth sophistication in an EOC—Eve of Construction—original.

The New York-based designer was an up-and-comer who already had Hollywood A-listers jockeying for the chance to own and wear her work. Faith thanked her lucky star that Magda had been able to arrange the loan of a very feminine, very form-flattering EOC evening gown in a shade of red that made her complexion glow.

She and Zander had spent every night for the past two weeks in her apartment, so Faith was excited to be out for a change. More than that, she looked forward to seeing Zander work live.

With no music to signal the start of the play, the dimming of the lights quieted the pre-curtain chatter and prompted a soft round of applause. Other than Zander and Kyla, the names of the cast had not been listed in the program. Because the actors would be working for free and on script, no one had known who the final cast would be until the actual performance. Faith recognized the actor playing Narrator when he lumbered onstage in jeans, a white shirt and a tweed jacket with leather elbow patches. He hadn't been seen onscreen in years, but he'd kept busy doing voice work since playing the beleaguered husband of an abrasive housewife on an old 90's sitcom.

He took a seat on a stool on the left side of the stage, and addressed the audience directly. "On the nice side of town in a quiet neighborhood called Sunnyside, seven residents meet monthly to discuss their gardens, in which they take an inordinate amount of pride. Ordinarily, these gatherings are quite dull, centering on talk of organic versus chemical fertilizers and the effectiveness of hollow-eyed garden owl figurines in scaring off small predators."

While the Narrator delivered his spiel, the cast of seven filed onstage to take seats in folding chairs that had been set up at a long, bare table. Two cast members lugged a big blue Coleman cooler, and one woman carried a wide platter heaped with pastries.

"While it all might seem dull to outsiders like us, the members of the Sunnyside Beautification Association could debate for hours the merits of pesticide versus duct tape in controlling gypsy moths," the Narrator continued. "But unlike previous meetings, this one is different. Flowers aren't the only things growing in Sunnyside. Secrets have grown there as well . . . And now, under the directorship of real estate agent Lottie Graball, we join the Sunnyside Beautification Association."

"Order! Order!" Lottie, played by an unknown middle-aged blonde, loudly demanded as the lights rose to illuminate the stage. "I hereby call this, the 182nd meeting of the Sunnyside Beautification Association, to order."

"What's on the docket today?" asked Sug Leadbetter, who was played by a heavyset actor known for his work in a national spaghetti sauce campaign.

"If you'd read this month's newsletter," Lottie began impatiently, "you'd know that Victor took time out of his busy schedule to join us this afternoon to discuss—"

"The proper way to stimulate vigorous growth, I hope," Kyla, as Desiree, broke in provocatively. "You know, Victor, I just whipped up a nice batch of stuffed mushrooms. I'd sure enjoy it if you came back to my place after the meeting and tried some. I grew them with the loose-soil pre-mix you gave me."

In the role of Billie, a shriveled, blue-haired actress unfamiliar to Faith interrupted with a loud harrumph.

"No, thanks," Zander said, giving voice to Victor.

Faith shuddered. Watching Zander perform live was far different than seeing him onscreen. Subtle changes in his tone and projection and a deliberate alteration in his posture were all it took to turn him into someone else. Into the flesh-and-blood Victor McIlwrath.

Zander might have spent a good part of the past ten years working and scraping to survive, but he'd studied his art too, and he applied his craft superbly.

"I have plans," Victor continued. "In fact, I'm flying out of town soon after this meeting, so perhaps we should get back to business."

Lottie loudly cleared her throat. "I agree. Our first point of order concerns the matter of the bamboo plantings with which Mr. Leadbetter chose to frame his rock garden."

The actors froze, a spotlight landed on the Narrator. "If the name Sug Leadbetter sounds familiar to you, then perhaps you're one of the many jazz fans who saw his history-making appearance on *The Tonight Show* with Jay Leno. Famous around the world for 'One Note,' a song he composed for his saxophone where he toots exactly one note every sixteen bars, Mr. Leadbetter is renowned in Sunnyside for being the most sedentary creature alive."

"The Beautification Association approved my bamboo wall and you know it, Lottie," Sug asserted, his speech sluggish, almost slurred.

"Yes," Lottie snapped. "They approved *your* wall, yet it's becoming *my* wall at an alarming rate. Your new shoots are taking over my hydrangeas. Unlike you, bamboo has a tendency to get a move on with life."

Sug grumbled in exasperation and rolled his eyes.

"Mr. Leadbetter had me install an underground border to keep the roots of his bamboo from sending new shoots onto your property, Mrs. Graball," Victor said.

"But he didn't pay to have the same border put on my side, to make sure my hydrangeas weren't overrun."

"You didn't pay for those hydrangea bushes, either," Sug muttered.

"Is there something you'd like to say to me, Mr. Leadbottom? I mean, Leadbetter?"

Billie timidly chimed in. "Well . . . Lottie . . . Mrs. Graball . . . when Victor offered the hydrangeas to the Association, they were supposed to be evenly distributed throughout all the properties. Not just yours."

"Every garden has its blossoms," said the Narrator. "Every garden also has its weeds. Billie Green, a retired teacher and spinster, has been a member of the Sunnyside Beautification Association since its inception, so one might say that her roots have run so deep there's no way of ever cleanly removing her."

"As president of the Association, it was up to me to decide the best use of Victor's generous gift," Lottie insisted.

"Even so," Billie muttered to herself, "those hydrangeas would have looked beautiful against the stucco on the south side of my house."

"I thought we were to hear from Victor today, not fight over three-year-old hydrangeas," Desiree said, winking at Victor.

Faith squirmed. Kyla Randall could have been the model for Venus at Venus Adonis. Her dark hair, big brown eyes and sun-toasted brown skin electrified the sparse set design. The seductive purr of her voice added to her appeal. If Faith hadn't known that Kyla had a handsome cardiologist husband and three gorgeous children in the audience, she might have leaped onstage and plucked the wink right out of her pretty brown eyes.

"Spa owner Desiree Calor is just as graceful and delicate as Spanish moss," the Narrator said, drawing Faith's attention back to the play. "And just as easily, she'll drape herself around something strong and handsome and slowly draw the life right out of it."

"Victor, I've been having the worst trouble with your big red cockscomb," Desiree said coyly. "It's shown no progress in nearly a month."

"I'll be happy to look into it later, Ms. Calor," Victor said icily.

"Whose turn was it to bring refreshments?" asked Hugo, a character who was being played by a Troy Theater member twice as round and heavy as the actor portraying Sug.

"Hugo Broadside has the biggest vegetable garden in Sunnyside," the Narrator said. "He produces the biggest tomatoes, peppers, cucumbers and carrots most people have ever seen. As you'll see, everything about Hugo is large, and always has been. Once he tipped the scales at 380 pounds, Hugo went on disability, collecting a paycheck from Uncle Sam . . . along with the paychecks he continues to collect as a freelance web designer."

"Did you bring the refreshments, Billie?" Hugo asked. In an aside to Sug, he sniped, "I hope not. Last time, she brought those nasty little pigs in blankets she buys by the case at the price club. They were still partly frozen when she served them."

"Yet you still managed to eat about two hundred of them," Sug said.

"Hugo, I brought the food today," announced Chele Metcalf in the role of Belle. "I brought a beautiful assortment of pastries from that new French *patisserie* downtown. I've got Meyer lemon tarts, crème brûlée popovers, pastry puffs, éclairs filled with chocolate imported from Belgium—"

After a longing stare at the blonde, blue-eyed Belle, the Narrator comically shook himself. "Belle Dellarosa, an interior decorator and a former Miss Pride of Springfield, has filled her garden with the lushest, most fragrant and most colorful blooms obtainable. And if you asked her, she'd consider herself the most beautiful one of all."

"—pecan diamonds dripping with honey, chocolate tazzas sprinkled with shavings of real gold—" Belle continued as if uninterrupted.

"Sounds luscious," said Desiree.

"Sounds expensive," Billie added.

"Well, nothing's too good for the Sunnyside Beautification Association," Belle said proudly.

Hugo grunted as he reached for the platter of pastries. "Pass that over here." The audience laughed at his gobbling and smacking as he devoured the tiny pastries. "Mmm! This is good stuff, Belle."

"Would someone please set the other tray of pastries over on the table next to my purse, far out of Mr.

Broadside's reach?" Lottie demanded. "And Mr. Broadside, would you mind not speaking with your mouth full?"

"That's the last we're gonna hear from him until he licks that platter clean," Sug said.

Hugo belched loudly, and Faith swore that she could smell the chocolate. Looking over her shoulder, she saw why she smelled chocolate. A young man in black was serving the audience from a platter just like the one onstage, but after watching Hugo's enjoyment of them, few people actually ate their pastries.

"Did you bring anything to wash this down with?" Hugo asked Belle.

"I brought the beverages, Mr. Broadside," Victor said. "There's a cooler full of bottled water and juice next to Mrs. Graball's things. It's a promotional giveaway from one of my suppliers, Hawthorne Custom Cuttings. They provided the eucalyptus you wanted for your fragrance garden, Ms. Dellarosa."

Another young man in black served bottles of water to the audience as the characters on stage passed around water and juice. Faith smiled, reading the label for HAWTHORNE CUSTOM CUTTINGS on her bottle.

"Victor, you should come by after the meeting and see how my fragrance garden has come along," Belle said blissfully. "On warm days, when I have my bedroom windows open, the breeze carries in the scent of the lavender and it just makes me feel all—"

"Victor, I've decided to reconfigure part of my yard to incorporate a fragrance garden," Desiree broke in. "I want an aromatic paradise, a Garden of Eden for the nose. Tell me, Victor, what scents are most passionate? Actually, I have a better idea. Why don't I come down to your office some night? We'll go through your sample books, maybe have a little dinner or something afterward, and plot my new garden. How's Friday for you?"

"Friday's no good for me. I have plans."

Faith got chills when Zander delivered his line directly to her.

"He's turning soil for my new herb garden," Billie pointed out.

"Oh, that can wait 'til Saturday," Desiree decided.

"No, it can't," Billie hissed.

Desiree left her chair to slink up to Victor. "She won't mind if we have our own little meeting. Can't one of your men turn her soil? You don't have to waste your time on a mundane chore like turning dirt."

"I've made another commitment, Ms. Calor, and in my opinion, a fragrance garden isn't really a vital part of your future."

She sat on the table, her butt near Victor's hand. "I'll decide what's vital, Victor, and I want to see your samples. Would you mind bringing your books to my place later this afternoon?"

"The last time I brought sample books to your place, I barely escaped with my life," Victor said quietly. "And I lost two buttons from my favorite shirt."

"I think I swallowed them after I bit them off," Desiree giggled.

Hugo suddenly grabbed his throat with one hand and banged the table with the other, knocking the platter to the floor. His face turning red, his eyes grew wider and wider as he struggled for breath.

"He's choking!" Belle cried. "Hugo's choking on a pecan tart! Oh, heavens, Hugo, you broke my pastry platter! It's genuine Waterford crystal!"

Gasping and gagging, Hugo stood and flopped backwards onto the table.

"Slap him on the back!" Lottie hollered.

"I wish I knew the Heimlich!" Billie fretted.

"You couldn't get those skinny arms of yours around him even if you did," Sug said.

"If you're not going to help me get him to his feet, Mr. Leadbetter, at least get out of my way so I can help!" Victor said, making his way to Hugo.

Desiree grabbed his arm as he hefted Hugo's huge frame into his arms. "Victor, you're so strong! Just look at these biceps."

"Hugo's just another sack of fertilizer for Victor," Sug said.

"Squeeze him hard, Victor!" Lottie screeched.

A loud, exaggerated spitting sound, like a stopper being expelled from an inner tube, erupted from Hugo, after which he breathed freely and deeply.

"Maybe you should try chewing your food before you swallow it next time," Billie griped under her breath.

"Thanks, Victor," Hugo panted. "I owe you my life."

Belle stabbed Hugo's chest with her index finger, and it sank down to the first knuckle into his flab. "*You* owe me a new Waterford crystal serving platter, Hugo."

"Ms. Dellarosa, would you get a bottle of water for Mr. Broadside?" Victor asked.

"Certainly. I think I could use a good stiff drink myself, but I suppose promotional cranberry juice will have to do."

"Would you pass a cranberry juice to me, too, Belle?" Desiree asked.

"I'll have orange, if there's any," Billie said.

"There's no more orange juice," Belle said. "Lottie grabbed all of them. How about grapefruit?"

"I guess that'll have to do."

"I owe you one, Victor. I really do," Hugo said as he and Victor resumed their seats.

"If everyone's okay now, what you folks owe is exactly what I came here to talk to you about," Victor said. "Some of your accounts are seriously past due."

"Let me handle this, Victor, seeing as I'm president of the Association," Lottie said, fussily clearing her throat. "Some of our members, Mr. Leadbetter for example, might not wish to have the severity of their debt to you revealed publicly."

"Actually, Madame President, you owe more than anyone else here."

"Perhaps we should adjourn for a moment so I can speak with Victor in private," Lottie suggested.

"No, Mrs. Graball, I think we've had enough diversions and distractions for one afternoon. What I have to say is short and sweet. I've provided a service to you folks. I expect to be paid for it. That's all."

Faith shifted in her chair. Zander's delivery had an undercurrent of menace that put her on the edge of her seat.

"And you know what, Victor?" Lottie said. "That's more than fair. It's about what's right. Everyone, Victor has provided detailed invoices, itemizing everything you all owe, so I'll just take the liberty of adding up the totals and dividing the sum six ways. Everyone pays an equal share and the accounts can be settled in one fell swoop with one Association check."

"Six ways?" Hugo asked. "There are seven of us. How do you figure a six-way split?"

Lottie's tone became overly sweet. "As you know, Mr. Broadside, the Sunnyside Beautification Association president is entitled to certain privileges that regular members aren't."

Billie's lips pursed so tightly they nearly disappeared. "Yes, you don't have to pay dues and you get the stall under the skylight in our communal storage shed. Those are the only privileges we voted to give you."

"When Mrs. Graball was elected president, she renegotiated the contract with my landscaping and gardening service. The association president—Mrs. Graball—receives my services and goods for free. The cost of her yard work is paid by the Sunnyside Beautification Association."

"That isn't fair!" Billie shrewishly shrieked. "That isn't fair at all! I've served the Association for six years longer than Lottie has, and I don't get anything out of it except aggravation. And now you expect me to pay for Lottie's imported Babylonian Bleeding Heart?"

"Lottie has done a lot as president," Belle offered in her defense. "She nominated my rose garden for the American Residential Botanical Award, after all."

"Oh, shut up, Belle!" Billie yelled. "Your rose beds and topiaries cost even more than Lottie's garden. A six-way split works out to your advantage almost as much as it does for Lottie. Sug and Hugo and I are the ones getting robbed!"

"Honestly, Billie, you're the one who's being unreasonable. It's not my fault, or Belle's, that you wanted mother-in-law's tongue and devil's pothos all over your yard, or that Sug chose a less labor-intensive rock garden. As for Hugo, he's actually profiting from his vegetable garden. He eats what he grows."

"So do you, Lottie," Hugo said. "Or have you forgotten the other privilege you wrote into your new contract, the one where you get to collect twenty percent of what each Association garden produces?"

Hugo's announcement began a chorus of disbelieving voices.

"What?"

"Are you kidding?"

"Is he serious?"

"She wouldn't dare!"

Lottie held up her hands. "Calm down, everyone. Calm down."

"You could take twenty percent of my award-winning roses?" Belle asked, her blue eyes wide in horror.

"Or twenty-percent of my Delilah irises?" Desiree demanded.

"You can have twenty percent of my gravel bed," Sug said. "I don't care."

"I'm not interested in anyone else's garden," Lottie said.

"Other than Hugo's tomatoes, cucumbers, peppers, carrots . . ." Billie interjected.

"Okay, enough of this, ladies and gentlemen," Victor said. "Obviously, you people have a lot to discuss with your president, and I wish you had time for it. I certainly don't. Please pay me what I'm owed, and you can continue your squabble over who pays what share."

"Let's vote on it," Lottie said.

Belle looked confused. "Vote on what?"

Lottie grinned. "All in favor of paying Victor now and re-distributing individual contributions, raise your hands."

"I move that each Association member pays his or her own itemized bill," Desiree suggested.

Clearly annoyed, Lottie said, "That's another way to do it, certainly."

"But you still get your work and materials for free?" Billie said.

"Of course," Lottie replied. "I'm Association president."

"All in favor of my motion!" Desiree announced.

"Fine," Billie snapped.

"Whatever," Sug shrugged indifferently.

"I guess so," Belle agreed dully.

"I abstain, as this vote does not affect me or my garden," Lottie said, a note of triumph in her voice.

"Hugo, how do you vote?" Desiree asked.

Hugo, his eyes glazed, chocolate coating his chin, didn't move.

"Mr. Broadside," she said, giving him a nudge. "It's your turn to vo—"

"Hugo, wake up and finish that éclair in your hand," Belle said loudly.

Billie peered closer at him. "He's so pale. I don't think he's sleeping."

Belle gasped. "He's not eating. He's not moving. He's not *breathing*!"

The actors froze in position, six of them leaning over the man playing Hugo, while the spot returned to the Narrator.

"The 182nd Sunnyside Beautification Association meeting has taken a tragic turn with the untimely death of Mr. Hugo Broadside," he said as the actor playing Hugo solemnly exited stage right. "It took a team of four emergency services technicians close to an hour to load Mr. Broadside's cold carcass onto a gurney as wide as a full-sized mattress. But the lone medical examiner who pronounced Hugo's demise spent only a few minutes determining that Mr. Broadside's death wasn't the result of natural causes related to his weight, or an accident resulting from his overindulging in Belle Dellarosa's pastries. As the surviving members of the Sunnyside Beautification Association are about to discover, Hugo Broadside was murdered, and right under their noses . . ."

"Poisoned?" Belle gasped. "Hugo was poisoned?"

"Constantly repeating it won't change it, Belle," Lottie nagged. "The coroner said that Hugo showed all the characteristics of a person who had ingested poison. A fast-acting one, by the look of it."

"He ate twenty-two pastries," Billie noted. "Maybe he was allergic to the pecan diamonds." Audience members who had selected pecan diamonds from the platter making the rounds tossed them back. Zander caught Faith's eye, and it was all Faith could do to keep from laughing.

"There has to be a logical explanation for what happened. I know *I* didn't poison him," Billie said.

"Are you implying that one of us did, Billie Green?" Desiree asked testily.

"Of course not."

"Yes, she is!" the Narrator whispered in a loud aside.

"Well, now that I think about it, I'm sure he didn't like giving twenty percent of his crops to Lottie," Billie speculated. "And if he threatened to expose her secret privilege, she might have gotten angry enough to drop something in his water bottle."

"How dare you accuse me, even indirectly!" Lottie railed. "Hugo and I were friends, neighbors, Association members and business colleagues, and I'd never harm a hair on his head. If I was going to poison anyone, it would be you, Sug, for letting your bamboo choke my hydrangeas."

"*Our* hydrangeas," Sug said. "They just happen to live in your yard."

"And if you'll recall, Billie, it was Belle who brought Hugo that tainted water," Lottie said.

"Tainted . . . !" Belle started indignantly. "Why are you so sure it was the water that killed Hugo? Only the murderer would know how the poison was administered."

"We all ate the pastries, and we're all still here," Billie said. "Hugo was the only one who drank water."

"I had a swig of Hugo's water," Sug admitted. "I didn't feel like getting up to get my own bottle. I'm still here, so . . . so . . ."

"Uh oh," interjected the Narrator. "Looks like Sug is about to go."

"Sug?" Belle pipped.

"Catch him, Victor, he's sliding off his chair," Lottie said.

"I think he just passed out from shock," Desiree said hopefully, helping ease Sug's bulk to the floor.

"Who passes out with his eyes open?" Billie snorted. "Unless Sug's too lazy to close his eyes when he faints."

"Is he dead?" Belle asked, her eyes twin circles of fear.

"Yes," Victor said, standing.

"You did do it, didn't you?" Desiree pointed at Lottie. "You killed Sug and you got Hugo, too! You said it yourself, that if you were going to kill anyone, it would be Sug, and now he's dead!"

"That was just talk and you know it!" Lottie yelled. "I'm not a killer. You ought to be pointing your finger at the person who brought the water."

"Victor brought the cooler," Belle said. "He told us it was a promotional item from Hawthorne Custom Cuttings."

"Victor," Desiree said, clutching Zander's arm, "you have to contact Hawthorne Custom Cuttings and tell them that their water has killed two people."

Victor laughed.

Zander's laugh was sinister, but it didn't frighten Faith. She knew that laugh—it belonged to their honors American history teacher.

"Well, I don't see what's so funny," said Billie.

"The water didn't kill Hugo and Sug," Victor said. "What was put into it probably did, however."

The actors, the narrator and everyone in the audience sat in stunned silence.

"Victor . . . did you . . . are you saying that you put something in that water?" Lottie asked.

"No," he calmly stated, "you're saying it. If this were to ever make it to court, that would be a very fine distinction."

"B-But Victor, why?" Billie stammered fearfully. "Hugo never did anything to you, and Sug never did anything to anyone."

Desiree finally put significant distance between herself and Victor. "I can't believe you killed them. Why?"

"Do you know what I do for a living, Ms. Calor?" Victor asked.

"You're a gardener, Victor," Lottie cut in. "Is that supposed to be a trick question?"

"I wasn't talking to you, Mrs. Graball, but since you've jumped into the middle of this, I'll answer you. No, it isn't a trick question. But clearly, you people of Sunnyside have no idea what a gardener does. I tend to life. I make our world more beautiful. And for the past ten years, I've watched the Sunnyside Beautification Association do everything in its power to undermine my good works."

"He's crazy," Billie said. "I'm calling the police. You're going away for a very long time, Victor."

Victor snickered again, this time giving Faith the chills. "Oh, I'm going away all right. To a gorgeous little island in the South Pacific, Darwin, to be exact. One with no extradition treaty with the United States."

"But why, Victor?" Belle asked. "Why did you have to kill Hugo and Sug?"

"The Lord is my Shepherd, Belle, but I've strayed from the rest of the flock. I've done what I believe needed doing. I killed Hugo and Sug for the same reasons that I've killed you, and Mrs. Graball, and Ms. Green and Ms. Calor."

"What?" the actors and the Narrator squawked.

"The poison wasn't just in the water," Victor said.

Daiyu, who had been drinking from her Hawthorne Custom Cuttings bottle, sprayed water all over the neck of the person seated in front of her. Faith again met Zander's gaze, and this time he couldn't hide an amused smile befitting his role as homicidal maniac.

"I also poisoned the juice you ladies were drinking earlier," Victor revealed.

Kyla Randall's performance up to this point had been great, but she showed the subtle mastery of her art through her facial expression as she said, "Tell me this is a joke, Victor. You wouldn't hurt me, would you? Not after we've been friends for so long?"

"I feel just fine," Billie said stubbornly. "I don't believe a crazy word of this. In fact, as far as I'm concerned, this meeting is . . . over . . ." Her last word fading, Billie went rigid and toppled out of her chair, landing on Sug's soft carcass.

A startled scream tore from Belle, and members of the audience jumped in their seats. "She's . . . Victor, you killed her! You killed *us*!"

"Victor, I've got $100,000 in Association funds stashed in an offshore account under a false name," Lottie said. "It's yours if you give me the antidote to the poison. I'm sure I don't have much time left, so—"

"How much do you really have in that secret account?" Victor asked softly.

"I told you. One hundred—"

"Tick tock, Mrs. Graball," Victor smiled.

"All right, all right! There's $200,000, and I'll transfer it all to you, I swear, if you'll give me the antidote!"

"What about me?" Desiree asked quietly.

"Make your own deals, honey," Lottie sneered. "What do you say, Victor?"

"Give me the account number and your wire information."

"Give me the antidote." Lottie held out her hand.

"Tick . . . tock . . ." Victor muttered as Belle slumped over dead.

Lottie rummaged through her handbag. She withdrew a small notepad and a pen, scribbled a few lines, tore off the sheet and thrust it at Victor. "Here! That's everything."

"Looks like Victor just hit the Lottie-ry!" the Narrator said, gleefully rubbing his hands together.

"Give me the antidote to the poison, Victor," Lottie demanded.

"The antidote for the poison in your system would have been generosity," Victor said. "But I'm afraid it's too late now, Lottie."

Shrieking, Lottie lunged at him with her fingers hooked into claws. "You son-of-a . . . *ACK!*"

Victor didn't move a muscle as Lottie's dead body landed right in front of him.

"I guess I'm the last to go, huh?" Desiree said, her voice quivering.

"It appears that the poison is taking its time with you."

"There is no antidote, is there?"

The chemistry Zander and Kyla had in *Burn* translated to the stage as well. The two played off each other so well, Faith didn't feel the slightest twinge of jealousy.

"I'm afraid not," Victor said almost tenderly. "You see, prevention is the only cure for what afflicted the Sunnyside Beautification Association. Each of your gardens was a beautiful representation of the very ugliest in each of you. Lottie's garden was packed with every flower she could get her hands on, including the hydrangeas I donated to the entire Association. There was no order, no design to her garden. It was merely a holding pen for what she acquired, whether she needed it or not. Lottie's greed was more than I could weed out."

"What about Sug? He was one of the nicest men I've ever known. He would give you the shirt off his back."

"Only if you unbuttoned it and removed it for him," the Narrator said derisively.

"Sug filled his garden with rocks and bamboo, and even then he was too lazy to tend it properly," Victor said. "A simple sweep of a brush now and then, and an occasional trim would have been all it took to show that he cared enough about the world around him to get off his butt once in awhile. I couldn't eradicate Sug's sloth."

"So you eradicated him. And Hugo?"

"His consumption was such that it threatened the livelihood of every living thing around him. Hugo was undone by his gluttony."

"You spent more time on Belle's garden than anyone else's. If you hated her so much, why did you make her garden so beautiful?"

"Everything about Belle was beautiful," Victor said. "She and I trimmed and pruned her roses perfectly; her topiaries were exquisite. Belle's pride in her appearance, her possessions and in her garden almost seduced me. I actually considered sparing her, until I realized that there was no humility behind Belle's pride. She wanted everything to be the best and most beautiful to inspire envy, not appreciation. I came close, but I didn't fall into Belle's trap."

"I'm feeling a little light-headed, Victor."

"I'm sorry about that. I was enjoying our conversation."

"Quickly, tell me why you killed Billie."

"Ms. Green spent so much time measuring her garden against everyone else's that she was never able to devote herself properly to what she had right in front of her. Her garden had the best light and the best soil, yet she spent hours talking about how she'd like to have Ms. Dellarosa's garden, and yours, and even Mrs. Graball's. I don't know which was more green—Billie or her garden."

Desiree weakly slumped in her chair. "And me, Victor. Why . . ."

"Because I'm not a man who likes to be mindlessly pursued," he said, a brittle edge to his tone. "If you'd shown half as much passion for your garden as you did toward me, perhaps . . ."

A sharp intake of breath followed by a long, slow exhalation signaled Desiree's demise, and Victor very gently rested her head on the table. He sighed heavily. "In case you were wondering, Ms. Calor, your garden was my favorite. I think you loved it. Just not the right way."

The lone spotlight remained on Victor as he moved about the table collecting bottles of water and juice, returning them to the cooler. He wiped down each chair he'd touched and the surface of the table. With a final caress of Ms. Calor's cheek, he picked up the cooler and stepped over Sug and Billie to exit stage right as the Narrator closed the play.

"And so, the 182nd meeting of the Sunnyside Beautification Association comes to an end, in every possible way. Victor, our avenging gardener and self-proclaimed lost sheep departs for places unknown, places where he hopes to find the beauty and virtue he sought in the residents of Sunnyside. But Victor isn't traveling alone, and his companion might again rear its ugly head. For Victor isn't without sin himself, and he knows it.

Unlike the dearly departed members of the Sunnyside Beautification Association, Victor McIlwrath's sin is as much a part of him as his own name. And wrath has a way of taking over when you least expect it to."

Zander posed for photos with Kyla Randall and the other cast members, and then he accepted kudos and thanks from the theater director and its members as he and the cast signed autographs. He wondered where Faith was, until he spotted her standing near the exit with her friend Daiyu, her cellphone pressed to her ear. Her head was down, and he couldn't read her expression until she looked up and saw him.

Zander's smile faded at the sight of her troubled expression, and when she clutched at her throat, he ran to her, flashbulbs popping around him.

"What is it?" he asked, stroking her arm. "What's wrong?"

"My mother . . ."

"Is everything okay?" Zander asked, concerned.

"It's storming in Dorothy," Faith whimpered.

CHAPTER 12

"You're leaving, just like that."

Faith had stripped off her designer gown the instant she walked into Zander's house, and he'd thought that she was thinking of doing the same thing he'd wanted to do every time he'd looked at her from the stage. When she quickly changed into blue jeans and a gauzy white peasant blouse, he knew that she had very different plans.

His accusation rubbed Faith the wrong way, and she visibly bristled when he gave her right shoulder what was meant to be a loving squeeze.

"Sorry," he mumbled, glowering. "But I just don't understand why you have to go."

"I don't *have* to, I *want* to." Faith continued tossing her clothes into her travel bag. "There's a difference."

"Do you want me to go with you?"

She spun to face him, a hesitant smile telegraphing her hope. "You would go back—"

"Hell no!" He said, giving the foot of his bed a savage kick. "You know damn well that I won't go back there!"

"Then why would you even offer?" Faith shouted.

"It was a simple question," he yelled, his volume matching hers. "I just wanted to know if you still had your crazy ideas about me ever going back to Booger Hollow."

"There's nothing crazy about a person going home when something bad is happening to her friends and family," Faith growled through gritted teeth.

"What friends?" Zander snorted. "Are you counting cheerleaders and dance classmates as friends? And as for your parents, you acted like they kept you under house arrest."

Her fur ruffled, Faith said, "I was a teenager, and as headstrong as my dad! Of course I butted heads with my folks. That doesn't mean I don't love them, that they don't love me. Things change, if you give them a chance. No, I didn't have a fan club back home when I was a kid, but there are a few people I grew close to over the years. Half the things I hated when I was a senior in high school are the things I love about Booger Hollow now." Flustered and impatient, her explanations jumbled. "Red Irv still serves awesome coffee, and his spaghetti and potatoes are the best! Some of our old schoolmates married each other, and they're my parents' neighbors now. I get the star treatment when I go home, because of my job. Even Bethany Brewer manages to find me and ask me what celebrities I've interviewed or written about. I still can't stand her, but just imagine what I could tell her this time!"

"When was the last time you were even there?" Zander asked.

"Christmas, damn it, only a few months ago! What difference does it make?"

"It just strikes me as crazy for you to fly off at a hair's notice to—"

Faith cut him off with, "What's crazy is someone who uses a natural disaster to sneak out—"

"There was nothing natural about that flood," Zander broke in. "Your father's company peeled that mountain like an overripe banana."

"—and lets the people who love him think he's dead for ten years!" Faith finished. "And don't you dare try to accuse my father of creating that flood! He didn't make it rain, you—!"

"What?" he snarled. "Say it." He stepped up to her. "There's nothing you can call me that I didn't hear a million times back East."

If he thought his height and breadth would intimidate her, Faith quickly disabused him of that idea. "I was going to call you a spoiled, egomaniacal, vindictive brat! Ever been called that?" Faith said nastily, pushing past him to sit on the foot of the bed.

She yanked on a pair of white socks and shoved her feet into her sneakers. She stood to furiously jam her hand into her low-slung jeans to tuck in her blouse, leaving it lopsided, one tail fully hidden, the other bunching at her hip.

His voice still at top volume, Zander railed at her. "You still refuse to see what it was like for me back—"

"Get over it!"

Faith's arms and legs stiffened from the force of her voice, her fingers splayed, her eyes fairly popped from their sockets.

"Damn it, already, Alex, just get the hell over it! People were mean to you back then, so what? SO

WHAT? People are mean to other people all over the world. You've got your revenge, and it's the best kind of revenge. You're handsome, you're rich, you're successful and you didn't have to demean other people to achieve your success. If you really want to punish all those dumbasses back in Booger Hollow who made you feel like you didn't matter, come back with me now and show them what they missed out on. Show them how stupid they were for not seeing what I saw all along!"

With no place to go, Zander's anger fled inward. His blood turned acid and seemed to burn all good sense right out of his brain. If for no other reason than to passively wound her, he very calmly said, "I hope the storms wash away Booger Hollow and Dorothy, West Virginia, for good this time."

Faith recoiled as if he'd struck her with more than words. She had nothing to say to him, couldn't even look at him, as she gathered her bag and left the house. Only after he heard the rattling clang of metal against metal of Faith's old Camry racing down his driveway did Zander sink onto the foot of his bed, his face in his hands.

Motionless but for the movement of his right thumb on the CHANNEL UP button of his remote control, Zander stared unblinking at the massive flat-screen television built into the wall of his great room. Brent, masquerading as the poster boy for L.L. Bean, sat in a nearby theater-style armchair, his feet in worn topsiders—no socks—wearing layered Polos in baby pink and Kelly green with matching patchwork Bermuda shorts.

"It's pretty bad out there," Brent said, his matter-of-fact tone contradicting the weight of his statement.

"Out where?" Zander responded flatly.

"You know where."

Zander flipped through all the pay-per-view and adult channels, worked his way through his HBO, Showtime and Starz movie channels, and blipped past MSNBC and the CNN family.

"Leave it there, please," Brent said, stopping him at The Weather Channel.

"You goin' somewhere?" Zander asked, noting that Brent had wanted to eye the Traveler's Advisory.

"Just leave it there."

Zander's mind wandered while Brent sat riveted to what Zander had decided was the most boring channel on his satellite system. He thought about getting up, showering and changing clothes after three days—or four—in the same jeans and T-shirt he'd been wearing when he last saw Faith. It occurred to him to get something to eat, as he'd already finished off the bowls of nuts that had adorned his tables.

Nothing tasted as it should have since he'd used his tongue to wound Faith, and quite frankly, he'd had no appetite. Not for food, anyway.

"Have you heard from her?" Brent asked, pulling Zander from his reverie.

"No."

"You haven't called her?"

"Why should I?"

"I thought you'd outgrown the sullen, son-of-a-bitch phase you were in when my mother discovered you."

"I'm not sullen," Zander said dispassionately. "I'm not going to chase a—"

Brent shushed him. The unsmiling anchors chairing the weather news had begun a report on the early April storms causing the floods that continued to bedevil West Virginia and Maryland.

Zander tried to ignore the report, but words like "severe," "disaster," "crisis" and "casualties" kept his eyes riveted to the screen. He had assiduously avoided anything that had to do with West Virginia in the years since he'd left. If anyone had asked him how many states were in the Union, he would have said forty-nine with a straight face.

As evidenced by the grim images provided by The Weather Channel, Zander saw that he might not be too far from wrong in the very near future.

He sat up, suddenly alert. Swallowing hard, he watched brown flood waters crash against trailer homes, snatching them clean off their moorings, using one to batter the next until walls collapsed to be pulled under the water. The Main Street that had existed only in his most troubled nightmares was half underwater. The plate-glass window of Red Irv's had been shattered by a car the raging water had hurled through it. Miss Lorraine's second floor dance studio was easily accessible by boat now that McGill's pharmacy was underwater.

An on-the-scene correspondent in a yellow slicker and dark green waders interviewed Duncan Blair, who had been mayor of Dorothy for as long as Zander could remember. He paid no attention to the interview; his interest was focused on the activity in the background. He recognized several residents of Dorothy despite the ten years they had on them: Travis Gates, one of many men and women soaked to the bone on a sandbag line, shoveled sand into a nylon bag held open by Art Brody Jr., the son of the man who owned the town body shop; Marjo Skipkey, the Lincoln High girls' athletic director, who had left her husband for another woman, slowly pulled a dinghy filled with cartons of Marlboro cigarettes, Busch beer and potato chips down Main Street; Tina Blair, the mayor's stout wife, still wore the bright red lipstick that, to Zander's eye, always made her mouth look like an open wound.

Zander had never known Mayor and Mrs. Blair personally, but he recalled the way Faith had made fun of Tina's "frooty" after she'd called Zander a "waste of space, like your father" after berating him for failing to clear her breakfast dishes fast enough after her Sunday morning feeding at the diner.

Upon asking for an explanation, Zander had learned that a frooty was Faith's name for the way Mayor Blair's wife's gut bulged against the center front seam of her elasticized pants. A frooty was a front booty.

"What's so damn funny?" Brent suddenly demanded.

Zander hadn't realized that he'd laughed aloud, but he quickly sobered when the scene on screen changed, and he caught a flash of an older African-American man directing sandbagging efforts at the rear of a big house that was all too familiar to him. Only then did Zander pay attention to the reporter's words.

"While local business owner Justus Wheeler coordinates efforts to protect his home and property from nature's next onslaught, locals fear that this may spell the end for the quaint mining community of Booger Hollow, West Virginia. Reporting live from Dorothy, West Virginia, this is—"

Zander hit the mute button. Resting his elbows on his knees, he sat forward, his head hanging between his shoulders.

"You can't run from your past forever," Brent told him. "I know it, my mother knows it and deep down inside you know it. As your agent, you know I have your best professional interests in mind. I know you don't want to hear it, but as your friend, I have to tell you that if you don't get off your ass and go to—"

"You're my agent," Zander said darkly. "That means you work for me. Get on the phone yourself, or get your mom's hired help to do it, but you'd better get me on the soonest possible flight east. Commercial, charter, corporate—I don't care. I gotta get home. To Faith."

The Lincoln High School gym was filled to capacity with most of Booger Hollow's five hundred residents taking shelter there. Army issue cots with thin mattresses and scratchy, grey wool blankets had been arranged in close, orderly rows on the floor where the Lincoln Black Bears had last won a state basketball tournament around the time Homer Hickam shot his last rocket off in Coalwood.

The Red Cross had set up relief stations for First Aid, but Red Irv, commanding the school's devoted phalanx of lunch ladies, had assumed control of the school kitchen. Their combined efforts and expertise had kept the town fed surprisingly well through the eight days of rain and resultant flooding, but supplies were dwindling fast.

Flood fatigue was the most damaging to the morale of the town, with everyone hoping for the best but expecting the worst from the latest storm, which had begun shortly after noon.

Exhausted, Faith had returned to the gym after a Saturday spent with her former schoolmates and neighbors building a sandbag levee along the mountainside border of Kayford Estates. Confident that the levee would hold, Justus Wheeler had decided that he and his wife would spend the night at home rather than join his daughter in the gymnasium.

Local authorities, his friends, even the Red Cross had pleaded with him to evacuate, but stubborn and certain of his ability to have things his way even against nature, Mr. Wheeler had refused.

Faith's confidence in her father's obstinacy was such that she believed he would be okay simply because he believed it. But she herself retired to the gym, if for no other reason than to show her solidarity with the town.

Sleep was hours away, if she would sleep at all. The sound of the rain, a lullaby in Fawnskin, sent frissons of terror through her as she sat crosslegged on her narrow cot in Dorothy.

She thought about going to the school library, the only place she had Internet access now that her smartphone had lost its charge, to see what flood news had made the online magazines. But Lincoln's current crop of students surrounded Faith, barraging her with questions about her job and the celebrities with whom she'd worked or had run-ins. Though she patiently entertained their questions, even telling them about the play she'd attended in Fawnskin a week ago, they did little to distract her from the worries weighing on her.

"Who's the biggest actor you've ever met?" asked a freckle-speckled redhead who grinned at her with a mouthful of corrective steel.

"Rick Fox," Faith answered. "He's six feet, seven inches tall."

"He's not an actor," the redhead groaned. "He's a retired Laker."

"Who's been in movies, so he's now an actor," Faith argued. "He's a very gracious interview, so don't knock my man Rick."

"Who's the meanest person you ever interviewed?" asked a young girl whose lank, dishwater blonde hair, still damp from her recent entry from outside, molded to the shape of her skull.

"Marjo Skipkey," Faith whispered. "She's a serious head case."

The students laughed, some even clapped.

"Who's your favorite actor?" cut a voice through the merriment.

Alexander Brannon, was the name on Faith's tongue, but she couldn't drive it forward.

"Are you okay, Miss Wheeler?" a middle-school student asked, sensitive to the change in Faith's posture and expression.

"Just . . . tired," she said. The last word faded as she noticed a rush toward the gym's double doors, where medics and townsfolk were surrounding the hunched figure of a bedraggled older woman, her thinning red hair a bright contrast to her wan complexion.

The students sitting with Faith turned to see what had captured her attention. The redhead's broad smile vanished. "Grandma?" he chirped before standing and trotting to the older woman.

Faith and the other residents of Dorothy had seen the woman's expression and posture too many times already since the sudden start of the flood, and Faith's eyes teared as she looked away from the redheaded kid in his grandmother's desperate embrace.

It didn't take long for the specific details to reach her. Herman Voss, one of Dorothy's oldest residents, had suffered a fatal myocardial infarction while trying to shore the Kayford Estates levee. His was the fourth life lost following two drownings and one death due to blunt-force trauma in the immediate aftermath of the initial flooding.

Mr. Voss had been a good neighbor, and Faith's pain at his loss was acute. Of all the things she remembered about him, the first that came to mind was her fourth-grade Halloween. Mr. Voss had dressed up as Angry Santa, a character who, jealous of the attention Halloween received, had set up booby traps in his front yard to snare unsuspecting princesses, cowboys, fairies, Power Rangers, superheroes, firemen and witches.

Faith had been one of his unfortunate victims, and she'd never laughed so hard as she and her fellow captives had watched their parents, garbed as genies, cavemen, clowns and gangsters, battle Angry Santa for their freedom. In the end, a ransom of Trick or Treat sweets had been paid, but Faith had never forgotten the sight of her dad, dressed as a ninja, fighting to free her.

"Dad," Faith gasped, sudden panic throbbing in her chest.

Tugging on her sodden overshirt and rain slicker as she ran, Faith tried to look past the grief-stricken huddle of the Voss family as she fled the gymnasium.

Hard raindrops hit her with the sting of BB pellets the second she raced through the outer doors of the gym. It didn't take long before the heavy rain freshly saturated her hair and clothing, and seemed to seep right through her skin to weigh down her limbs.

"Miss, the roads are closed," a waterlogged National Guardsman told Faith, catching her arm as she tried to move past his post at the double doors. "We're advising residents to—"

"Let go!" Faith demanded, wrenching her arm free.

"Faith, it's not safe, hon," said a Dorothy Police officer. "You—"

"Is this town under martial law?" Faith asked.

"No," the officer started, "but I don't want to see anyone putting herself in harm's way for no good reason."

Without wasting time to explain her reason for heading out, Faith carefully picked her way down to Main Street.

The high ground upon which Lincoln stood leveled out all too quickly, and Faith had to borrow one of the boats moored to the parking meters. She chose Mayor Blair's, confident that it probably had the best motor and a full tank of gas. The four life jackets strapped to the bench seats gave her added comfort as she ripped the cord and started away from the impromptu pier.

It had been a long time since Faith had last taken a boat out on open water, and her journey to Kayford Estates assured her that she never again would. Her weight did little to anchor the slight boat, and her muscles ached from the strain of steering it as wind and rain conspired to drive her into flooded businesses and homes, and run her aground atop submerged SUVs. Short of capsizing, nothing would drive her back to the school until after she had collected her parents.

Brown, roiling water filled with debris tossed her about like a toy while overhead, grey-black clouds violently emptied their contents onto a town that had already suffered far too much. Beneath the rush of the river now coursing down Main Street, the hiss of the rain and the cry of wind, Faith heard the raspy voice of the mountain as the rain slashed open a fresh vein, generating a new flood to give further strength to the existing one.

The water had no place to go other than Kayford Estates.

"Dad!" Faith shouted as her childhood home came into view.

Justus Wheeler, as stubborn as he was successful, was on the roof of the five-bedroom home he'd struggled so valiantly to save from the flood. A dutiful captain determined to sink or sail with his beloved vessel, Justus had set up a tent for two on the roof. Thinking to further protect them from the storm, he'd set it in a protected groove between two angles of the roof. Justus had underestimated the strength of the unpredictable winds and failed to secure the support ropes accordingly. Two of the tent walls angrily whipped at him and Faith's mother as they huddled together. Too far from any of the upper windows that would have returned them to the flooded interior of their home, Justus and Emiline Wheeler were trapped on a precariously angled section of the roof.

"Jump!"

Emiline was the first to hear her daughter's shout. She didn't hesitate. Pulling out of her husband's arms, she eased onto her bum and gingerly scooted to the edge of the roof. She dangled there, buoyed by the water and her life vest until Faith navigated the boat near enough for her to let go of the expensive covered gutters the Wheelers had installed the previous spring.

"Em!" Justus cried, reaching for his wife when she landed roughly in the boat, her right shin making painful contact with the edge.

Justus had little time to react to his wife's condition, not when his own footing had become so tenuous. He slipped, one of his galoshes flying into the night sky as he landed hard on his backside and ingloriously slid down the roof toward a certain dunking.

"Damn it, Dad," trembled from Faith's lips upon noting that, while her father had surely insisted that Emiline wrap herself snugly in a life jacket, he himself had neglected to wear one. The boat lurched Emiline onto its floor as Faith motored in a quick reverse to catch her father. Justus landed in a sodden heap close enough to Faith for her to hear the finale of the rant he'd started on the roof.

"—willful and stubborn, and I don't know where you get it from! This water is toxic, or haven't you been paying attention to the toxicology reports? I've been stuck here in the middle of nowhere, and even I know how stupid and dangerous it is for anyone to be out here in a boat made of tin and wishes!"

"Dad!" Faith yelled, struggling with both hands to turn the boat against a viciously strong wind. "I'm the captain of this ship, and if you don't buckle on a life vest, strap yourself to a seat and shut the hell up, I swear to the sweet baby Jesus I will toss you into the drink myself! Do you understand me, Daddy?"

Faith was tempted to cut the engine and threaten to keep the boat exactly where it was until Justus agreed to every one of her conditions, just as he'd done to her on road trips a few times in her childhood. Faith imagined that her father was seeing a female replica of what she used to see in the rear view mirror: a pair of menacing brown eyes as dark and rich as freshly brewed espresso, a deep furrow between black eyebrows as fine as his had been thick. She hoped that her own furious gaze also reflected what his had: the love that had motivated the threat in the first place.

"Damn rainwater," Justus grumbled, using the heels of his palms to grind at his eyes. "Emiline, honey, is this thing on the right way around?"

While her mother adjusted the straps at the back of his orange life vest, Faith took care of the ones in front, tightly bundling her father. "Does this feel okay?" she whispered near his ear.

Faith found herself wrapped in her father's sodden embrace. "Thank you, baby girl," he said, pressing a kiss to the curls plastered to her left temple. "I love you."

"I love you, too, Daddy," Faith smiled.

For the first time ever, Justus Wheeler was first to break an embrace with his daughter. "Ahoy, captain," he said, "let's get underway before we get washed away!"

"What's going on?" Emiline Wheeler asked, clutching at her daughter and husband. "Something's not right."

There were new boats moored at the heads of the parking meters lining the part of Main Street leading to the hill upon which sat Lincoln High. The dull gray boats had been used to motor in waterproof camera equipment and makeshift signal spires that bobbed along with the boats containing them.

"It's Herman Voss," Faith said. "He had a heart attack."

In her concern for her parents, Faith had forgotten about Mr. Voss. But now that the media had gotten wind of the fourth death in tiny Booger Hollow, the reality of her neighbor's loss weighed heavily on Faith.

Emiline's tears mingled with rainwater as Justus helped her from the boat, which Faith had quickly secured. She helped her parents up the steep path to the gymnasium, dreading the spectacle surely unfolding within the dry warmth of the town's sanctuary.

Local newsfolk were probably interviewing somber townspeople, who would regret being filmed in the unforgiving wash of overbright light from the newscameras.

Mayor Blair and his wife—who was lugging a frooty even bigger than the one Faith had first labeled—sidled into every shot they could, their grief as prefabricated as the overinsured double-wide trailer they had lost to the flood.

The excitement coloring the activity within the gym caught the Wheelers entirely by surprise. A huge crowd tightly surrounded someone centered beneath one of the idle basketball hoops. The voices of reporters overlapped and competed to be heard while camera technicians held their cameras high and strained to hold microphones on long booms over the center of the crowd.

Faith caught a single strand of words, and they drew her forward. Like an All-American linebacker, she shouldered her way through the townspeople and media, fighting her way to the man holding everyone's attention.

"Would you repeat that please, Mr. Baron?" a female reporter was asking as Faith burst into the center of the group.

"I said," Zander started, "that nothing is ever as bad or as frightening as it seems. All you need is . . . Faith."

His eyes found her, and for a moment, Zander thought his legs would give out. He hadn't realized how tense he'd been over the past twenty-four hours until he found himself snatching Faith's weary, bedraggled form into his arms. Holding her as tightly as he could, he cupped the back of her head, mashing down the drenched mass of spiraling curls he found there.

"I love your hair like this," he murmured, his face partially hidden in her hair.

"You smell like pond water," Faith teased.

"All of Booger Hollow smells like pond water," Zander said.

"Mr. Baron?" came a female voice. "Mr. Baron, are—"

"Zander Baron is my stage name," he announced after reluctantly pulling his face free of Faith's hair. "A few of the people in this room know me by my real name." Perhaps subconsciously drawing on her for strength, his arms tightened around Faith. "It's Alexander Brannon. I was born and raised right here, in Booger Hollow, West Virginia."

"Okay, I knew that your big announcement would cause a reaction, but I didn't know that it would be frickin' pandemonium," Brent chuckled.

274

Looking as though his floodwear had come straight from an Abercrombie & Fitch Disaster Chic catalog, Brent pulled Alex and Faith in closer as they stood in a huddle atop an empty section of the bleachers.

"Lookit Harry, Hermione and Weasley up there!" Red Irv shouted as he strolled by, fresh smears of pasta sauce on his white apron making it look as though he'd recently slaughtered half the lunch ladies. "You kids make sure you come down and get some grub. It's psghetti and patabas!"

"What the—?" Brent asked.

"Spaghetti with red sauce and boiled new potatoes with olive oil and rosemary," Alex translated. "That was my favorite Saturday night dinner at the diner." Moved, Alex stared at the aluminum floor of the bleachers to hide his eyes.

"Sounds good to me," Brent said. "Will you guys be okay while I go for some grub?"

Alex chuckled at Brent's ease in Booger Hollow. For all his affinity for the finer, and to Alex, most ridiculous, things in life, Brent had adjusted to Booger Hollow instantly. He'd arrived in champion-protector mode, determined to keep Alex safe from the snaggle-toothed, inbred Appalachians who'd dared make the first nineteen years of Alex's life a misery.

Upon seeing his former schoolmates and neighbors, Alex saw rather plainly what Faith had promised: time and gravity had wrought their own revenge upon his antagonists.

Leland Birch, who had run his father's used car dealership into bankruptcy, had put on fifty pounds all between his neck and hips, and appeared to be using some sort of clear adhesive to make sure that his last five strands of hair remained affixed to his dome.

Ritchie Platt never finished college and returned to Dorothy, where he worked odd jobs, when he worked at all. Until the flood, he'd lived alone in a trailer very close to the one the Brannons had formerly occupied.

Tina Blair's frooty had grown to the point where if she were standing in profile and had her head turned to one side, one couldn't clearly discern if she was turned forward or backward.

Not everyone had fallen into such disrepair. Travis Gates was tall, strapping and handsome, though he had a way of shrinking somewhat when his shrill wife Bethany appeared. And Red Irv, but for a little extra gray at his temples, had the same humor, good cheer and common sense that Alex had known and from which he had benefited.

After the thirty seconds of complete silence that had followed his announcement, Red Irv had been the first person Alex had approached and apologized to for his disappearance. In his inimitable and unfailing acceptance of any act committed by someone he loved, Red Irv, openly weeping, had attempted to murder Alex by gathering him into a hug so tight that Alex nearly lost consciousness from lack of oxygen.

The town's general humility and shame at its memory of how it had treated Alex softened Brent's heart, and he came to view Booger Hollow for what it was—a small town with the attendant problems and promise of any other town in the world. In mistreating one of its own who had gone on to forge his own incredible path far outside their watch and with none of their assistance, Alex had proved what might have inspired their resentment and dislike from the get-go—that he had been the best and brightest star among them all along.

Where folks had once shunned Alex, calling him names to his face and insulting his family, they lined up to shake his hand and meet him for the first time all over again.

Many of the younger kids had never heard of the Brannons, so they were fully and typically star-struck. But the oldtimers, the perpetrators, sheepishly welcomed Alex back into the fold.

"This really couldn't have gone better," Brent said, returning with a paper plate heaped with spaghetti and potatoes. "Calls are coming in from all over the United States. The Red Cross had already sent out pleas for disaster relief aid to this area, and supplies have been trickling in. But your arrival has started a flood—I couldn't resist that—of donations of food, water, clothes, generators, toys, building supplies. Alex, dude, I'm your agent, and I had no idea that you were this big of a star."

"Hm," Alex said, his noncommittal grunt drawing Brent's attention from his tasty heap of carbohydrates.

"What's the matter?" Faith asked, turning to follow Alex's line of sight.

It was the redheaded kid. He sat on the opposite side of the gymnasium on a bleacher bench just as high and alone as Alex had been when she and Brent had climbed the seats to join him.

"Guys, excuse me," Alex said before beginning his descent.

Faith tracked him through the crowd, watched him receive pats on the back, kisses on the cheek and distrustful or envious stares. Alex paid little attention to them as he made his way to the redheaded kid and sat down beside him.

Alex had used the last catastrophic flood to end his life in Booger Hollow. Smiling sadly, Faith wondered what he could be saying to someone who had actually lost a loved one in this latest one.

Whatever Alex said made the redheaded kid sob, which led Alex to offer the manly comfort of a squeeze to the back of the kid's neck. Alex's words eventually dried the boy's tears, and even earned a slight smile, a high five and a neat little fist bump that left Faith feeling much better herself. Alex might not have wanted to come home, but he was certainly doing a good job of making himself at home.

"I like that," Travis Gates said, studying the front cover of the most recent issue of *Newsweek*. "Movie Hero Turns Hometown Hero."

"They used the whole piece, right down to the headline." Faith was so proud of her first national news story that she kept it under her pillow—in plastic, to protect the fragile cover from the scratchiness of the overstarched army-issue pillowcases.

Two weeks after the first rain, and most of Booger Hollow was still living in the Lincoln High gymnasium. All the homes and businesses at the base of Kayford Mountain had suffered irreparable damage, and Kayford Estates was a total loss. One of the most striking and memorable photos accompanying Faith's article had come from Brent's cellphone, and it featured her father's roof, which had been smashed into a pile of kindling that had been carried two miles from the rest of Kayford Estates.

Alex had lived up to the title of Faith's article. He had rolled up his sleeves and helped salvage the town with the same enthusiasm and determination as any other native, perhaps working harder than anyone else since he'd come into the fight late and totally fresh.

"Like Rhett Butler in the middle of *Gone With the Wind*, when he decided to leave Scarlett and Melly and enlist in the Confederate army," Faith had cooed when Alex told her that he'd decided to stay in Booger Hollow and help any way he could. "He knew the cause was lost, but—"

Alex had pulled her into his arms and had given her a kiss that rivaled the one Rhett had given Scarlett prior to his departure for the war. Unlike Scarlett, Faith had wanted more after melting into that passionate good-bye.

Brent had arranged for more comfortable accommodations in Whitesville for Alex and Faith, but both had refused his offer to be airlifted round-trip daily by a National Guard helicopter. Alex had spent the past several nights on a cot in the gym, the most unpleasant part of which was the fact that nightly it was moved between those of Emiline and Justus Wheeler, to the great amusement of old acquaintances like Travis Gates, who had stopped by Faith's cot to compliment her on the article that had put the ordinary human face on Booger Hollow and all its heroes.

"It was him, wasn't it."

Alex sat facing Faith on her mother's cot. His remark had been phrased as a question, but it had clearly been a statement of assumed fact. And Faith knew exactly what he referred to.

"It only happened once. I was home for Christmas break, my freshman year at NYU," she began, holding his gaze. "I—"

"Never had a chance."

Travis had circled back to return Faith's copy of *Newsweek*, and his comment left Faith and Alex both confused.

"I never had a chance," Travis reiterated. "I'd been crazy about this girl, but her heart went with you, Alex. I was there when she needed someone, and I'll be there if she ever needs me again. But she was always yours. Always."

Alex watched Travis return to the cots grouped under the scoreboard, where his wife Bethany, three sons, parents and in-laws awaited him. Travis had always treated Alex with respect and kindness. To be fair, Alex had to admit that Travis had attempted to befriend him, only to have been ignored because of the company he'd kept, specifically that of Leland Birch.

Growing up, Travis Gates had been the guy Alex had wanted to be, and Travis now lived the life that Alex had once thought was perfect.

He knew better now. He knew that Faith, wherever he found her, was the one thing that would make his life perfect. That would make it worth living. He watched Travis' family swallow him up and head off to the cafeteria for lunch, and he envied him nothing, not even that he'd been the man to whom Faith once had turned for solace.

He had Faith now. That was all that mattered.

"Are you okay . . . with everything?" she asked hesitantly.

"No, I'm not." He stared her dead in the eyes, his expression unreadable, his body language revealing nothing.

"Alex, it was a long time ago, and it never would have happened if—"

"If I hadn't been so stupid," he finished for her.

"I wasn't going to say that."

He scooted off Emiline's cot and onto his knees between Faith's. "What were you going to say?"

"I . . . shoot . . ." It was so difficult to remember with Alex's mouth so close to hers, his hands resting at her hips.

"Let's get married," he said simply. "Today. Right now."

Her fingers splayed, her arms bent at her sides, Faith opened her mouth and her lungs and filled the gym with a sound that rang through the entire Lincoln High school campus. Almost as quickly as Faith's scream, the news of Alex's proposal traveled from cot to cot until it raced out the doors and through several classrooms, where students had grudgingly returned after almost two weeks of flood vacation.

By the time Faith had composed herself, it seemed that all of Booger Hollow was awaiting her answer.

Faith cleared her throat in the unnatural silence of the gym. "I'm sorry," she said. "But what did you ask me?"

Alex cleared his throat, camouflaging his sudden nerves with a dry chuckle. "Faith Wheeler," he started, "will you marry me?"

"It depends," she replied, earning a chorus of groans from onlookers. "Who are you? Are you the man I love, or are you the Hollywood fiction?"

"My name . . . I'm . . ." He had to clear his throat again, but no matter how hard he tried, he couldn't dislodge the uncomfortable lump of emotion threatening to close his windpipe.

Faith took his hands and held them to her heart.

"I'm Alexander Orrin Brannon," he said, speaking to her as though they were the only two people in the world. "I'm from Booger Hollow, West Virginia, and I'm in love with you, Faith Wheeler. I love you, and I want to spend today, tonight, tomorrow and the rest of forever with you. Will you marry me?"

Faith couldn't work words out just yet, so she nodded until she could whisper her acceptance in his ear as he embraced her, lifting her off her cot.

Applause traveled through the gymnasium, and Red Irv's eardrum-stinging stadium whistle increased the intensity of cheering and clapping.

"Hold on, now, wait a damn minute," Justus Wheeler demanded, emerging from the crowd gathered around his family's cots. "You can't marry my Faith."

"Oh yes, he can, Daddy," Faith said decisively. Her eyes roamed the crowd hoping to spot her mother and enlist her support.

Wagging a finger at Alex, Justus directed his next words to him. "I told you ten years ago that you weren't to get involved with my little girl!"

Faith's eyes widened in surprise; the muscles in Alex's jaw hardened. Emiline Wheeler's right hand went nervously to her throat. Onlookers scattered, but they didn't go far.

"Daddy . . ." Faith started softly, looking from her father to Alex and back again. "Alex . . . What . . .?"

Hundreds of people in the gym managed to keep totally silent as they watched a real-life drama played out before them.

"Do you want to tell her, or should I?" Alex said, his gaze fixed on Justus.

"Somebody better tell me what the hell you two are talking about!" Faith demanded.

"What's done is done, baby girl," Justus insisted. "We need to deal with the here and now, not the—"

"Tell her, Justus," Emiline Wheeler said firmly. "Tell her, or I will."

Justus, his arms folded across his chest, his shoulders hunched in consternation, looked every bit the willful child refusing to open his mouth for lima beans.

Desperate for answers, Faith appealed to her mother. "Mama, what's going on?"

"Alexander," she began quietly, "Alex," she corrected, tipping her head toward him, "came to the house one day while you were at school."

Faith's head whipped back toward Alex, who stared resolutely at Justus, a tiny muscle flexing at the hinge of his jaw.

"He asked to speak with me and your father," Emiline continued. "He wanted permission to take you to a matinee."

"*Armageddon*," Justus grunted. "I got your Armageddon, all right. Bruce Willis had it right. You don't let just anybody come after your baby girl."

"Your father . . ." Emiline cleared her throat, brought a hooked finger to her eye to wipe away a tear. "Your father told Alex that he wasn't to ever set foot on our property again. And that he was to stay away from you, Faith."

Faith knew her parents well enough to know that Emiline had presented the blandest, most watered-down version of what her fiery-tempered father had likely said to Alex. "When was this?" she asked.

Emiline's face collapsed in pain. "Two weeks before the last big flood."

Framing his neck in her hands, Faith forced Alex's gaze from her father to her. Too many emotions—anger, frustration, pride, love, relief—moved through her, and she took him tightly in her arms. "You didn't leave because you hated this town," she whispered. "You left because you loved me." She balled her hands and gave him a light punch. "If you'd only waited, you could have come with me! You could have—"

"Talk about the melodrama of youth," he said, pulling her away just enough to see her face. "Your father told me that I had no chance with you, that I had nothing to offer you. He said that you deserved better than Alexander Brannon."

"She did!" Justus grunted defiantly.

"I didn't want to be the wedge that drove you further from your parents back then, Faith," Alex said. "You were already fighting with them over college."

"She didn't listen to us about that, either!" Justus pointed out.

Faith would have turned on her father if Alex hadn't intervened.

"All I had back then was Faith, and when you told me that I couldn't see her . . ." Alex winced, reliving the pain of that moment. "I wanted to die. So I did. Faith brought me back to life. I thought I was being respectful back then by asking for your permission to date your daughter, but Faith no longer lives under your roof, and she doesn't need your permission to get married. I won't ask you for her hand because it's no longer yours to give. I won't ask for your blessing, either, because I don't want it if you can't give it with a free and willing heart. I love your daughter, Mr. Wheeler. Nothing means more to me than her happiness, and I'm gonna make damn sure that I spend the rest of my life making her happy. Do we have your blessing?"

Justus cycled through a series of defiant sputterings and gesticulations that left a few spectators chuckling.

"He came back from the dead for her," Red Irv called out. "Give 'em your blessing, you old goat!"

"Shut your ass up, Red!" Justus responded angrily. "When you get a little girl, then you can come up on me, telling me what's best—"

"Justus, stop it!" Weeping openly, Emiline shifted her gaze from her daughter's hurt to her husband's anger, and then to the love Alex bestowed upon her daughter. "Don't make the same mistake twice, Jus. We might lose both of them this time."

"Tell me one thing, Alex," Justus said. "Do you have a house?"

"Yes," Alex said. "I want to turn it into a home."

"How many bedrooms?"

"I've got a four-bedroom, six-and-a-half bath A-frame on five acres in Fawnskin, California. Big Bear Lake is in my front yard, the San Bernardino mountains surround me and it rarely rains. It's all paid for."

"Hold on, you said it's all paid for?"

"That's right."

"You're thirty years old and you don't have a mortgage," Justus said.

"Alex makes a good living," Faith added. "He invests wisely."

"Got your own house at thirty," Justus said, appreciation mingling with his anger and annoyance. "You want that blessing in writing, or will a handshake do?"

EPILOGUE

"Who's this?"

"You know who this is," Faith said, smiling. She ran her fingers through the overlong honey curls of the three-year-old at her hip. "That's Daddy."

"Who's this?" the child asked, moving his finger from the man in the picture to the woman he held in his arms.

"I don't know," Faith said, tapping her chin. "But she looks familiar, doesn't she?"

The little boy rolled his big hazel eyes in exaggerated circles. "That's you, Mama. Only not so fat as you are now."

"Thanks," Faith laughed, giving him a playful shove. "This isn't fat." She used both hands to trace the massive swell of her belly, where her second child currently resided. "This is your baby brother or sister."

Brent Justus Brannon, never particularly enthused about talk of his impending sibling, turned back to the framed photo propped on the fireplace mantel. "Where am I?"

Faith pointed to the photo in which her abdomen was pressed to Alex's. "You're still in there."

"I'm a flood baby!" B.J. announced proudly.

B.J. had been conceived shortly after Alex's proposal, most likely during one of his and Faith's secret trysts in the Lincoln High audiovisual room. Or one of the music practice rooms. Or on the floor of the dance studio . . . Faith couldn't be exactly sure which location had been the scene of the crime, as it were. After a quick ceremony performed in the school auditorium by Mayor Blair and a reception catered by Red Irv in the cafeteria, the whole town had danced the night away in the gym to tunes spun by Herman Voss' grandson, a right little DJ in the making.

In between assisting with Booger Hollow's recovery efforts, Faith and Alex had honeymooned all over the school. Magda Pierson had sent Daiyu Lin to Dorothy to photograph Zander Baron's impromptu nuptials, and the photo Faith now looked at with her son was her favorite, even though it had nothing to do with the marriage ceremony.

Daiyu had been shadowing them as they had participated in a salvage effort to recover what could be rescued from Red Irv's Diner. Faith's hair was a bush, mud had dried on her face, hands and rain slicker. Alex's hair, dark with floodwater, hung in his face. His jeans and boots were caked with mud and one of the sleeves of his shirt had been torn by a piece of digging equipment, but neither figure in the photo seemed to see anything other than the beauty of the other.

Belly to belly and hips to hips, they stood on high ground, Kayford mountain hazy in the background, the receding water line sharp and ugly in the foreground. Their hands told a more complete story than any words could. Alex held both of Faith's in his, pressing his lips to one while pressing the other to his heart. Faith gazed at him, her eyes bright and lovely, her smile beatific.

Daiyu had captured their ooze, and the photo was displayed prominently in their home in Fawnskin.

"Can we call Daddy?" B.J. asked.

"Absolutely."

Faith waddled into the kitchen, B.J. on her heels. He hopped onto a tall stool near the phone stand while Faith dialed the number Alex had given them.

Alex answered on the first ring. "Is it time?"

"No, honey," Faith smiled, putting him on speaker. "B.J. just wanted to hear your voice."

"Hi, Daddy!" he piped. "Where are you?"

"I'm in Oahu, Hawaii, baby. I filmed a scene where I got to fight with a dragon."

"A real dragon?"

"A computer dragon," Alex said. "I did all my sword fighting and the computer guys will put the dragon in later."

"Okay, Dad, bye!" And with that, B.J. scurried off into the great room.

"How are you, honey?" Alex asked. "Any action on number two?"

"I saw the doctor this morning. I'm still only two centimeters dilated, but nothing else is going on. I'm not having this baby until you get back, so quit thinking you're going to get out of the delivery."

"I'm not trying to—"

"Alex, you vomited twice and passed out once when B.J. was being born," Faith said. "I know you're not looking forward to the big show. Why else would you take off so close to my due date to do location shots so far away?"

"Say the word, and I'm home," he challenged.

"You're in the middle of the ocean," Faith laughed. "You're just gonna pick up and pack up and come running back to me if I tell you to?"

"Not if you tell me," Alex clarified. "But if you ask me."

"Alex, darling," she started, "will you please come home to your big ol' wife and one and a half children?"

There was no answer.

"Alex?"

Still no response, only muffled voices from the other side of the world.

"Alex!"

As Faith listened, the voices became sharper. "Damn it, he's doing it again!" wailed a male voice with a distinct accent.

"Where's he gone?" asked an American voice.

"Hell if I know. Ask *him*, if you can catch him this time!"

"I think he's going home," offered a faint female voice.

"For cripes' sake, not again!" screamed the native accent. "That's the second time since we started filming!"

Laughing so hard she had to hold her belly, Faith leaned against a countertop. Her laughter became a gasp of pain when a contraction seized her. It wasn't the pleasant, gentle tightening and release of a Braxton-

Hicks, but the real deal. Once it passed, she disconnected the phone and glanced at the clock. The second one didn't hit her until fifteen minutes later, with a third coming fifteen minutes after that.

Faith calmly called her obstetrician before calling Brent, who immediately went into panic mode.

"We've got to get Alex back here," he said. "And we've got to get someone to keep B.J. Damn it, I wish I still had the Fleming Viper. It'll take me two hours to get to you, Faith."

"Brent, it's under control," Faith assured him. "Grover Dylan is on-call for B.J., and I'll meet Alex at the hospital."

"Meet—? What?"

"Alex is on his way," she said. "He'll probably get here before you do. He left the island about an hour ago."

"He walked off the set?"

"Yep."

"Again?" Brent growled.

"Yep."

"Why this time?"

"For the same reason he does it every time." Faith caressed her belly, and closed her eyes to better hear the faint music of her son singing to himself as he played with his toy dragons. "Because he loves me."

The End

AUTHOR BIO

Tempting Faith is Crystal Hubbard's seventh romance novel for Genesis Press. She is also an award-winning children's book author. The mother of four, Crystal resides in St. Louis, Mo. She spends her free time promoting cancer awareness and conducting writing workshops for grade school students.

2009 Reprint Mass Market Titles

January

I'm Gonna Make You Love Me
Gwyneth Bolton
ISBN-13: 978-1-58571-294-6
$6.99

Shades of Desire
Monica White
ISBN-13: 978-1-58571-292-2
$6.99

February

A Love of Her Own
Cheris Hodges
ISBN-13: 978-1-58571-293-9
$6.99

Color of Trouble
Dyanne Davis
ISBN-13: 978-1-58571-294-6
$6.99

March

Twist of Fate
Beverly Clark
ISBN-13: 978-1-58571-295-3
$6.99

Chances
Pamela Leigh Starr
ISBN-13: 978-1-58571-296-0
$6.99

April

Sinful Intentions
Crystal Rhodes
ISBN-13: 978-1-585712-297-7
$6.99

Rock Star
Roslyn Hardy Holcomb
ISBN-13: 978-1-58571-298-4
$6.99

May

Paths of Fire
T.T. Henderson
ISBN-13: 978-1-58571-343-1
$6.99

Caught Up in the Rapture
Lisa Riley
ISBN-13: 978-1-58571-344-8
$6.99

June

Reckless Surrender
Rochelle Alers
ISBN-13: 978-1-58571-345-5
$6.99

No Ordinary Love
Angela Weaver
ISBN-13: 978-1-58571-346-2
$6.99

296

2009 Reprint Mass Market Titles (continued)

July

Intentional Mistakes
Michele Sudler
ISBN-13: 978-1-58571-347-9
$6.99

It's In His Kiss
Reon Carter
ISBN-13: 978-1-58571-348-6
$6.99

August

Unfinished Love Affair
Barbara Keaton
ISBN-13: 978-1-58571-349-3
$6.99

A Perfect Place to Pray
I.L Goodwin
ISBN-13: 978-1-58571-299-1
$6.99

September

Love in High Gear
Charlotte Roy
ISBN-13: 978-1-58571-355-4
$6.99

Ebony Eyes
Kei Swanson
ISBN-13: 978-1-58571-356-1
$6.99

October

Midnight Clear, Part I
Leslie Esdale/Carmen Green
ISBN-13: 978-1-58571-357-8
$6.99

Midnight Clear, Part II
Gwynne Forster/Monica
Jackson
ISBN-13: 978-1-58571-358-5
$6.99

November

Midnight Peril
Vicki Andrews
ISBN-13: 978-1-58571-359-2
$6.99

One Day At A Time
Bella McFarland
ISBN-13: 978-1-58571-360-8
$6.99

December

Just An Affair
Eugenia O'Neal
ISBN-13: 978-1-58571-361-5
$6.99

Shades of Brown
Denise Becker
ISBN-13: 978-1-58571-362-2
$6.99

2009 New Mass Market Titles

January

Singing A Song...
Crystal Rhodes
ISBN-13: 978-1-58571-283-0
$6.99

Look Both Ways
Joan Early
ISBN-13: 978-1-58571-284-7
$6.99

February

Six O'Clock
Katrina Spencer
ISBN-13: 978-1-58571-285-4
$6.99

Red Sky
Renee Alexis
ISBN-13: 978-1-58571-286-1
$6.99

March

Anything But Love
Celya Bowers
ISBN-13: 978-1-58571-287-8
$6.99

Tempting Faith
Crystal Hubbard
ISBN-13: 978-1-58571-288-5
$6.99

April

If I Were Your Woman
La Connie Taylor-Jones
ISBN-13: 978-1-58571-289-2
$6.99

Best Of Luck Elsewhere
Trisha Haddad
ISBN-13: 978-1-58571-290-8
$6.99

May

All I'll Ever Need
Mildred Riley
ISBN-13: 978-1-58571-335-6
$6.99

A Place Like Home
Alicia Wiggins
ISBN-13: 978-1-58571-336-3
$6.99

June

Best Foot Forward
Michele Sudler
ISBN-13: 978-1-58571-337-0
$6.99

It's In the Rhythm
Sammie Ward
ISBN-13: 978-1-58571-338-7
$6.99

2009 New Mass Market Titles (continued)

July

Checks and Balances
Elaine Sims
ISBN-13: 978-1-58571-339-4
$6.99

Save Me
Africa Fine
ISBN-13: 978-1-58571-340-0
$6.99

August

When Lightening Strikes
Michele Cameron
ISBN-13: 978-1-58571-369-1
$6.99

Blindsided
Tammy Williams
ISBN-13: 978-1-58571-342-4
$6.99

September

2 Good
Celya Bowers
ISBN-13: 978-1-58571-350-9
$6.99

Waiting for Mr. Darcy
Chamein Canton
ISBN-13: 978-1-58571-351-6
$6.99

October

Fireflies
Joan Early
ISBN-13: 978-1-58571-352-3
$6.99

Frost On My Window
Angela Weaver
ISBN-13: 978-1-58571-353-0
$6.99

November

Waiting in the Shadows
Michele Sudler
ISBN-13: 978-1-58571-364-6
$6.99

Fixin' Tyrone
Keith Walker
ISBN-13: 978-1-58571-365-3
$6.99

December

Dream Keeper
Gail McFarland
ISBN-13: 978-1-58571-366-0
$6.99

Another Memory
Pamela Ridley
ISBN-13: 978-1-58571-367-7
$6.99

Other Genesis Press, Inc. Titles

A Dangerous Deception	J.M. Jeffries	$8.95
A Dangerous Love	J.M. Jeffries	$8.95
A Dangerous Obsession	J.M. Jeffries	$8.95
A Drummer's Beat to Mend	Kei Swanson	$9.95
A Happy Life	Charlotte Harris	$9.95
A Heart's Awakening	Veronica Parker	$9.95
A Lark on the Wing	Phyliss Hamilton	$9.95
A Love of Her Own	Cheris F. Hodges	$9.95
A Love to Cherish	Beverly Clark	$8.95
A Risk of Rain	Dar Tomlinson	$8.95
A Taste of Temptation	Reneé Alexis	$9.95
A Twist of Fate	Beverly Clark	$8.95
A Voice Behind Thunder	Carrie Elizabeth Greene	$6.99
A Will to Love	Angie Daniels	$9.95
Acquisitions	Kimberley White	$8.95
Across	Carol Payne	$12.95
After the Vows	Leslie Esdaile	$10.95
(Summer Anthology)	T.T. Henderson	
	Jacqueline Thomas	
Again My Love	Kayla Perrin	$10.95
Against the Wind	Gwynne Forster	$8.95
All I Ask	Barbara Keaton	$8.95
Always You	Crystal Hubbard	$6.99
Ambrosia	T.T. Henderson	$8.95
An Unfinished Love Affair	Barbara Keaton	$8.95
And Then Came You	Dorothy Elizabeth Love	$8.95
Angel's Paradise	Janice Angelique	$9.95
At Last	Lisa G. Riley	$8.95
Best of Friends	Natalie Dunbar	$8.95
Beyond the Rapture	Beverly Clark	$9.95
Blame It On Paradise	Crystal Hubbard	$6.99
Blaze	Barbara Keaton	$9.95
Bliss, Inc.	Chamein Canton	$6.99
Blood Lust	J. M. Jeffries	$9.95
Blood Seduction	J.M. Jeffries	$9.95

Other Genesis Press, Inc. Titles (continued)

Other Genesis Press, Inc. Titles (continued)

Other Genesis Press, Inc. Titles (continued)

Icie	Pamela Leigh Starr	$8.95
Illusions	Pamela Leigh Starr	$8.95
Indigo After Dark Vol. I	Nia Dixon/Angelique	$10.95
Indigo After Dark Vol. II	Dolores Bundy/ Cole Riley	$10.95
Indigo After Dark Vol. III	Montana Blue/ Coco Morena	$10.95
Indigo After Dark Vol. IV	Cassandra Colt/	$14.95
Indigo After Dark Vol. V	Delilah Dawson	$14.95
Indiscretions	Donna Hill	$8.95
Intentional Mistakes	Michele Sudler	$9.95
Interlude	Donna Hill	$8.95
Intimate Intentions	Angie Daniels	$8.95
It's Not Over Yet	J.J. Michael	$9.95
Jolie's Surrender	Edwina Martin-Arnold	$8.95
Kiss or Keep	Debra Phillips	$8.95
Lace	Giselle Carmichael	$9.95
Lady Preacher	K.T. Richey	$6.99
Last Train to Memphis	Elsa Cook	$12.95
Lasting Valor	Ken Olsen	$24.95
Let Us Prey	Hunter Lundy	$25.95
Lies Too Long	Pamela Ridley	$13.95
Life Is Never As It Seems	J.J. Michael	$12.95
Lighter Shade of Brown	Vicki Andrews	$8.95
Looking for Lily	Africa Fine	$6.99
Love Always	Mildred E. Riley	$10.95
Love Doesn't Come Easy	Charlyne Dickerson	$8.95
Love Unveiled	Gloria Greene	$10.95
Love's Deception	Charlene Berry	$10.95
Love's Destiny	M. Loui Quezada	$8.95
Love's Secrets	Yolanda McVey	$6.99
Mae's Promise	Melody Walcott	$8.95
Magnolia Sunset	Giselle Carmichael	$8.95
Many Shades of Gray	Dyanne Davis	$6.99
Matters of Life and Death	Lesego Malepe, Ph.D.	$15.95

Other Genesis Press, Inc. Titles (continued)

Other Genesis Press, Inc. Titles (continued)

Peace Be Still	Colette Haywood	$12.95
Picture Perfect	Reon Carter	$8.95
Playing for Keeps	Stephanie Salinas	$8.95
Pride & Joi	Gay G. Gunn	$8.95
Promises Made	Bernice Layton	$6.99
Promises to Keep	Alicia Wiggins	$8.95
Quiet Storm	Donna Hill	$10.95
Reckless Surrender	Rochelle Alers	$6.95
Red Polka Dot in a World of Plaid	Varian Johnson	$12.95
Reluctant Captive	Joyce Jackson	$8.95
Rendezvous with Fate	Jeanne Sumerix	$8.95
Revelations	Cheris F. Hodges	$8.95
Rivers of the Soul	Leslie Esdaile	$8.95
Rocky Mountain Romance	Kathleen Suzanne	$8.95
Rooms of the Heart	Donna Hill	$8.95
Rough on Rats and Tough on Cats	Chris Parker	$12.95
Secret Library Vol. 1	Nina Sheridan	$18.95
Secret Library Vol. 2	Cassandra Colt	$8.95
Secret Thunder	Annetta P. Lee	$9.95
Shades of Brown	Denise Becker	$8.95
Shades of Desire	Monica White	$8.95
Shadows in the Moonlight	Jeanne Sumerix	$8.95
Sin	Crystal Rhodes	$8.95
Small Whispers	Annetta P. Lee	$6.99
So Amazing	Sinclair LeBeau	$8.95
Somebody's Someone	Sinclair LeBeau	$8.95
Someone to Love	Alicia Wiggins	$8.95
Song in the Park	Martin Brant	$15.95
Soul Eyes	Wayne L. Wilson	$12.95
Soul to Soul	Donna Hill	$8.95
Southern Comfort	J.M. Jeffries	$8.95
Southern Fried Standards	S.R. Maddox	$6.99
Still the Storm	Sharon Robinson	$8.95

Other Genesis Press, Inc. Titles (continued)

Other Genesis Press, Inc. Titles (continued)

Order Form

Mail to: Genesis Press, Inc.
P.O. Box 101
Columbus, MS 39703

Name _____
Address _____
City/State _____ Zip _____
Telephone _____

Ship to (if different from above)
Name _____
Address _____
City/State _____ Zip _____
Telephone _____

Credit Card Information
Credit Card # _____ ☐ Visa   ☐ Mastercard
Expiration Date (mm/yy) _____ ☐ AmEx ☐ Discover

Qty.	Author	Title	Price	Total

Use this order form, or call
1-888-INDIGO-1

Total for books	_____
Shipping and handling:	
$5 first two books,	
$1 each additional book	_____
Total S & H	_____
Total amount enclosed	_____

Mississippi residents add 7% sales tax